'Gracious, I must fly!'

Verity sped to the door and dashed out, only to collide on the threshold with someone who was about to enter. He crashed to the floor in an ungainly heap.

'Oh, I am so very sorry,' she uttered contritely. It was evident from the way the poor man was gripping his underlip between his teeth that he was in a good deal of pain, but he managed a faint laugh.

'You are determined—to see me—humbled, are you not? I trust this may be—lowly enough for you!'

Dear Reader

Despite an unavoidably long gap since JUST DESERTS, Elizabeth Bailey is back again with a beautiful and touching story set in Tunbridge Wells in the 1790s. AN ANGEL'S TOUCH gives us Verity, determined to do her best for the Marquis and his children. . . Mary Nichols returns with THE DANBURY SCANDALS, a marvellous love mystery where both the hero and heroine belatedly discover their connection to Viscount Danbury, and get into trouble because of it!

The Editor

Elizabeth Bailey grew up in Malawi, returning to England to plunge into the theatre. After many happy years 'tatting around the reps', she finally turned from 'dabbling' to serious writing. She finds it more satisfying for she is in control of everything; scripts, design, direction, and the portrayal of every character! Elizabeth lives in London and teaches drama to GCSE students.

Recent titles by the same author:

JUST DESERTS
SWEET SACRIFICE

AN ANGEL'S TOUCH

Elizabeth Bailey

First published in Great Britain 1992
by Mills & Boon Limited

© Elizabeth Bailey 1992

Australian copyright 1992
Philippine copyright 1992
This edition 1992

ISBN 0 263 77951 3

Masquerade is a trademark published by
Mills & Boon Limited, Eton House,
18–24 Paradise Road, Richmond, Surrey, TW9 1SR.

Set in 10 on 11 pt Linotron Times
04-9212-77464

Typeset in Great Britain by Centracet, Cambridge
Made and printed in Great Britain

CHAPTER ONE

THROUGH the window of the slow-moving coach, a patch of bright colour in the valley below caught at the traveller's idle, wandering gaze. Leaning forward in her seat, Miss Verity Lambourn discerned a clutch of gaily painted wagons grouped about a neat clearing, from the centre of which emanated a plume of smoke.

Since this sunny afternoon in mid-July was fine and warm, it was to be inferred that the fire was lit for the purpose of cooking the gypsies' dinner, rather than the provision of illumination for a night of wild revelry to the strains of a fiddle and the beat of a rhythmic drum.

But the young lady whose clear hazel eyes were devouring the peaceful serenity of the scene was of an imaginative turn of mind. Already she had conjured up a mental image of a dusky, raven-haired beauty, of voluptuous mien, improbably attired in a flouncing petticoat of violent hue, dancing with wicked abandon about the flickering flames, while her handsome counterpart looked on with a brooding, sullen passion that boded ill to his erring inamorata.

For in such manner was Miss Lambourn prone to enliven the tedium of her days, and in particular the hours of enforced inertia on the present journey to Tunbridge Wells. The heavy old-fashioned coach made but ponderous progress from one stage to the next, even though drawn by six horses. They had of necessity had to traverse a cross-country route from their home village of Tetheridge in the county of Hampshire, and the roads, being less well-kept than the main pike thoroughfares, were not conducive to speed. Then, too, Lady Crossens had declared that she would not rattle her old bones more than she need, and the journey had occupied five days at a snail's pace when two might well have sufficed.

They had joined the main road from London to Tunbridge Wells at Sevenoaks, however, on this last leg of the journey, and the smoother ride had encouraged her ladyship to sink into slumber, her chin resting on her chest, leaving Miss Lambourn free to the indulgence of her visions.

So Verity leaned from the window to people the gypsy camp with the creations of her vivid imagination. Her ideas were perhaps ill-informed, culled as they had been from the products of the pens of more experienced observers than herself, and she had the wit to realise it.

But perhaps they were not so far removed from the truth, she thought with an inward smile, as her glance found the nearer figure of a man very much like the sultry figment of her mind, and, by his rough clothes and the spotted handkerchief about his neck, clearly a member of the gypsy clan from the encampment in the valley below. And those two children there, below the big tree by the roadside—a small boy, not much older than her little brother at home, who guarded with both hands an infant as yet unbreeched, who might be of either sex. Were they not gypsy urchins? Her hero's bairns perhaps? she wondered amusedly as she saw the gypsy man halt in his way and turn to look at the two.

Then, as Verity gazed on the scene from the window of the passing coach, it was as if a curtain lifted, dissolving the dream and presenting her with several incontrovertible signs of stark reality. She took them in all at once, her thoughts racing to a swift conclusion.

The children's attire bore the unmistakable stamp of gentility. Sporting a well cut frock-coat and breeches,

a neat neckcloth and boots, the boy was every inch the
miniature replica of a country gentleman. And no
gypsy child would be swathed in that baby bonnet or
the plain white round gown, embroidered and laced.
The infant was whimpering, little hands clutching at
the other small body whose protective arms now gathered it to him, in his face a look of fear as he stared at
the gypsy not twenty yards away.

Almost without conscious decision, Verity was up,
grabbing at the little window above the forward seat by
means of which the passengers might converse with the
coachman and the groom by his side, and pushing it
open.

'Stop! Oh, please, Brading, stop *at once*!'

It took a moment or two for her anxious voice to
penetrate the ears of the coachman on the box above,
and by the time the vehicle came to a standstill the
little drama being enacted was several yards behind it.

But Verity did not wait for the wheels to become
completely motionless. She thrust open the door, gathered up her skirts, and sprang somewhat hazardously
down into the road. She stumbled a little, for the coach
doorway was some few feet off the ground. But in her
anxiety for the children she made nothing of it, righting
herself swiftly, and not even hearing the sleepy but
exclamatory tones of Lady Crossens from behind her.
'What. . .what. . .? What is amiss?'

Then she was running back and in seconds saw that
her surmise was correct. The gypsy had started towards
the children, and the boy was backing away, having
inexpertly lifted the infant in his arms, hampered by
the added burden of its weight from taking to his heels.

Verity, calling out, came hurtling towards them, and
she saw all eyes turned on her in amazement. The
gypsy halted, staring, and the boy looked as if he
feared equally an attack from this new quarter.

'Gracious, where have you been?' gasped Verity in mock exasperation as she arrived out of breath at his side. 'We have been hunting for you all over!' Then, leaning down to him a little, she dropped her voice. 'Are you in trouble? May I be of service to you?'

The boy blinked at her and clutched closer to his inadequate bosom the infant, who now began to cry in earnest. Under cover of this fresh noise, Verity added, 'Don't be afraid! I will help you if I may. Let me first get rid of this man.'

Then she turned to the gypsy and called out. 'So foolish of my little friends! They lost their way. But they will be safe now with me.'

The gypsy's face darkened with a flush, whether in anger or shame Verity could not tell. He stared hard at the little group for a moment or two, and then his eyes went past them just as Verity heard a footfall behind her. She turned to see that the groom, who had come down from his perch on the box of Lady Crossens' coach and followed her, had taken a step or two forward as if to offer his protection.

'Pray don't!' she said to him softly. 'There is no need for alarm, I am persuaded.'

'Maybe not, miss,' muttered the groom gruffly, 'but I'll be keepng me place beside you all the same.'

It was impossible to tell whether the gypsy overheard this exchange, but he shrugged slightly and turned away, walking unhurriedly off in the direction of his camp. Within a short time, he disappeared from sight as he descended into the valley.

Miss Lambourn, satisfied and not a little relieved, turned back to her protégés. She was forestalled, however.

'Her ladyship says as how you're to come back at once, miss,' the groom told her apologetically.

'Yes, yes, I shall do so directly,' Verity said

impatiently. 'I must first see how we can assist these poor young things.' Then without further ado, she began to speak to the boy.

'Tell me, if you please, how I may help you. You are lost, perhaps? I know you cannot be out here all by yourselves on purpose.'

The boy shook his head, his initial fear fading. Whether it was her friendly manner or the presence of the burly groom, he was visibly relaxing, though Verity noted that his thin shoulders were still shaking.

'It was Peggy,' he said in a grudging tone, as if the explanation were forced from him, indicating with a dip of his chin the small child he still clutched to his meagre chest.

Peggy was wailing so loudly that Verity felt impelled to do what she might to stem the flood before she could expect to converse with any degree of coherence. She crouched down, therefore, and addressed soothing blandishments to the little girl.

'There now, little one, don't cry so! You will be home directly, darling, I promise you. Come, now, come. All will be well, you'll see.'

Surprise arrested the child's sobs, and she stared at the stranger out of big blue eyes, luminous still with her tears. But when Verity held out her hands and would have taken the infant into her arms, Peggy pulled back and turned her face into the boy's chest.

'Tittoo,' she uttered plaintively. 'Tittoo! Tittoo! Peddy want Tittoo.'

'She means her nurse,' the boy translated, seeing Verity's puzzled look. His young arms were tiring and he set the little girl down. Though she clung to his slim torso, Peggy made no protest, but eyed the strange lady with interest, whimpering for 'Tittoo' now and then.

Had she had any knowledge of such things, Peggy

would have noted that Miss Lambourn was far from fashionable. She was neatly turned out in the forest-green greatcoat dress of linen that had been made for her for travelling, and a pretty tall-crowned beaver hat embellished with ribbon. The feather tippet and muff for extra warmth against draughts had been discarded in the coach, but the ensemble lacked that touch of elegance that would have taken from it a countrified air.

Miss Lambourn was no beauty, either, though regular features in a fresh complexion, taken together with her candid direct gaze and the dark curls rioting under the hat, had an attraction all their own. That was, for those ready to overlook the defects of a plump bosom, and height a little below the average. She had, however, an uncommon degree of animation and a very friendly smile, which no doubt encouraged the waifs she had encountered to extend to her their trust.

'Peggy is your sister?' Verity guessed.

The boy nodded again. 'Yes. She was in the garden with Kittle—that's her nurse—and I saw her run off towards the woods.'

'Didn't—er—Kittle see her?'

'She weren't watching. Gossiping with one of the gardingers, she was,' the boy said, with an austerity that sat uneasily on his small person.

'How very shocking!' Verity commented primly, suppressing a smile. 'But could you not have called out to her?'

'I *did* call out,' protested the boy, tossing his head indignantly so that the straight fair locks that rested on his shoulders flicked about his cheeks. 'I called *plenty* times. Only I was quite far off, you know. And Peggy can go ever so fast when she wants, though she is not much above two years old. I had to run myself, but she was into the woods before I could catch her. And she would not stop when I shouted, not she!'

'But you did catch her, after all,' Verity said admiringly. 'You *did* do well.'

'Course I caught her!' scoffed the child. 'I am near seven myself, you know. And I *am* a boy.'

'Of course you are. How silly of me! I beg your pardon,' apologised Verity hastily. 'But then why did you not take Peggy back at once?'

The boy flushed and looked away. 'I—I *should've*, I know. But—but I thought p'raps it would teach her a lesson. Kittle, I mean. If—if she thought she had lost Peggy for a bit.'

'Ah, I see,' Verity nodded understandingly. 'I dare say you were right. She must have had a severe fright.'

'Yes,' agreed the boy dubiously, looking shamefaced. 'Only I—I don't know the woods well. I'm not allowed in them mostly. 'Cause of poachers, you know.'

'But you do manage to spend some time in them, for all that,' she suggested with a twinkle.

He reddened again. 'Well, yes. But not enough to—to know them as I'd like, and—and. . .'

'And the long and the short of it is that you missed your bearings and became lost. And who shall blame you for that? Gracious, what a misadventure! I think, though, we should get Peggy back home as fast as we are able, don't you?'

'Yes, but they'll come for us soon, I think,' the boy announced, with an unconcern that, together with his self-possessed air and his very grown-up manner, spoke more eloquently than his clothes of a privileged background. 'That's why I made for the road. They are bound to come looking this way, for this is all *our* land. We are out of the 'state grounds here, though.'

Even as he spoke there came the sound of many

hoofs, and Verity turned in time to see several horsemen approaching from behind the coach. She noticed
as well old Lady Crossens' gaunt features peering out
at her, and urged the groom to run back and reassure
her that she would rejoin her in a moment. But the
groom was mindful of her ladyship's orders. 'For
heaven's sake, Dogget,' she had uttered distractedly,
'get after her and fetch her back! And mind she comes
to no harm, for she is in my care, and if I must face
dear Grace and the Vicar with the tale of a vanished
daughter, I shall likely go off in an apoplexy!' He chose
therefore to remain stalwart by Miss Lambourn's side
until it should please his mistress's oddly behaved
young guest to recover her sanity and get back into the
coach.

There was no time for Verity to persuade the groom
to do as she asked, or herself to call out a reassurance
to the old lady, for the horsemen were upon them,
reining in and dismounting in a flurry of exclamatory
comment.

'Good God, my lord, what a dance you have led us!'
called a slim, youthful individual with a gentlemanly
air.

'You have her safe, me lord!' came from a thick-set
man in fine livery. 'God be praised!'

'Your lordship had best come quick. Fat's in the fire
now, and no mistake!'

The last words, muttered by a lad with the look of a
stablehand, who had flung off his horse the first and
was closest to the boy, were accompanied by a significant jerk of the head.

Verity, following the direction of his gaze, saw that a
phaeton had drawn up a few yards away. It was driven
by a slight young man who turned a lean countenance
set in lines of severity upon the errant children, and

handed his reins to the middle-aged groom who sat beside him.

The group about her fell silent, and Verity watched with interest as the man descended, slowly and with apparent difficulty, from the phaeton into the road. The groom handed him a cane and as he advanced towards them, a pair of dark angry eyes fixed intimidatingly on the boy, it was to be seen that he walked with a pronounced limp, seeming to drag his hip over a stiff right leg.

No one spoke as he came up, and the boy met that menacing eye with a look of sullen apprehension in his own.

'Well, Braxted?' the young man demanded in a quietly controlled tone. 'Have you anything to say for yourself?'

The boy's eyes, big and blue like his sister's, flashed momentarily, and then sank. He compressed his lips firmly together and steadfastly regarded the ground. But Verity saw his small hands tighten on the shoulders of his little sister, whose arms still clung about him.

Peggy let out a squealing protest which drew all eyes. The young man looked at the gentlemanlike member of the entourage of three.

'Inskip,' he said quietly. The man addressed immediately leaned down and prised the infant's hands from about her brother's person. The boy instantly let her go and stepped back a pace. The little girl was swung up as the man in authority added, 'Take her to the phaeton. Hoff may hold her. I will not be above a moment.'

The other nodded briefly, and went off with Peggy. The other men took the opportunity to retreat a step or two. Verity could not blame them. There was such a heavy charge of held-in fury emanating from the authoritative young man that it was almost tangible.

She found it uncomfortable, and oddly inapposite. For he looked so insignificant a man.

He was quietly, if respectably dressed in a green frock-coat over buckskin breeches and top-boots, cravat neatly though unimaginatively knotted, and a plain, round-brimmed beaver over a quantity of rich brown locks drawn back and tied in the nape of his neck. His features were good, though marked, young as he was, with lines of suffering that ran down to a well-shaped mouth, tight-lipped at this moment, and a resolute chin. It was his eyes, so dark as to be almost black, that were his most striking attribute, attractive even as they burned with the anger that he turned back on the boy.

'Well, Braxted?' he repeated, in a voice that was not the less threatening for its quiet control. 'Your pranks are one thing, and to be discussed between us at some more convenient time. But to be involving your little sister in them goes beyond the line of what may be tolerated.'

He paused, but the boy, though he raised his blue orbs to stare defiantly up into that smouldering gaze, had nothing to say.

'I trust,' continued the man softly, 'I make myself plain?'

'Yes, sir,' the boy asserted gruffly.

'Upon my word!' ejaculated Verity, suddenly entering the lists, as the implications of this speech burst in upon her. 'And I trust, sir,' she said, rounding on the young man in righteous indignation, 'that you will take the trouble to enquire more particularly into this affair before you inflict the dreadful punishment that I suspect to be in your mind!'

Taken aback, the young man jerked round to face her. He almost tripped up in his clumsy haste and had to support himself with his cane. The liveried servant behind him sprang forward to his assistance, but he waved him away without a backward glance. It was evident that he had not even noticed Verity standing there, but the look of surprise was swiftly succeeded by one of scarcely veiled annoyance.

'And what, ma'am,' he demanded icily, 'has this affair in any way to do with you?'

'I will tell you!' Verity declared at once, not in the least deterred by his manner. 'I happen to be in possession of the true facts of the matter, having come upon the scene a few moments before yourself. I would have supposed, sir, that anyone with the least degree of common sense must perceive at once that the boy is far too protective of his sister to be likely to implicate her in any pranks he might play. And in this instance, as you would have known had you troubled yourself to *ask* the child before *flinging* accusations at his head in that—that *brutish* fashion, there was no *prank* in the case!'

Then, without giving her astonished auditor an opportunity to open his mouth, Miss Lambourn dropped to her knees before the boy and grasped him urgently by the shoulders.

'My dear young friend, do, I beg of you, *think* for a moment. I dare say it is all very brave and *manly* for you to take the blame for something which is in no way your fault, but you cannot have thought the question through. Only consider! Another time you may not be at hand to see the danger, and what if the nurse should be so careless when you are not by to dash so gallantly to the rescue? Then you would have cause to blame yourself indeed! For by your keeping silent, you know, the nurse will *never* be corrected, for I cannot think that she will confess her fault.'

The boy Braxted looked much struck by this, and, grasping his hands and smiling coaxingly at him, Verity

added, 'What good can it possibly do for you meekly
to accept a punishment which you have done nothing
to deserve? Indeed, only misery can come from such a
gross injustice. To you, perhaps to your sister and the
nurse. And indeed——' with a fleeting glance up at the
stern countenance above her '—to your mentor himself. I wish, *dear* friend, you will think better of it and
tell him *everything*!'

Braxted now also cast a quick look up at the young
man standing silently by. He noted that the features
had relaxed, and the dark eyes had lost their fire. His
stiffness melted and he grinned suddenly.

'Well, I will, then. I like to have a friend like you.'

Verity smiled and pressed his hands before releasing
them. 'I am glad. I hope we may meet again.'

She rose to her feet and turned to look again at the
young man. Like Braxted, she saw that the anger had
vanished from his eyes, to be replaced by a gleam
which she strongly suspected to be of amusement. An
amusement she deprecated, for his conduct had been
disgraceful! Then he spoke, and his words disarmed
her.

'It is apparent that I owe you both apology and
thanks,' he said, adding with an ironic little bow, 'I
have certainly been put very firmly in my place.'

Verity bit her lip on a laugh, her outrage dissipating
fast. The implication was not lost on her. There was no
doubt she had been extremely uncivil. 'I have to beg
your pardon, sir.'

'Pray don't,' he pleaded, and Verity thought there
was a lurking twinkle in the black depths of his eyes.
'You have done me a signal service—albeit unwittingly, for I do not flatter myself that such was your
intention!—and I am only sorry that I cannot stay to
express my thanks more suitably. You see, I must get
Margaret home.'

'Margaret?' repeated Verity, vexed to feel herself blushing at the implied rebuke. How unhandsome of him when she had already apologised!

'Peggy, he means,' chimed in Braxted.

'Oh, yes, of course. Do go at once!' Verity begged, thankful for the excuse that would afford instant relief from her embarrassment, and feeling rather guilty for forgetting the infant's needs while championing the boy Braxted.

But when she looked up at the phaeton she saw that Peggy seemed quite contented in the competent arms of the middle-aged groom who managed both to nurse her and hold the horses without apparent difficulty. It crossed Verity's mind that perhaps the child was more often to be found in the arms of servants than in those of her own mother. She had certainly called in her distress for 'Tittoo', her nurse Kittle, rather than for 'Mamma'.

There was no time for further speculation, however, for the young man, having muttered some words of farewell that she scarcely heard, was already climbing laboriously into the phaeton, while Braxted hopped nimbly up to take his own place, squeezing in between the groom and his father.

His *father*? Verity supposed he must have that identity. Though he did not behave in the least like a father should. Admittedly, he had owned himself at fault, but his attitude to the children had been far from loving! And then, too, though everyone had addressed Braxted as 'my lord', none had offered a similar courtesy to the young man. Perhaps he was merely Braxted's tutor. He certainly acted more in the manner of a schoolmaster than of a father! she thought with severe disapprobation.

'You may tell me your tale on the way, Braxted,' she heard him say to the boy as the phaeton started forward, in a tone that lent credibility to her last theory. Especially as the childish treble did not pipe up in response as it ought to have done at a parent's bidding. At least not to Verity's ears. Or perhaps it had been drowned by the clatter of the horses' hoofs, she thought, trying to be charitable.

To the obvious relief of Lady Crossens' groom, who had been hovering on the fringes of the group all this while, she began to walk back to where the old coach stood waiting. The groom hurried ahead of her to let down the steps and hold open the door.

The phaeton and its accompanying horses were already lost to sight as Miss Lambourn, apologising to the groom for keeping him waiting all this time, climbed into the coach. She was greeted by the querulous voice of her patroness.

'And now, miss, if I might trespass upon your valuable time, perhaps you would be so obliging as to tell me the meaning of this extraordinary conduct?'

It took some time to persuade Lady Crossens of the justice of her actions. But although Miss Lambourn patiently explained the circumstances, she could by no means subscribe to her ladyship's freely expressed view that she ought to learn to mind her own business.

'You would not have had me drive on and leave those poor little mites to their fate?' she exclaimed, shocked.

'If this is not precisely of what your dear mama warned me,' complained Lady Crossens, ignoring this home question. 'Impulsive, that's what she said of you. Impetuous and impulsive!'

'I dare say I am, ma'am,' Verity admitted, in her honest way, 'but even Mama would not, I am persuaded, denounce my having interfered in the matter. And Papa——'

'Oh, you need not tell me what *Papa* would say!' uttered her ladyship crossly. 'I am well able to imagine it for myself. If he had his way, he would doubtless clutter up the vicarage with a score of waifs and strays. As if there were not enough of you as it is!'

This was undeniable. The Reverend Harry Lambourn might count himself blessed in the possession of his seven surviving daughters, and in particular of his last-born and most treasured only son, but his adored and adoring wife was at her wit's end to know how to dispose suitably of this bevy of maidens.

Faith at twenty-eight was a matron with children of her own, having snaffled the most eligible of the local gentlemen to become the village doctor's wife. Prudence, already on the shelf at twenty-four, had been sent to Kingsclere to stay with her mother's brother, in the hope of contracting a suitable alliance. For Patience, just a year younger, had achieved a respectable engagement on a visit to her more prominent Lambourn cousins in Winchester. Lady Lambourn, however, with two daughters of her own to be suitably established, was hardly likely to saddle herself with any more of the sisters at present.

Mrs Lambourn had greeted with heartfelt thanks, therefore, Lady Crossens' kind suggestion that Verity, now eighteen, should accompany her to Tunbridge Wells when she went, as had long been her custom, to take the waters during that no longer fashionable six-week season in the summer. True, when both Prudence and Patience, in their turn, had gone there with her ladyship a few years earlier, Mrs Lambourn's high hopes had not been rewarded. But with three more girls already in their adolescence, a needy parson's wife ought never to look a gift horse in the mouth. So she had argued with her spouse when the reverend gentleman had demurred.

'You would not have it thought, Mr Lambourn, that we are ungrateful for her ladyship's kind offices on our daughter's behalf.'

'My dear,' protested the gentleman, 'we are already so much beholden to Lady Crossens for so many kindnesses that I hesitate, I do indeed, to add to the burden of indebtedness.'

'Good gracious me, Mr Lambourn, there will be nothing of that sort, I do assure you! Why, how in the world do you suppose poor Lady Crossens could manage without some young attendant to run her little errands, and perform those offices so very arduous to a woman in her declining years?'

Mr Lambourn suggested that Lady Crossens' servants, her maid in particular, might be employed upon such work. But this foolish idea was summarily disposed of.

'As to that, her ladyship's woman is always permitted to take a holiday at this season. And well does she deserve it! I never knew a female so cantankersome as our kind patroness.'

'I hope you are not suggesting that Verity should go to Tunbridge Wells in the capacity of lady's maid!' objected her husband in accents of disgust.

His fond helpmeet cast him a look of scorn. 'Nothing of the sort. Lady Crossens will employ a local girl, of course. But apart from her coachman and groom, she will have none of her own people about her. Verity's assistance will therefore be invaluable to her and in such a cause I should not care to refuse to allow our daughter to go. Prudence and Patience did so well by her that it is not to be wondered at that she should be anxious to secure Verity's company. Indeed, I do not know how she will go on otherwise! I may add, you made no objection to *their* going.'

'If that is your recollection, my dear, I can only say

that it is not mine,' said her spouse with an ironic look. 'Be that as it may, and indeed taking the case of Prudence and Patience into consideration, I am doubly reluctant——'

But Mrs Lambourn had all her ammunition at her fingertips and loosed a shaft that silenced the enemy once and for all. 'Do you tell me that you would put a bar in the way of your daughter's pleasure? Why should not poor Verity also see something of the world? And that she deserves this treat, you will scarcely deny!'

Mr Lambourn was far from denying anything of the kind. He was well aware that to Verity's lot had fallen the care and entertainment, and to some extent the education, of her three younger sisters for the last few years, for Mrs Lambourn's attention had been almost entirely taken up with anxious solicitude over her one and only son in his infant days. For it was in these early years that she had lost several of those seemingly endless baby girls, as they succumbed to various ailments that proved beyond the power to mend even of the zealous practitioner who had at length become her son-in-law.

That she was assisted in this delicate task by every one of her daughters, all of whom adored their baby brother, in no way mitigated the good lady's conviction that young Master Lambourn was the child most in need of maternal devotion.

The reverend could not acquit himself of an almost equal devotion to his only son, and consequently went through periodic torments of remorse at the neglect from which he imagined his girls to be suffering. If he suspected his wife's chief motive in packing her fourth daughter off to Tunbridge Wells, he said nothing of it, merely agreeing that Verity deserved her good fortune and taking care to thank Lady Crossens in suitable style.

Her ladyship's manner of receiving these thanks, however, left him in no doubt that the whole scheme had been concerted between the two ladies for one purpose only.

'I'll do my best to get her off your hands, Harry, but, as I told Grace to her face, I don't hold out much hope. Tunbridge ain't what it was, but if any eligibles under sixty come within hailing distance I'll spread my net, never fear!'

It was on the tip of Harry Lambourn's tongue to withdraw his consent, his sense of what was fitting revolting against the idea of any of his daughters being given in matrimony to a man his own age or older. But he knew her ladyship to affect an exaggerated form of speech and so held his peace.

In truth, for all her crochets and complaints of Harry Lambourn's boundless and reckless charity, for he could ill afford it, Lady Crossens was very fond of the vicar of Tetheridge parish, which came largely under her patronage as the major landowner of the area. She had early become an ally of poor Grace Lambourn in the formidable task confronting her with so many female offspring, and had often enough lamented to her that she had no son or grandson who might take one of them to wife and so provide for the rest. Whether in fact she would have permitted such an unequal alliance had such been the case, Mrs Lambourn privately doubted. But in fact Lady Crossens had ever been childless and had no suitable nephews or near connections whom she might have offered up on the altar of matrimony to succour one of the Lambourn sisters. And her husband's heir was already a family man. Nor, since she had been invalidish for many years, was she part of the fashionable social whirl, and could not therefore take a stray Lambourn under her wing for the season in London.

What she could do, however, she did with a good heart, and, if some little return for her generosity was to be made out by services in kind, who could cavil at it? So Prudence and Patience had both had their chance in the admittedly limited opportunities of Tunbridge Wells.

And now there was Verity, who had most fortunately reached an appropriate age just when Lady Crossens should feel well enough once more to attempt the journey after some four years' absence from that favourite haunt of her golden youth.

For to Lady Crossens, as to others of her generation, Tunbridge Wells was steeped in nostalgia, and she could derive almost as much pleasure in the early nineties in talking with her cronies of the dear old days as she had enjoyed in the reality of its heyday in the forties and fifties when Beau Nash reigned supreme.

By the time the coach rumbled into the town, and fetched up outside the coach office, the questionable behaviour of Lady Crossens' protégée had given way to an argument over the identity of the man who had incurred Verity's wrath.

'From what you have said,' offered her ladyship, 'I should guess this boy Braxted has come into his inheritance a minor, and this person is his guardian.'

'Yes, that is quite possible,' Verity agreed. 'I suppose he is an uncle or cousin. He certainly exhibited the sort of breeding that would suggest a genteel background.'

'But that would not preclude his taking a post of tutor or secretary,' argued Lady Crossens. 'Indeed, one would employ none but a gentleman born on such work.'

Verity thought about this. 'I must say I should be glad to know him for something insignificant of that sort, for his conduct towards those poor children was quite abominable, and I am still very much out of charity with him! But I must confess that the other men treated him with a deference that argued against it. I am inclined to think you are right, Lady Crossens. Let us suppose him a guardian—and a remarkably bad one at that!'

'Pish! What should he do? Fawn all over them and indulge them to death like another I could——' Her ladyship broke off, belatedly recognising the infelicity of this retort.

But Verity was not in the least offended and she knew very well what the old lady had intended to say. 'Like Papa, you mean. Yes, I know he indulges us. He is the best and kindest of fathers!'

And the most sentimental, her ladyship might have added. But she did not. There was a degree of intimacy in the Lambourn family that in truth she envied a little, in spite of her strictures, and she could readily appreciate Verity's disgust at the quite different circumstances that apparently prevailed in this boy Braxted's household.

But Miss Lambourn, having settled to her satisfaction the probable station in life of her late antagonist, had moved on to indulge her ready imagination in a fantastic flight of fancy. In her mind's eye she was turning the limping, angry young man into a hideously deformed and ravening monster, who coveted his young ward's title and lands and was even now plotting to eliminate him and bury his bones in the dried-up moat surrounding his sinister castle.

Lady Crossens' voice recalled her from a scene of terror in the young lord's bedchamber, where the grotesque figure of the murdering guardian leaned over the angelic sleeping child, dagger raised ready to strike.

'Here we are!' trilled the old lady excitedly. 'Oh, do but look about you, child! Isn't it heaven? I can hardly believe it. I am back at last. Back at the Wells!'

CHAPTER TWO

'MAY I say what an inestimable pleasure it is to welcome your ladyship back among us? You have been sorely missed these last years.'

The speaker, a dapper, middle-aged gentleman with a manner that nicely blended respect with an air of self-importance, nevertheless spoke in all sincerity. Mr Richard Tyson, the present master of ceremonies for Tunbridge Wells, had a healthy fondness for any and all of the wealthy and high-ranking patrons who still chose to grace his domain in the summer. Especially those like Lady Crossens who, although holding fast to old customs, still cared to dress with the times and so keep the Wells a little in fashion.

Her ladyship had put off her travelling dress and arrayed herself for the evening in an open robe of figured French lawn over a muslin petticoat with a large cross-over handkerchief that effectively concealed her scanty bosom, and was sporting a dashing feathered turban over powdered hair which was suspiciously lush for her years.

It was not perhaps a costume that would have made fashionable London stare, but it was quite good enough for this watering place and had evoked lavish compliments from Mr Tyson. For he, and many like him, depended on this custom for their livelihood, although the increasing number of new residents was beginning to boost the hitherto meagre pickings during the rest of the year.

'You will find us very little changed,' Mr Tyson said comfortably, 'though we have done what we may to improve the amenities. The Walks have been repaved this year, you know.' He coughed and, with a sly sideways glance at Lady Crossens, corrected himself. 'The *Parade*, I should say, for so it has now been decided to designate it.'

'Parade? Parade?' echoed her ladyship in disbelieving tones. 'Bless me, Mr Tyson, whatever next?'

The master of ceremonies shrugged and spread his hands, uttering in a self-deprecatory tone belied by the smirk about his mouth, 'Wiser heads than mine, Lady Crossens, wiser heads than mine!'

'Pish and tush! "Parade" indeed! They shall never hear such a nonsense on *my* lips, I promise you.'

'Are you speaking of the Pantiles?' asked Verity, rather at a loss.

'The *Walks*, ma'am,' explained Mr Tyson, 'was used to be the official title.'

'Pho!' ejaculated the old lady. 'The Pantiles it has ever been, and will so continue, mark my words! All these new-fangled ideas. I dare say I may find every pleasant custom overset, never mind that poor old Nash may be turning in his grave!'

'By no means, I assure you, dear lady,' said Mr Tyson reassuringly. 'You will find everything just as it used to be. We still have our little pleasures in the Rooms—our concerts and balls, and *cards*, as I know you will be glad to hear.'

'Ah!' sighed Lady Crossens with satisfaction. 'Yes, I have missed my whist. Of balls you may speak to my companion. I am not going to make a figure of myself in the minuet at my age!'

The master of ceremonies turned obligingly to where Verity was seated, by the windows of the little parlour from where she was enjoying a view of the main thoroughfare of Tunbridge Wells. For the lodgings that Lady Crossens had taken, as she always did, were only a couple of doors down from the coach office, in a suite of first-floor rooms situated directly over the paved walkway affectionately known as the Pantiles.

The effect in the still light summer evening was very pretty. On the pavings below a number of persons, in pairs and groups, were strolling gently. Across the way ran an avenue of graceful trees concealing to some degree the buildings on the other side. A theatre was visible, though clearly just now uninhabited, and a species of large hall from which plentiful light streamed. There was a small musicians' gallery, with trellis barrier and pretty columns and, looking down the Pantiles, there could just be seen the end of the colonnade that Verity had been told ran the length of the street under the low roofs below her. There was a sound of music and an occasional trill of laughter floated up to the open window.

A rising thrill of pleasure fluttered in Verity's breast as she accepted with a word of thanks a copy of the master of ceremonies' rules and regulations as Mr Tyson enumerated the entertainments on offer.

These appeared to be considerable to one accustomed to the quiet backwater that constituted Tetheridge village. Verity hoped her modest wardrobe would be adequate to meet the demand likely to be placed upon it. Unlike her patroness, she had donned a simple chemise undress gown of sprigged cotton and threaded a bandeau through her dark curls.

But it looked as if she must soon delve into her supply of more formal attire. The programme promised two balls a week with minuets, a cotillion and country dances, as well as recitals and theatrical entertainments. All this besides chatting with the company in the coffee-rooms and meeting at the spring to drink the waters of a morning.

'Not that I should suppose, with so charming a

complexion, you have any need to do that,' said Mr Tyson gallantly.

Verity laughed. 'No indeed! I am in excellent health. Though I shall be surprised if it does not break down in all this gaiety. Upon my word, I had not looked for such a round of dissipation!'

'Well, well,' the gentleman uttered, visibly gratified. 'I believe we are not quite in a decline.'

'Decline! I dare say I shall be obliged to leave you all to your revels and take to my bed with a good book within the week!'

Laughing heartily at this pleasantry, Richard Tyson assured her that in that case she might surely find some suitable tale on the shelves of one of the two circulating libraries.

'I recall your sister—Miss *Prudence*, I think?— partaking very lavishly of such delights some years ago.'

'Oh, yes, Prue told me how happy she was to find all the latest published novels immediately to hand. I shall certainly follow her example.'

It did not take many days for Verity to become familiar with all there was to do and see in the social centre of Tunbridge Wells. She very quickly became acquainted with everyone, residents and visitors alike, and so was instantly able to pick out an alien face as she hurried from the Assembly Rooms to execute a commission for Lady Crossens.

A light drizzle was falling and, clutching her pelisse about her, she ran quickly across the Walks towards the shelter of the colonnade on the other side. She stood for a moment, shaking off the drops and pushing her hood back off her dark curls. She caught sight as she did so of someone standing before one of the shop windows, looking at the wares displayed there.

At once she knew he was a stranger, and choked back the automatic greeting with which everyone saluted one another as they met in the street. The place was all but deserted on this inclement morning, and she hesitated a moment or two, uncertain whether to proceed. Then the man turned his head at some slight sound she made and shock rippled through her chest.

It was he! That same pale face under the plain beaver hat. She could not mistake! And as her eyes dropped down as if to verify the fact, she noted the cane, which had been slightly hidden by the folds of his greatcoat, on which he leaned a little.

She saw the startled recognition leap into his eyes and knew a moment of sheer panic. Should she greet him? What could she say? That awkward meeting at which she had not hesitated to lash out at him! And the brief, sardonic comment he had made that showed how mannerless he had thought her conduct!

The whole, almost forgotten scene flashed back to her in vivid detail and she felt her cheeks grow hot with embarrassment. Heavens, she must get away!

Her errand was to Mr Sprange's place and her way unfortunately led past the shop where the gentleman stood. Lowering her gaze to the paving, she began to move. But, in spite of herself, she could not resist a peep up at him as she passed. It was a mistake.

Her eyes looked straight into those black ones and her feet stopped of their own volition. It was only for a brief moment she hovered thus, but he lifted a hand to his beaver and doffed it, bowing slightly.

Verity's cheeks flamed anew. She gave the tiniest of nods in response and hurried on, her heart thudding so hard that she felt breathless.

Absurd! What in the world was the matter with her? The man was a monster! Had she not intervened, he would undoubtedly have beaten that poor little boy

Braxted. She had no reason to feel discomfited. It was, on the contrary, he who should feel mortified, meeting once more the stranger who had been obliged to take him to task!

It occurred to her suddenly that there had not been any sign of discomfiture, either in this brief glimpse she had just had of those black eyes, or at the time. Had he been chagrined? Abashed? He had not! Instead he had had the temerity to laugh at her!

Arrived in Mr Sprange's shop, it was with the words and smiles of an automaton that she responded to the lad who served her, requesting the playbill for Mrs Baker's next theatrical presentation with scarcely a thought to what she was about. Fortunately there was little chance of the assistant mistaking her needs, for there was only the one theatre in Tunbridge Wells and Mrs Sarah Baker had a monopoly on the productions that were staged there.

She dawdled over the various prints and bills of coming events, hoping desperately that the young stranger would go away. There was no sign of him when she eventually came out of the shop, but as she made her way back to the Assembly Rooms she was conscious of a slight feeling of disappointment.

The capacious building she entered was the central meeting place and the venue for most of the season's events. The rooms were large and airy, with huge columns and marbled ornamentation after the fashion of those in Bath. But they contrived, perhaps because of the many knots of people seated in the alcoves made by settees and well-placed screens, to appear remarkably cosy. Yet when the main room was cleared for dancing, its size showed to advantage.

In one of the corners near to the adjoining card-room, the lady's favourite haunt, Verity found Lady Crossens deep in conversation with an elderly widow,

Mrs Polegate, whom Verity had already come to know well. For this crony of her patroness was an almost constant companion, and it had been obvious to the young lady when Mrs Polegate visited them on their first evening that her two elders were ripe for a high old time.

A greater contrast to Lady Crossens could not have been found than this lifelong friend. She was a dewy-eyed sentimental dame, with the mind of a butterfly, who took the world as it presented itself to her eyes, never troubling to look beneath the surface. She had none of the shrewdness that characterised her friend, but equally none of her acerbity. Inveterately though she gossiped, she had not a particle of malice in her nature, and this trait endeared her to her friends even while the more discerning among them dubbed her a fool—including Lady Crossens, who did not scruple to call her so to her face.

'Dear Emilia, I was quite overcome with happiness when you wrote you was coming at last,' she had fluttered that night, her plump countenance wreathed in smiles that crumpled the remnants of an erstwhile prettiness into a multitude of wrinkles. 'I declare, it has been a desert here without you! And last year in particular, when we had such frolics and jaunterings about—so delightful!'

'If it was so delightful, my presence can have only been superfluous,' said Lady Crossens drily, unimpressed by the worth of her friend's protestations.

'Oh, yes, but your being there would have added so much to our pleasure,' uttered the other lady sincerely.

Biting back a laugh, Verity wondered if Mrs Polegate was merely impervious to irony or quite incapable of recognising her own inconsistencies. Lady Crossens had no such doubts.

'Your wit has not improved in my absence, at any rate, Maria.'

'Oh, but I am not at all clever, Emilia. You know I am not.' She looked across at Verity. 'I never was, you know. Poor Emilia has had much ado to put up with my silliness all these years.'

'Pish!' scoffed her ladyship, adding gruffly, 'You're a good-hearted girl, Maria. And that, believe me, counts for a deal more than a sharp tongue.'

To hear her patroness address a lady quite her own age as a *girl* almost overset Verity, but she contrived to keep her countenance, smiling kindly at the visitor.

'Very true, ma'am. But I wish you will tell me, Mrs Polegate, how you became acquainted.'

'Oh, I know what you mean! So unlikely a friendship, don't you feel?' said the lady, displaying so unexpectedly accurate an understanding of Verity's thought that she felt herself redden a little. But Mrs Polegate did not appear to notice. 'You may say we are *Wellsian* friends, I suppose, for we met here, both in our very first season. What days they were! Dancing on the green! Do you not remember, Emilia?'

'Do I not! I ruined my best satin shoes and lost a diamond buckle!'

'How your mama did scold!'

Like all the elderly habituées of Tunbridge Wells, the two ladies were forever to be heard reminiscing about the 'dear old days'. Today was no exception, and while they rattled on Verity had time to recover her poise, which had been very much overset by the unexpected encounter with the angry young man of her adventure.

She therefore greeted the sight of the widow's plump, unsuitably clothed figure with relief now. For in spite of Lady Crossens' freely expressed criticisms, Mrs Polegate arrayed herself always in the chemise gowns she loved, exposing a good deal of bosom and demonstrating the girth of her thickened waistline all too clearly with the gathered-in style, and the sash that all but vanished between the rolls of flesh above and below. She was addicted, moreover, to large mob-caps which most unflatteringly framed her round pink face and only added to the unfortunate impression of mutton dressed as lamb.

'And of course you recall that dreadful Mrs Montagu and her blue-stocking set,' she was saying to her friend. 'So clever! I never could understand the half of her discourse.'

'That woman!' Lady Crossens snorted. 'She was not near so clever as she would have us believe. Setting herself up for a queen to all the men of letters! I was never so happy as when her coach overturned.'

'Oh, no, ma'am, how uncharitable!' exclaimed Verity, startled out of her preoccupation.

'Oh, yes, Emilia,' echoed Mrs Polegate. '*Poor* Mrs Montagu! Not but what the coach did not in fact overturn. But she was very much shaken.'

'Poor Mrs Montagu indeed!' said her ladyship impenitently. 'You had as well say poor Miss Chudleigh!'

'If I had not forgotten her!' shrieked Mrs Polegate. 'Scandalous, shameless woman!'

'Why, what did she do?' asked Verity, glad of something sufficiently diverting to keep at bay the intrusive memories of a certain gentleman.

'What did she not do?' countered Lady Crossens.

'Well, my dear,' began Mrs Polegate, with an air of unfolding a great mystery, 'Elizabeth Chudleigh was an extremely beautiful lady and the gentlemen were mad for her, but in the end she married the Duke of Kingston. And *then* it transpired that she was already married!'

'And so it all came out,' put in Lady Crossens. 'She was tried for bigamy by the House of Lords.'

'And convicted?' asked Verity, quite shocked.

'Oh, yes,' said Mrs Polegate. 'But they could do nothing about it, for she *was* a peeress! She was ruined, naturally. But she went abroad——'

'Taking, so it was said, the Duke's money with her.'

'Yes, but, Emilia, he *was* dead.'

Verity was betrayed into a choke of laughter. 'Gracious! I had no idea Tunbridge Wells was such a den of vice!'

'Oh, but all *that* occurred in London, you know,' said Mrs Polegate excusingly. 'She behaved *quite* respectably here. And she was very beautiful.'

'Does that make it any better?'

'Beauty and wit may generally excuse a good deal,' said Lady Crossens shrewdly. 'Not that there has been much of the latter in evidence at the Wells.'

'But, Emilia, only think of the Water Poets!' protested the widow. 'Some of the verses were very witty. And so elegant and pretty.'

'Who in the world are the Water Poets?' demanded Verity.

'Anyone who could turn a verse. Or, indeed, who *thought* they could,' her ladyship explained.

'They were used to write verses in a book kept at the bookseller's on the Walks. We—I mean the ladies, for they were nearly always written in compliment to one of us—were used to go daily to read them.'

'Yes, and afterwards scratch out the eyes of those so honoured, or, if one should be oneself chosen, peacock about the place well set up in one's own conceit.'

Verity smiled. 'Now I understand why you return here year after year, dear ma'am. Tell me, did Lord Crossens address such verses to you?'

Her ladyship's lips twitched, for anyone less romantic

than her bucolic lord would be hard to imagine. 'Oh, I was no subject for such fripperies. Too tall, too skinny. Always was. But Maria had many an admirer pen his ardour thus.'

'Oh, Emilia!' protested the good lady, blushing.

'Well, you were an uncommonly pretty girl, Maria, I will say that for you. But Mr Polegate—God rest his soul!—who was *not* the handsomest of men, nevertheless carried her off in the teeth of them all.'

'Oh, yes,' sighed Mrs Polegate. 'Dear William! What days they were!' Her smiling face reached Verity's and fell suddenly. 'But how dull it must be for you, poor Miss Lambourn! Alas, we have no water poets now!' She shook her head sadly so that the frill of her ridiculous mob-cap rippled. 'Scarcely any young persons at all, let alone eligible gentlemen of rank and fortune. I am afraid you must find it sadly flat.'

'Oh, no,' Verity disclaimed at once. 'Though I must say it seems sadly expensive. Why, there is a fee and a gratuity to be dropped at every hand!'

'Very true. They are shocking robbers!' agreed Mrs Polegate in a hushed voice, casting glances about as if she expected to be set upon there and then.

'Don't be ridiculous, Maria!' scolded Lady Crossens in a lowered tone. 'You know very well all the servitors depend upon gratuities for their livelihood.'

'So they do!' Mrs Polegate said, apparently struck, although in fact she regularly tipped lavishly without giving the matter a thought.

'And you need not concern yourself with such matters, Verity,' added her ladyship. 'I will take care of all that.'

Miss Lambourn could only be thankful. The Vicar was not a poor man, but his small personal fortune and the stipend of his profession had been very much dissipated by the exigencies of keeping a large family, and all the girls had been bred in habits of the strictest economy. To have been obliged to defray the innumerable little impositions of such persons as water-dippers, waiters, sweepers and even the minister who attended the King Charles Chapel, not to mention the master of ceremonies himself, would have seriously embarrassed her slender purse.

It seemed, a day later, that she might do so in quite another matter. She was idling in one of the toy shops that abounded under the colonnade. These places provided all the little knick-knacks, both useful and merely decorative, that anyone might require: snuff-boxes, ivory notecases, thimble-holders or pincushions; metal buckles or brooches, candlesnuffers and scissors, corkscrews, needle and bodkin cases; and little pieces of gilt jewellery. Any sort of oddment, in fact, that might be fashioned in a pretty way to delight or amuse. But they also sold the wooden goods that had come to be known as Tunbridge Ware, and which Verity so much liked that she had already whiled away a good many moments examining them.

Having been greeted by the friendly proprietor, she spent some time looking with great interest at a number of writing-cases and boxes of one sort and another, all beautifully made with designs of inlaid wood in a variety of colours.

She had just picked up a large box and, on opening it, had found it to contain another, smaller version, when the shop door opened. Turning her head, Verity saw first a cane, and then the neatly garbed figure of a young man limping through the doorway.

It was *he* again!

She gasped with shock, and the box fell from her agitated fingers, breaking open on the floor and scattering its inner secrets in every direction. To Verity's horrified eyes, it appeared as if there were broken boxes everywhere she looked in the confined space of the shop, although in fact the nest was composed only of four.

'Oh, gracious heaven!' she uttered distractedly, bounding forward and stooping to retrieve them.

The proprietor, tutting distressfully, came out from behind his little counter to assist.

'No, no, madam. Allow me!'

'So stupid!' Verity muttered, aware of burning cheeks. 'I am so very sorry!'

'No matter, no matter.'

The unwitting cause of the commotion stood quite still, one hand resting on the doorknob, the other grasping his cane as he watched the two of them scramble for the boxes. As they began to fit them back together, he let go the handle of the door and gently reached out to touch Verity's arm. Her clear gaze came up to meet his in an enquiring look, though her heightened colour demonstrated her intense embarrassment.

'I beg your pardon,' he said quietly, 'but this last little errant knave appears to have escaped your notice.'

So saying, he poked with his cane at a very small box which had stayed intact and had come to rest by the door. Easing it into the room, he added, 'I regret that I am unable to perform the correctly gallant action and pick it up for you.'

But the proprietor was already seizing the box from the floor as the spontaneous smile sprang to Verity's lips.

'Oh, pray don't trouble yourself on that account! Indeed, it was shockingly careless of me.'

'I had rather have said it was careless of me—to have so unkindly startled you, I mean.'

'You didn't—it wasn't——' Verity stammered, flushing again.

She was rescued by the proprietor, requesting her to hand him the remaining box she still held.

'I hope they are not damaged,' she said anxiously. 'Such a beautiful piece of workmanship!'

The shopkeeper was examining the boxes with a sharp eye for any scratches, but at length he somewhat grudgingly professed himself satisfied that no harm had been done.

'Thank goodness!' Verity said, with a sigh of relief. She could not but have offered to buy the boxes had they been spoiled, and she knew the price of them to be well beyond her means, and was thankful to be spared the necessity of making such an offer.

But it was plain from the proprietor's expression that he thought she should have done so in any event. Before he could say anything, however, the young stranger intervened.

'I have no doubt that the boxes are as good as ever,' he said in the quiet well-bred tone that seemed to be habitual to him. 'Wood, you know, can stand a great deal of wear and tear.'

It crossed Verity's mind fleetingly that he looked rather meaningfully at the proprietor as he spoke, but as she was only too anxious to encourage this point of view, the thought quickly passed away.

'That is very true. Though perhaps, as it is inlay work, it might be a trifle more delicate?'

'Not at all,' said the gentleman instantly, responding to the note of appeal in her voice. 'I have known whole tables and armoires of inlay that have lasted a good century and more. The wood is no less durable for being put together in small pieces, you know.'

'I devoutly hope you are right,' Verity said frankly.

'Unlike the other day,' he returned smoothly, 'when you very definitely felt me to be wrong!'

The betraying colour rushed into Verity's cheeks and she stared up at him in mingled dismay and indignation. How could he bring that up now? Just when she was beginning to warm to him! And there was that gleam again in the depths of his black eyes. He was laughing at her! She drew herself up.

'You must excuse me,' she said stiffly. 'I have an errand to perform.'

'No, pray——' he began, putting out a hand.

But Verity had already stepped past him to the door. She wrenched it open and saw his hand drop. Next instant, she had left the shop and was hurrying away down the colonnade.

Until this moment, she had thought of her actions that day as perfectly justified. Now, suddenly she saw them as they must appear in the eyes of this man. A strange young woman, escorted only by a groom, accosting him in the middle of his legitimate business and taking him to task in front of a number of servants. By rights he should have been either angry or ashamed. Or both. But it was evident that the episode was to him merely amusing. He must take her for a very odd sort of a female, she supposed. Indeed, considered from his point of view, she imagined her conduct must have seemed positively eccentric! How mortifying it was to reflect that the man she had been busy despising had been enjoying a laugh at her expense all this while! Had she righted a wrong about which the perpetrator remained quite undisturbed?

These worrying thoughts occupied her, all that day and into the next morning, almost to the exclusion of all else, so that it was perhaps fortunate that she was obliged dutifully to escort Lady Crossens from one place to the next. It seemed in her preoccupation that the same conversations took place over and over again, only with different persons. There were few young people about, those in evidence mostly, like herself, in attendance on their elders unless, as with a few, a slow carriage or wan features dictated an obvious reason for their presence.

But Verity had not lacked company, for although she could not believe that Lady Crossens' acquaintance were particularly anxious to meet her—for she was no beauty!—the master of ceremonies took his duties seriously, and made it his business to perform introductions.

On this particular morning, after they had gravitated to the Assembly Rooms, she had just seen her ladyship settled and was moving away, when she was accosted by a gentleman whom her patroness always stigmatised an old bore, for all that he had been presented as the resident Wellsian playwright. It appeared that he had seen her reading the playbill for Mrs Baker's forthcoming productions.

'Are you a lover of the theatre, Miss Lambourn?' demanded Richard Cumberland.

'I regret that I have had no opportunity to find out,' Verity answered candidly. 'I have never been farther afield than Winchester before, you see.'

'Do you mean to say that you have never witnessed a theatrical production?' asked the gentleman, shocked.

'I believe I did so once as a child,' Verity said, feeling as if she ought to be apologising for this lack in her education.

But Mr Cumberland beamed. 'Then it will be our privilege to introduce you to the greatest pleasure a man may enjoy.'

'The greatest? What of reading?'

'Pshaw! Mere books, Miss Lambourn, are nothing

compared to the live rendition of words! It shall be my happiness, ma'am, to prove this to you. Yes, yes, I shall read you one of my own plays.'

'God help you!' murmured a voice close to Verity's ear.

She turned her head to find standing rather too close to her an old gentleman who was another of the local residents. For all his age, Sir John Frinton was something of an exquisite. Although he refrained from adopting the extravagant costume of a dandy, he was always elegant, as today, in suits all of a piece with the exception of his waistcoats, which were flowered or striped. But he adhered both to his wig and his powder, and was always rouged with a provocative patch, in spite of fashion's decree against such an outdated adornment.

'Really, Cumberland,' he went on, addressing the playwright, but with a wink at Verity, 'enough to put the poor girl off for life!'

'Sir!' uttered the playwright, outraged, his cheeks reddening. 'You are offensive!'

'I am sure Sir John is funning,' Verity put in quickly. She found Sir John's nearness cloying and edged away a fraction. 'For my part, I should be happy to hear one of your plays, Mr Cumberland, though I would be loath to trespass upon your time.'

'I should not grudge a moment of it,' responded the other, gratified.

Verity bestowed her friendly smile on him. 'You are very kind, sir.'

'There now, Cumberland, you are amply rewarded,' said Sir John, thrusting his tall person rudely between them. 'You may take yourself off now and leave Miss Lambourn's entertainment to me.'

Mr Cumberland, his features darkening, compressed his lips, bowed to the lady and moved away, leaving

Verity wondering whether this acceptance of defeat
sprang from a dislike of quarrelling before a lady or
the fact that Sir John was his social superior, not to
mention the undeniable advantage of his slim, tall
figure as against the playwright's portly frame. Sir
John, meanwhile, smiling at her in triumph, was calmly
possessing himself of her hand.

'His plays are tedious in the extreme, Miss Lambourn,
and so I warn you! You will find my company far more
amusing.'

'Will I indeed?' said Verity politely, removing her
fingers from his clutch. 'How is that?'

A pair of thin lips curved in a smile that must once
have been ravishing, and which still had some power to
attract. 'Long practice, my dear.'

Verity had to laugh. But she said severely, 'And do
you always practise on ladies who might well be your
grandchildren?'

'Naturally,' said Sir John suavely, not in the least
abashed. 'Or at least, whenever possible.'

'I take it that is not very often in Tunbridge Wells.'

'Alas, no. And there is always a duenna to spoil
sport.'

He sighed as he spoke, looking over to where Lady
Crossens sat, glaring across at him. He turned back to
Verity, ruefully grinning.

'She knows I am not a marrying man, you see.
Otherwise, I dare say I should receive all kinds of
encouragement.'

'My dear sir, I assure you I am not on the catch for
a husband,' Verity said indignantly. 'And if I
were——'

'Emilia would scarce consider me an eligible parti
for you,' he finished, laughing. 'But she would, you
know. There are so few of us bachelors at the Wells.'

'Well, even if *she* did, I would not!' declared Verity frankly.

'Ah, so you *are* on the catch for a husband!' teased the old man.

'I am nothing of the sort!' Verity said, rather flustered, as she tried to banish from her mind the picture of a pale-featured face that had unaccountably jumped into it. 'I have quite other plans, as it happens.'

He looked intrigued and would have enquired further into the matter, but that Lady Crossens was making unmistakable signs for Miss Lambourn to go over and join her.

'Your guardian is growing anxious,' he said with a twinkle, 'so I must let you go. I shall look forward to another such exchange.'

Verity only smiled and left him, but her eyes followed the old man as he wandered about the room in search of other prey. Her imagination was afire: the attractive smile on his thin lips spreading rapidly into a wolfish grin as he towered over the shrinking form of the young and lovely heroine, manoeuvring her into a corner while the flickering candlelight played tantalisingly over the white swell of her bosom where his lascivious eyes rested.

Her thoughts were interrupted by her patroness's voice. She turned to find that Lady Crossens was on the fidgets.

'Bless me, if I had not forgot to warn you about John!' she was saying in an urgent undervoice. 'It was most remiss of me! Now you must be on your guard, Verity.'

'Against what, ma'am? Surely you cannot think me so foolish as to fall in love with a man who must be old enough to have sired my own father.'

'There is no saying what young girls will do,' said her ladyship acidly. 'Do not be taken in by his amusing ways, child. He is a confirmed rake and has been so from a boy!'

'Have no fear, ma'am! If I was to be taken in, it would be by—by someone far other than Sir John Frinton!'

Lady Crossens' attention was claimed then by one of her friends, so that she did not notice the telltale colour that had crept into her protégée's cheeks.

Murmuring an excuse of having forgotten something at their lodging, Miss Lambourn sneaked quietly out of the Assembly Rooms and wandered under the shade of the trees beside the Pantiles where the market women sold fruit and vegetables. Her thoughts were very far from the vendors crying out their wares as she passed.

That man! How dared he force his way into her mind, cutting up her peace? Just because a gentleman had a pair of black eyes that seemed to pierce a path into a person's very soul, was that any reason for him to come barging in where he was least wanted? As if there was any danger of her being 'taken in' by such a man! How idiotic it was of her even to think of him in such a connection!

Her aimless feet had taken her to the end of the tiled walkway, and as she turned to retrace her steps, a familiar sound broke her absorption. Just as she identified the dot and carry tapping of a cane on the pavings, she saw the limping leg from the corner of her eye.

Turning, she looked up just as the young man stepped forward to intercept her.

'Oh, no!' she uttered faintly.

'I do beg your pardon,' he said a little diffidently, 'but I must beg the favour of a word.'

Confronted so suddenly with the subject of her thoughts, confusion engulfed Verity, and she responded so curtly as to be almost rude. 'Well, what is it?'

A frown came into his eyes. 'I will not keep you long, ma'am. Though I came here today expressly to find you.'

'To find me? Gracious heaven! But why?'

'For a sufficient purpose, which you will learn if you will give me a moment of your time.'

Nettled by his manner, Verity snapped, 'Well, sir?'

His tone became much less cordial. 'It is nothing very much. Merely that I thought you might care to take possession of these.' He held out a package towards her.

Verity's eyes widened, for the size and shape was all too familiar. 'Is that——? I hope that is not——' She broke off, staring at him in rising indignation. 'Are you offering me that nest of boxes I dropped yesterday?'

'Well, yes, ma'am. I really have no use for them and——'

'Upon my word!' Verity burst out. 'After all you said about wood and—and inlay lasting so well! You have actually gone and purchased the wretched things!'

'It is usual in such circumstances,' he said coldly. 'But I could see very well that——'

'That I was reluctant to purchase them myself!' Verity finished furiously. 'And so you have shown me up to be either mean or poor in the eyes of that man, and I shall never be able to enter his shop again!'

The gentleman's face fell ludicrously. 'Good God, ma'am! I never intended anything of the kind!'

'No! Just as you never intended to make a mistake in the matter of poor Braxted. Never have I come upon a more high-handed, arrogant manner of conduct!'

The black eyes sparked sudden fire, but the calm voice was like ice. 'Indeed, ma'am? Then it ill becomes me to force it upon you further. I will wish you a very good day.'

Turning on his heel, the gentleman limped off across the Pantiles, the cane echoing his uneven step as it sounded an overloud tattoo on the pavings.

Verity stood watching him go, fighting an irrational urge to chase after him with a mouthful of apologies.

CHAPTER THREE

PULLING herself together, Miss Lambourn straightened her shoulders and walked quickly back to the Assembly Rooms, her mind in disorder.

Why should she apologise? she thought crossly. Was it not he who was guilty of an unpardonable liberty? Without so much as a by your leave, he had taken it upon himself to compensate the proprietor of the toy shop—and now she thought of it, remembering the look he had bestowed upon the man, he had planned it at the outset!—for a piece of negligence that had nothing whatever to do with him. It was *her* responsibility, and, if she saw no need to buy the boxes, what right had he to interfere? And then to offer them to her, positively rubbing her nose in her own blunder!

Here, however, Miss Lambourn's innate honesty intervened. No such malice had been intended, she knew. It might have been more tactful to have kept his charitable act to himself, but at least the man had meant nothing but kindness. He had evidently perceived—how she could not begin to guess—that she was unable to recompense the owner of the shop herself, and had stepped in to relieve her of the necessity. For if he had thought her merely tight-fisted he would not have tried to bestow the boxes upon her. And now, she reflected, a trifle conscience-stricken, the poor man was stuck with a set of perfectly useless items!

As she decided, rather reprehensibly, that it served him right, a giggle escaped her.

'What an age you have been, child!' came the voice of Lady Crossens, startling her back into awareness.

As Verity's gaze focused on the old lady's face, she saw that she was being sharply scrutinised.

'You look positively impish, girl! What mischief are you brewing?'

'None, upon my honour, ma'am,' Verity said earnestly, but there was a telltale colour in her cheeks.

'Don't tell me! *Something* has occurred to bring that look to your face. And you were chortling as you came in. I heard you.'

To her confusion, Verity found herself the cynosure of several pairs of eyes, Lady Crossens' remarks having been clearly audible to the friends she had about her. She noted with dismay that not only was Mrs Polegate looking at her with avid interest, but the teasing eyes of Sir John Frinton were also fixed upon her. Miss Lambourn, unused to society, and brought up imbued with her reverend father's conviction of the efficacy of the virtues of truth and honesty, was quite unable to prevaricate.

'If you must have it, ma'am,' she said as if the words were forced from her, 'I have had another encounter with that man we met on the road.'

For a moment Lady Crossens looked blank. 'What man?'

'With the children, ma'am. On our way here, remember?'

'Oh, him! Bless me, you have not quarrelled with the wretched fellow again, I hope!'

'Well, yes, ma'am, I am afraid I have,' Verity confessed. 'It was all rather unfortunate. But quite an accident and very much my own fault.'

'But what in the world. . .?'

'Dear ma'am, do not ask me!' Verity begged in a

low tone, with a significant glance cast at the people about them. 'I will tell you the whole presently.'

'Heavens, yes!' uttered her ladyship, recollecting herself. 'What am I about? Here, John, don't you go asking any awkward questions! Nor you, Maria.'

'Oh, Emilia, as if I would!'

'Well, mind you don't!' conjured Lady Crossens, unimpressed. 'I know you, Maria. Gossip mad, you are!'

She turned to Sir John, but he met the challenge in her eyes with a bland smile. 'I am silent as the tomb, dear Emilia. I would not for the world embarrass Miss Lambourn.' He gave his arm to Mrs Polegate. 'Come, Maria. Let us take ourselves off and leave the ladies to converse in private.'

'I don't know how he conceives the Assembly Rooms to be private,' said Lady Crossens as they strolled away. 'You had better tell me everything over dinner.'

But when in due course Verity told the story, she had had sufficient time in which to calm down and the fluent account she gave of the brief meetings that had occurred was so prosaic that the elder lady had nothing to say, beyond a wry comment that she could not see what Miss Lambourn had found to amuse her.

Mrs Polegate, however, proved less reticent than her old friend had hoped. The next day being Sunday, Verity was up betimes to take herself to early morning service while Lady Crossens joined the daily routine of drinking the waters.

The Tunbridge Wells social scene being entirely encompassed in the area of the Pantiles, it was impossible for Verity, walking to and from the King Charles Chapel at the far end of it beyond the well itself, where the water-dippers dispensed their glasses of health-giving liquid, to miss the early morning ceremony of taking the waters.

It was amusing to see all the valetudinarians wandering about in their dishabille. The ladies were in undress gowns, chemise robes closed from bosom to hem with buttons or ribbon ties, worn with or without a sash, their hair tucked into mob-caps or turbans. The gentlemen sported brocaded dressing-gowns of virulent hue, full length and tied with a girdle, or, in the case of Indian banyans, falling to the knee and magnificently frogged. Their shaven heads were covered by velvet nightcaps, except for those modern-minded gentlemen, who had fallen into the coming fashion of wearing their own hair, some of whom saw fit to twist their greying locks into rag curlers which stuck out all over their heads.

The company seemed quite unconcerned at the extraordinary picture they presented, and it was, to Verity, a question whether they came there to partake of the health-giving chalybeate spring, or to meet their acquaintance. For the chatter and laughter quite outdid the groans at their aches and ailments and complaints of the bitter taste of the waters. Lady Crossens was in her element, her scrawny figure almost darting about as she greeted some newly arrived old friends with enthusiasm and traced in exhaustive detail their several meanderings in the intervening years since her last visit.

After a hearty breakfast, once Lady Crossens was more comformably dressed, they went over to the ladies' coffee-room for another bout of gossip, and again, when that palled, passed across the Pantiles to the Lower Assembly Rooms for yet more of the same, for there were no dances and no card playing on the Sabbath. Verity found a chair a little way behind that of her patroness, and here she was very soon joined by the plump form of Mrs Polegate.

'Poor Miss Lambourn! Are you dreadfully bored?' began that lady, innocently enough.

Verity turned to find the widow had seated herself with a rustle of her wide taffeta petticoats, and was regarding her with a kind of wistful pity.

'Not at all, ma'am,' she said smiling. 'There is no occasion for you to worry yourself on my account. I am doing very well.'

'Oh, I do hope so,' said the lady mournfully. 'It is so melancholy to see young people moped quite to death.'

'Gracious me, ma'am, I promise you I am nothing of the kind!' She saw that the lady looked unconvinced and added cheerfully, 'One must of necessity be quiet on a Sunday, you know.'

'That is true. I abominate Sundays for that very reason, do not you?'

'Being a clergyman's daughter, ma'am, I cannot say that I do,' Verity replied, twinkling.

'Of course, yes. How silly!' laughed the widow merrily. 'I suppose you would not look for excitement and adventure at all.'

'Oh, I am not the less anxious for them on that account, believe me!'

'No, of course you are not! How should you be, so young and full of life as you are?' Her expression changed as she leaned closer and said on an enquiring note, 'And as to adventure, you rather hinted at some such thing yesterday, I think.'

'Oh, that!' Verity said offhandedly. 'Well, you could call it that. Really, it was nothing.'

'Do not say so! A *man*! And children, was it?' asked Mrs Polegate, her eyes avid with anticipation in their frame of white lace. 'Did it happen on your way here?'

'Well, yes,' confessed Miss Lambourn, sure that her patroness would disapprove. But she was incapable of deception and knew not how to parry the other lady's probing without discourtesy. Moreover, she was by now quite anxious to know the identity of the man who would persist in crossing her path, and she thought perhaps Mrs Polegate might be able to enlighten her.

She told the tale as briefly as she could, and, although the widow did not listen without a good deal of exclamatory comment, she no sooner heard the name Braxted than she identified it at once.

'Mercy! They must have been Salmesbury's children!'

'Salmesbury, ma'am?'

'From Braxted Park,' announced the lady, as if this must explain all. 'The Marquis, you know.'

'*Marquis*! But the boy——'

'Oh, the boy is the Earl of Braxted. An honorary title, of course.'

'Oh.' Verity blinked. 'We quite thought he must have come into his inheritance a minor.'

'Oh, no, indeed. The Marquis is still a young man, I believe. Not that I know him. I doubt if anyone here does, for no one of that sort comes to the Wells any more,' she said regretfully.

'But then, the man who took charge of him.' An appalling thought came into her mind. But no! No, it was not possible! 'Mrs Polegate, he *surely* cannot have been the Marquis?'

'I should not think so at all. I dare say the Marquis is at Brighton. These great men, you know, are rarely at home. No, no. Some minion, no doubt, entrusted with the care of the estate.'

Which summarily disposed of that dreadful suspicion! thought Verity thankfully. She must otherwise have died of mortification! Of course he could not have been the Marquis! These men of high estate had better things to do with their time than to chase after errant children, had they not? Why, he and the Marchioness must of course be *far* too occupied with—with balls and—and routs and the like, to bother their august heads with poor Braxted and his sister Peggy! No, indeed. That sort of mundane consideration fell into the far from amiable hands of this steward, or secretary, or whatever he might be.

Here Verity's conscience intervened. She was unjust. He had shown himself to be both thoughtful and amiable, to *her* at least. Indeed, she could almost find herself liking him, were it not for that wickedly quizzing gleam in his eye! It would give her a great deal of satisfaction to tell him what she thought of his misplaced amusement! Not that she supposed he would ever speak to her again, she acknowledged wryly, after the manner of their last parting.

This thought was so unpalatable that she tried to shake the whole memory of the black-eyed young man from her mind and force her thoughts into other channels.

A day or so later, having dismally failed in this object, sheer exasperation drove her to *take steps*. Accordingly, she left Lady Crossens to indulge in a lie-in, for the old lady's chancy constitution was beginning to wilt a little under the dissipations she was enjoying.

'Shall I fetch a physician to you, ma'am?' Verity had asked her worriedly.

'Don't dare! I won't have any of those old fossils fussing about me: I have enough to bear of that at home!'

'But if you are ill, ma'am——'

'Pho! I am nothing of the kind. Merely a little tired. Don't fidget me, girl! I shall rest a little longer today, and get up only in time to catch up with Maria at the Rooms.'

Verity looked doubtful, but as her ladyship was insistent, ordering her from the room at last, she gave up and took herself to Baldock's library which was situated towards that end of the colonnade nearest to the chalybeate spring.

She spent an agreeable hour browsing amongst the books on offer there, hesitating between the latest Gothic novel, a form of literature of which she was inordinately fond, and one of Dr Smollett's tales which had not previously come in her way. Remembering how much she had enjoyed the adventures of Roderick Random, she at length decided in favour of Smollett's story about Peregrine Pickle, feeling that with such a name it was probable that the hero's activities would be calculated to amuse. The idea of the Necromancer might attract her, but she knew from past experience that it would only set her imagination working, and there were far too many daily engagements here at the Wells for her to have time to spare for her little hobby. No, Peregrine Pickle let it be!

Taking the volumes, she gave her name to the librarian, who had a word to say about her choice as he always did to all who came there. Verity stayed chatting a moment or two until she noticed by the clock on the mantelpiece that she had overstayed her time.

'Gracious, I must fly! Lady Crossens may need me to help her dress for the Assembly Rooms.'

She sped to the door and dashed out, only to collide on the threshold with someone who was about to enter. The impact was severe, knocking the breath from her body and causing her to drop her books and grab at the door-jamb to prevent herself from falling.

The other party was less fortunate. He staggered back, shoved a leg behind him to save himself, and threw out a hand to clutch at air. The cane flew from his grasp and clattered to the pavings, and his bad leg, unable to take the unbalanced weight, crumpled under him. He crashed to the floor in an ungainly heap, losing his hat in the process.

'Oh, no!' gasped Verity as, with a sudden lurch of the stomach, she recognised the pale features. 'Not *you*!'

A servant in livery, who happened to be passing at that moment, started forward to the gentleman's aid. At the same time, the librarian, who had witnessed the accident, came running out. But Verity was before them both, crouching down and seizing the gentleman's arm.

'Oh, I am so very sorry,' she uttered contritely. 'Have I hurt you very badly?'

It was evident from the way the poor man was gripping his underlip between his teeth that he was in a good deal of pain, but he managed a faint laugh.

'You are determined—to see me—humbled, are you not? I trust this may be—lowly enough for you!'

'Oh, pray do not! I did not mean it!' Verity cried, distressed. 'Let me help you, sir.'

But it was in fact the two men who lifted him to his feet, while Verity scurried to catch up his cane and hat. He took them from her with a word of thanks, but visibly winced as he put his weight on the injured leg.

'You *are* hurt!' Verity said anxiously. 'You must sit down at once.'

Without hesitation, she moved to his side and slipped an arm about him. 'Lean on me, sir. We will go back into the library.'

'No, no,' he said at once, reddening and trying to shake her off. 'I will be perfectly well in a moment.'

'You will be nothing of the sort,' argued Verity firmly. 'Why, you are looking absolutely white!'

He grinned slightly, and his tone was faintly apologetic. 'I always do, you know.'

'You are *much* paler than usual,' Verity assured him,

and looked at the other two men who were hovering about them. 'Please help the gentleman into a chair.'

She stood back to allow them access. In their zeal to be of service, they crowded either side and half carried him, protesting, into the library, where they placed him tenderly in an easy-chair. Verity, belatedly recalling the volumes she had dropped, collected them and dusted them off, relieved that they also were undamaged. Ever helpful, once in the library she took away the gentleman's cane and hat and laid them aside, and then directed the servant to go in search of a doctor. An easy task in this town where physicians were two a penny.

'Good God, no!' ejaculated the poor young man with some vehemence. 'I assure you I do not need a doctor! If I may just rest here a moment, I shall be quite well presently.'

'Are you certain?' Verity asked worriedly. 'You may have damaged something, and I could never forgive myself if you were to be disabled all through my fault!'

'My dear girl,' he said, in a tone somewhere between amusement and exasperation, 'my *disability* is entirely my own doing. I am quite used to it, you know. Have no fear. I would feel it if anything had gone seriously amiss. But if it will make you happy, let me assure you that I will have my own physician examine the limb thoroughly when I return home. Will that content you?'

'I suppose it must,' Verity said reluctantly. She smiled at the servant. 'Thank you so much for your trouble. We will not detain you any longer.'

'No trouble, madam,' said the man. 'I only hopes as the gentleman takes no lasting hurt.'

'Indeed, so do I!' Verity said devoutly.

The man went off and the librarian asked if there was anything more he could do.

'No, I thank you,' said the gentleman with a smile. 'Don't let me keep you from your work.'

The librarian bowed, and, bringing forward a straight-backed chair, he set it for Verity. 'Pray call me, ma'am, if I may be of any further assistance.'

'Thank you, you are very good,' she said warmly, sinking on to the chair and placing the books on her lap.

'He is indeed,' echoed the gentleman, low-voiced. 'If he had not brought that chair, I should have felt impelled to offer you this one.'

'Oh, stuff! As though I should care for punctilio at such a moment!'

A faint smile curved his lips. 'No, I fancy a too-rigid adherence to the rules of etiquette is not your besetting sin!'

Verity's own lips quivered, though the ready colour tinged her cheeks. 'I—I have been impolite, I know,' she faltered. 'I—I have wanted to—to beg your pardon for——'

'Pray do nothing of the kind!' the gentleman interrupted instantly. 'You have nothing for which to beg my pardon, I assure you.'

'But I have!' she protested. 'I said *such* things and——'

'*No!*' he snapped, quite roughly. 'I will hear no apologies from you! Believe me when I say that I require none!'

Verity bit her lip on a sharp retort, for a frown creased his brow on the words and he closed his eyes briefly as if a spasm of pain had attacked him. Instead she gazed anxiously into his face, and spoke with unwonted diffidence.

'Are you sure you do not need anything? You are dreadfully pale still! A glass of water, perhaps?'

A grin lightened his sudden severity. 'From the

chalybeate spring, I suppose? No, I thank you. I am not yet in such straits.'

She gave a choke of laughter. 'Oh, dear, I hope not! Though I dare say the waters would do you all the good in the world. I don't blame you for refusing them, however. My patroness—the lady I am with, I mean—says they taste excessively nasty.'

'So I am led to believe,' he agreed.

There was a pause. Constraint returned. There was so much to unsay, so much awkwardness in this encounter. Every word that rose to Verity's lips seemed inappropriate, and she felt unusually tongue-tied. The more so because this was the first time she had seen the man without his hat, and she was struck both by the luxuriance of his long hair which was a trifle dishevelled—rather endearingly so—from the late clash, and by the pale countenance now exposed to her sight. In spite of the lines of suffering, his features were pleasing, she realised with a sense of shock. And she had thought him a monster!

She was glad suddenly that she had chosen to wear the pink gingham gown and the flower-trimmed hat of chipstraw, for she knew them to be becoming. The thought made her blush as she glanced at him and found his black eyes were upon her, roving, it seemed, over her features.

He smiled. 'Are you enjoying your visit here?'

'Very much,' Verity said warmly, seizing thankfully on the neutral topic. 'There is so much to do, and the company is very amusing.'

He stared at her. 'Amusing? Good God!'

She smiled. 'Oh, I know they are mostly advanced in years, but to tell you the truth I have been so much in the company of children of late that I am enjoying the change.'

'It seemed to me,' said the gentleman, his black eyes

showing that suspiciously reprehensible gleam, 'that you like children.'

'Yes, I do,' Verity replied slowly, eyeing him warily. Was he mocking her? 'But constant association with them can be very wearing.'

'So I should imagine.'

She frowned. How oddly he spoke! Though perhaps these words bore out her suspicion that he spent little or no time with young Lord Braxted and his sister Peggy. Before she could formulate any of her thoughts into a question, however, he spoke again, on quite a different subject.

'What book have you there? The latest romance?'

'Certainly not! I hate romances.'

His eyebrows lifted. 'Indeed? I know you to be quite unlike the normal run of young ladies, but you cannot be as different from them as that!'

'Can I not?' Verity said indignantly, by no means pleased by this fresh reference to the unconventional way she had behaved towards him. She ignored the gambit, however, and pounced on another point. 'Pray why should you suppose that just because one is a female one should care only for such nonsense as that?'

'I beg your pardon,' he said with a suspiciously demure lowering of his black eyes. 'I see I have gauged the situation quite wrongly. Do tell me, then, what is the *serious* matter of the book you have chosen. A history, perhaps?'

'No such thing——' Verity began, and stopped. He was looking at her again and the glint was more pronounced than ever. In spite of herself, she felt a rueful smile curve her own lips, and she held out one of the volumes for him to see. 'As a matter of fact, it is by Tobias Smollett. One of his humorous adventure books. But before you say a word, let me tell you that I *almost* picked one of those Gothic horror things, to which I will confess I am positively addicted. Now tell me how like all my sex I am in enjoying such arrant nonsense!'

The gentleman grinned. 'I should not dare! Particularly as I have a predilection for such novels myself. In my defence, let me say that most females of my acquaintance are more inclined to sigh over Sir Charles Grandison and Lord Orville than young Master Peregrine Pickle.'

'What, those dead bores!' cried Verity, making him laugh out. 'It is shocking of me to say so, of course, because my father is a clergyman, you must know, but I have always found these romantic heroes quite tediously virtuous.'

'And the heroines quite tediously lachrymose. Yes, I agree with you. How much more exciting to read of villainous monks and terrifying castles with their evil inmates ready to trap the unwary!'

Verity, remembering all at once the way she had woven just such a plot in her head about him, found herself stricken to silence. Fortunately, the gentleman himself saved her from the necessity of continuing the discussion.

'Tell me! Do you think our several rather unfortunate contretemps justify an exchange of names?'

'Oh, of course,' Verity gasped thankfully. 'How very rude of me! I am Verity Lambourn.'

He inclined his head. 'My name is Haverigg. My family name, that is, Miss Lambourn.'

'Oh, I am not *Miss* Lambourn,' Verity explained. 'There are two sisters still unwed before me, you know. Although I suppose as I am alone here, there is less need for such accuracy.'

'There are three of you?' he asked politely.

'Three! We are seven sisters, sir.'

'Good God!'

'You may well exclaim. My mother is in despair! For how in the world is she to establish us all suitably?' Her friendly smile dawned and she added merrily, 'Now, if real life were anything like a novel, you, Mr Haverigg, instead of being a sober married man with two children, would turn out to be the prince in disguise!'

Mr Haverigg gazed at her blankly. 'But I am not——'

'Oh, gracious!' Verity ejaculated suddenly. 'I was forgetting. Of course, you are not those children's father at all!' She smiled confidingly at him. 'I quite thought you were at first, you know. But then you spoke to poor Braxted in *such* a way, and paid scarcely any attention to little Peggy, that I knew you *couldn't* be their papa. Naturally, it is not your business to be *fawning* over them, as I am assured by Lady Crossens—oh, she is the lady who so very kindly invited me to come here with her, by the way—is the case with *my* papa. Have you children of your own?'

Mr Haverigg appeared to be struck dumb. His face was paler than ever, and the black eyes held a sombre expression that gave Verity pause.

'I—I beg your p-pardon,' she stammered. 'I am speaking quite out of turn.'

'Not at all,' he said quickly, still with that strange look. 'I am—I am afraid I cannot—I can't——'

Verity suddenly thought she understood, and the colour flooded her cheeks. The poor man was a cripple! He was probably not even married, never mind having any children. She started to speak again, hardly aware of what she said, concerned only to cover up the dreadful *faux pas* she had made.

'Are the children well? I do hope so. And none the worse for their adventure, I trust.'

'I—I hardly know,' responded Mr Haverigg. He seemed dazed. 'I have not seen them.'

'Not seen them!' echoed Verity, astonished out of her confusion. 'But how is this? You are not Braxted's tutor, I take it. But surely if the Marquis is away, it is your responsibility to——' She broke off in consternation. 'Have I been mistaken? I quite thought you were the great man's steward, or secretary, or some such thing.'

There was an inflexion of a question in her voice, but Mr Haverigg still hesitated, looking away. Good God, what could he say?

'I am not his secretary, nor his steward,' he said slowly. 'The fact is. . .you see, Miss Lambourn, I——'

He glanced at her again and found her cheeks aflame. Another attack of conscience? he wondered.

'I'm sorry,' she said contritely. 'I did not mean to be vulgarly inquisitive.'

'Not at all,' he murmured politely, feeling the words to be hopelessly inadequate.

He tried to think of something appropriate, some way to rescue her from her obvious embarrassment. But Miss Lambourn was rising from her seat and putting out her hand.

'I must leave you now, Mr Haverigg. I hope you will suffer no ill effects.'

He took her hand and began to push himself forward.

'No, please don't get up!' she begged quickly. 'Pray remember me to Lord Braxted, if—if you should see him. I don't suppose Peggy will remember me. They are delightful children. So pretty. Their parents must be so proud of them! Goodbye!'

She turned on the words and walked quickly out of the library, leaving him gazing after her, ashen-faced and dumb.

Thank God she had not waited! For he could think

of nothing to say. Not a word! How could he answer? What could he possibly say? She had entirely misread the situation, but good God, how could she not do so? And yet it was not her misconception that had almost annihilated him. In a few simple sentences she had stripped him bare, exposed his every failure, rent the protective skin he had grown and left him prey to the promptings of the still, small voice within.

Sighing deeply, he reached for his cane and hat, placed the latter on his head, and rose painfully to his feet. The librarian rushed to his assistance, but he politely and firmly fended him off, and made his way out into the street, down past the springs and across to the edge of the common where his phaeton waited in the charge of Hoff, the middle-aged groom.

This worthy took one look at his face and began tutting and scolding with the freedom of an old retainer.

'There now, if it ain't just as I said it would be! You've knocked yourself up, me lord, and no wonder!'

'Don't fuss, Hoff!' said the gentleman wearily. 'I have taken a fall, but it is nothing.'

'A fall!' exclaimed the groom, shocked. 'And you've called no doctor to you, I'll be bound!'

'Of course I have not. But I shall send for Claughton to look me over.'

'Aye, that you will, me lord, if I've to fetch him to you meself!' promised his henchman grimly. 'Now just you wait while I find a boy to hold the horses and I'll help you up, me lord.'

'Don't be a fool, man!' snapped his lordship. 'I can manage very well.'

But he winced as he hoisted himself into the phaeton, a sign of pain that was not missed by his anxiously watching attendant, who lost no time in deprecating this foolish independence in a spate of heavy sarcasm.

'Aye, that's right, me lord. You go for to make everything worse for yourself with your obstinate ways! Don't you pay no mind to them as has nursed you through all those tricksy times when your lordship never thought to walk on your legs again!'

'Damn you, Hoff, be silent!' begged his master, closing his eyes tight shut against the memories that these words brought crowding in.

The groom, seeing the reins held in his master's competent hands and the horses quietly standing, ventured to let go their heads and leap nimbly up to take his place in the phaeton. The gentleman was leaning one elbow on his good leg and had shaded his eyes with his hand. The groom's gruff tone entirely failed to conceal his anxious concern.

'Do you pass over them reins, me lord, afore you falls out of this here rig!'

His lordship brought his hand down, rapping out, 'I am quite capable of driving this vehicle to Braxted Park, and I'll thank you to mind your place and your tongue!'

The curt tone was alien both to him and to his faithful attendant.

'As your lordship pleases,' said Hoff stiffly, drawing himself up into the erect posture of the perfect servant.

His master turned to look at him. Hoff had been with him since his own childhood, and was devoted to him as he well knew. He realised that this unaccustomed and undeserved harshness had deeply hurt the man.

His hand went out to briefly touch the groom's arm and, when the servant looked round, he gave him a rather wan smile.

'Forgive me, Hoff. I am not myself. But I *must* drive. I need—I need occupation.'

'Well, o'course, me lord, I understand,' said the

groom, unbending at once. 'Just you let me have the reins whenever you feel yourself tiring.'

All the same, he kept a sharp watch and held himself in readiness to intervene at need. He knew his master, and if something had not happened to bring back that dark period—those days when the whole household feared at times for his lordship's reason, let alone his life!—then his name was not Samuel Hoff!

The groom was perfectly right. The Marquis of Salmesbury, struggling with his own particular demon, was indeed remembering the appalling events of two years ago, when his careless haste had cost his children their mother's life and had left him a cripple.

CHAPTER FOUR

MISS LAMBOURN, hurrying away to her lodging, with her mind all chaos, was shocked, but secretly relieved, to hear from the maid hired for the season by her patroness that her ladyship had got up from her bed and gone with Mrs Polegate to the ladies' coffee-room.

'She said as she would see you in the Assembly Rooms later, miss,' added the girl.

Verity thanked her and escaped to her little bed-chamber, glad of a few minutes of solitude to collect her disordered thoughts.

How much more discomfiture must she bear on account of this wretched Mr Haverigg? She could scarce open her mouth in his presence without letting fall some incautious word that resulted in her own confusion. Was she so tactless? Or was he merely touchy?

No, that was unfair. After all, who would not be a trifle out of temper after being knocked so violently to the ground? Poor Mr Haverigg had taken it remarkably well, she was forced to admit. It had not been *that* which had caused him to clam up and look so—so— yes, *bleak*, poor man! If ever anyone looked to be in the grip of care, it was this pale-faced young gentleman just before she had left him. All had been well until *she* had mentioned marriage and children, reminding him no doubt of his infirmity and how it had destroyed his chances of connubial happiness.

Come to think of it, she was obliged to admit that on the whole the difficulties that had arisen between them had been all of her making. *She* had attacked him on the first occasion. *She* had dropped the boxes, precipitating the next unfortunate encounter——

Here her thoughts suffered a check. But no! He had come specifically to Tunbridge Wells to find her. He had said so! Just to give her that nest of boxes. She frowned at her own reflection in the glass where she had been absently looking, prinking her dark curls back into order and straightening her bonnet.

Was that all you wanted of me, Mr Haverigg? she wondered. A pulse leaped suddenly in her throat, and she felt her heartbeat quicken. How odd! The idea that he had deliberately sought her out gave her an obscure kind of pleasure. As if she had not positively taken him in dislike at their first meeting! And he had returned today. But—but she did not dislike him! How could she, when he had shown himself to be both pleasant and forbearing?

Verity gave herself a mental shake. What was she thinking of? Of course he had come, just as she had, to find a book at the library. The recollection left her feeling curiously flat. However, the likelihood was she would not see him again, she decided, turning away from the mirror. It was pointless to think about the man. If there was a nagging suspicion at the back of her mind that his absence would make the Wells seem sadly empty, she resolutely declined to acknowledge it.

It was with a determined air of cheerfulness, therefore, that she went down to the Assembly Rooms in search of her patroness, still concerned about her health. But she found her happily engaged in her favourite pastime, indulging in a rubber of whist with the old nabob Martin Yorke, another lady and Sir John Frinton. Lady Crossens brushed her anxious solicitude aside with scant words, her eyes on the cards in her hand. Verity abandoned her questions. All four players were so deeply engrossed that even Sir John, whose love of cards was seen to surpass his propensity for dalliance, merely called a greeting before turning back to the game.

But Mrs Polegate, no card player, was fidgeting from group to group, clearly at a loss. She no sooner saw Verity than she made a beeline for her.

'Miss Lambourn, I have been on the look-out for you.' She grasped Verity's arm and lowered her voice, her eyes fairly dancing with excitement. 'I have *such* news!'

'Why, what, ma'am?' asked Verity, startled.

But the widow had first to drag her away to sit in a quiet corner. 'For if we look to be absorbed in our conversation, no one will venture to disturb us.'

'I bow to your worldly-wise knowledge, Mrs Polegate,' Verity laughed. 'But what in the world is this about?'

'It is the *Marquis*,' whispered Mrs Polegate in thrilling accents. 'So dreadful! I knew you must be interested after meeting his children so opportunely.'

'Do you mean this Lord Salmesbury? What of him, ma'am? What has occurred?'

'Oh, nothing *now*. It is just what Sir John told me. I happened to mention his name, you know,' she said airily, making a business of arranging the ruffles about her neck, for she had on a tippet lavishly trimmed with ruches of ribbon.

Did you indeed? Verity thought to herself grimly. Aloud, she said, 'And did Sir John know him?'

'Oh, yes, he knew all about it. And so should I have done, only that it was the year I did not come here, and so I knew nothing at all of the matter.'

Verity blinked in bewilderment. 'Mrs Polegate, I have not the remotest understanding of what you are saying!'

'Of course, yes, how silly!' fluttered the lady, open-

ing her fan and plying it with energy. 'I declare, I am
so much overset, I scarce know myself what I am
saying! The thing is, when dear Emilia did not come
here, I missed her so dreadfully that I vowed I should
not set foot in the place the next year. Nor I did. But
that was just when it happened and so of course I heard
not a word about it, for by the following year it had
been forgotten. As everything is, you know, for old
events must give place to new!'

'But what *was* it?' Verity demanded.

'I am coming to that,' said the widow, and her face
crumpled into sorrowful lines. 'Such a tragedy! The
poor poor Marquis!'

'What, ma'am? *What*?'

'His *wife*, my dear,' uttered Mrs Polegate in accents
as stricken as if she had herself suffered the loss. 'The
Marchioness. She was *killed*. A carriage accident, they
say. So young, too. Barely three and twenty years of
age she was, it seems.'

'How—how *terrible*!' Verity said faintly. 'Those poor
children!'

'Yes indeed. The little girl was but a babe—a few
months old.'

Miss Lambourn was looking quite appalled. No
wonder Peggy had only wailed for 'Tittoo', as she
called her nurse! She had no mama. Had been mother-
less almost from birth. And Braxted! Her heart ached
for the child. She knew what it was to lose one close to
her, for her sister Constance, but a year her senior,
had been taken from them at the age of twelve. It had
been painful even when the infant girls had died. How
much more so must it have been for that lonely boy,
who had not even the comfort of siblings to assuage his
grief. For Peggy could not have offered the easing that
her own sisters had done in their shared loss. And from

what she had been privileged to observe it did not appear that his father was of much help. Unless. . .?

'Mrs Polegate, what of the Marquis himself? Was he——?'

'Oh, my dear, that is the worst aspect of the whole business!' declared the widow. 'The poor man was so devastated that he shut himself up in Braxted Place and has not been seen since!'

'He did *what*?' Verity demanded in accents of strong indignation. 'How abominably selfish!'

'Oh, no, dear Miss Lambourn, how can you say so? Such a romantic devotion!'

'Romantic fiddlesticks! How should his shutting himself up serve anyone at all? Pray did *you* find it necessary to make such a ridiculous charade out of your grief?'

'Oh, no, indeed no!' said Mrs Polegate, somewhat flustered by this severity. 'But then, you know, dear William had enjoyed *many* years of a very good life. And he was so ill at the end that one could not but feel it a *mercy* when he did leave us.'

'Yes, I dare say, ma'am,' Verity said, brushing this aside, 'but my sisters enjoyed scarcely *any* life, and yet we continued about our business. It—it was hard, it is true,' she conceded, tears standing in her eyes, 'but I cannot think we could have made it easier by moping in solitude! And what of those poor little children? They are surrounded only by servants, and must bend to the will of that heartless Mr Haverigg, who I suppose is busy about the Marquis's affairs, while the great man indulges himself in this foolish fashion in his ridiculous ivory tower!'

The same conclusion had been reached by the Marquis himself as he drove back to Braxted Park. The dreadful truth had been laid out for him by that slip of a girl who had shoved herself and her opinions into his life. Her low—*deservedly* low, God help him!—opinion of his role as a father had thrust on him the realisation that he was as bad as no father at all! Buried in his own sorrow, his own guilt, he had deprived his children of himself as well as of their dead mother.

Miss Lambourn. . .what had she said her name was? Verity? Yes, Verity for truth. How apt! Miss Verity Lambourn had begun by showing him how much at fault he was in jumping to conclusions about Braxted's supposed prank. And scarcely had he stopped smarting from that rebuke when she had all unwittingly delivered another. A blow more violent than she had any idea of! She had realised that he could not be their father because, if you please, he had 'spoken to poor Braxted in such a way, and paid scarcely any attention to little Peggy'. Good God, she must have supposed him utterly indifferent to his children! *Indifferent*! God help him, if only he were!

But Miss Lambourn could not know how closely Braxted resembled his mother, how so exactly his small features caught her every expression, so that he could scarcely bear to be in the child's presence for the constant reproach that his countenance made to the Marquis's sorely troubled conscience. And then there was Peggy, equally the image of the mother she had hardly known and whose name she bore. How could he have endured to hold that innocent little body in his arms, knowing that he had as good as slain her natural protector?

Such had been the cause of his distancing himself from his blameless offspring. Only now did he see how selfish and inhuman an act this had been. Remorse gnawed at him, more painful than any of the bodily hurts he had sustained this day.

Small wonder he had been unable to correct the false

impression Miss Lambourn had acquired of him! She knew, evidently, or had found out, that Braxted was the son of the Marquis of Salmesbury. How could he tell her that he was the same Marquis, after the strictures she had uttered? Already so much had been said, so much had occurred to produce misunderstanding between them. If he now told her his true identity, he did not know which of them must be the more embarrassed!

No. Better he should remain 'Mr Haverigg', as she had mistakenly called him. After all, it was unlikely that they would meet again. He had only to keep away from Tunbridge Wells. That should not be difficult. He was already something of a recluse. Let him become more so. But not, he decided suddenly, as he turned his horses into the gates of Braxted Park, to his children!

Accordingly, he accosted his butler as that worthy opened the big double front doors to his master.

'Cradoc, where shall I find Lord Braxted at his hour?'

The servitor, far too well-trained to betray his stupefaction, nevertheless opened his eyes a little. 'Lord Braxted, my lord?'

'Yes—my son!' said the Marquis impatiently.

The butler eyed him uncertainly.

'Well? Have you gone deaf, Cradoc?'

'I beg your lordship's pardon, but has Lord Braxted incurred your lordship's displeasure?' ventured the butler.

'Good God!' ejaculated the Marquis. 'Have you run mad?'

Cradoc prudently held his peace, but Salmesbury was shocked. Was he so formidable a father, then, that he had hitherto only sought out his only son—his heir, damn it all!—to scold him for some fault? He had not thought himself so harsh a parent. But perhaps it was true. Contrary to all appearances, he had rarely had occasion to chastise the child, but until now he had not realised that virtually the only contact he had had with the boy had been when there was a homily to be delivered. So much so that apparently even his butler felt it necessary to protect the child against him.

'The boy has done nothing, Cradoc,' he said quietly. 'I would like to see him, that is all. Now where may I find him, if you please?'

The butler bowed, evidently satisfied. 'I believe he will be in the schoolroom with Mr Eastleigh, my lord.'

Thanking him briefly, the Marquis limped away towards the grand staircase that dominated the huge open hall of Braxted Place. It was typical of the ornate building which had been erected by the present Marquis's grandsire after the Italian fashion. A vast baroque structure, with high domed ceilings and spacious rooms, decorated throughout with a profusion of carved plaster cornices, with angels and demons peering from odd corners, and marble statues nestling in every niche.

The Marquis, inured to the splendours that had surrounded him from birth, traversed the long gallery above without once glancing at the paintings that hung there, and made his way to the corridor that led to the upper floors where the children and servants dwelled out of sight.

As he opened the door into the schoolroom where he had himself been tutored, he did not fail to notice the look of apprehension that came into his son's face when he glanced up to see who had entered. Clearly, Braxted shared the butler's fears.

Mr Eastleigh, a gentleman in orders of late middle age, who was chaplain to the Haverigg family as well as tutor to the hope of the house, looked almost as surprised as the boy himself.

'My lord!' he uttered faintly.

'Good morning, Eastleigh,' said the Marquis quietly, but his eyes were on the boy's face. God, how like Margaret he was! With an effort, he dragged a smile on to his lips. 'Good morning, Braxted.'

'Sir!' uttered the boy, springing to his feet, the wary look more pronounced than ever.

What have I done? What have I done? thought Salmesbury in silent anguish. Aloud he said, 'What are you studying today?'

Braxted blinked. 'G-Greek, sir.'

'*Greek*?' The Marquis frowned, looking at the tutor. 'Isn't he a little young for Greek?'

'Oh, no, my lord,' Eastleigh said earnestly. 'If a boy has the aptitude, it is never too early to begin. Master Wystan—my lord Braxted, I should say—has a most superior understanding. Most superior! He is quite a scholar, my lord.'

'Is he indeed?' said Salmesbury, looking at the child with a new interest. How little he knew of the boy! 'I am—delighted to hear it. But I wonder if I may be permitted to—to interrupt his scholarly activities for a short while.'

'But of course, my lord. You are the boy's father, after all. Naturally, you may order his studies as you see fit.'

Yes, I am his father, thought the Marquis. Yet he seems a stranger to me. As I must to him, poor child!

'Thank you,' he said quietly. 'Braxted. . . Wystan. . . Would you care to—to walk with me a little?'

Braxted's jaw fell open and he stared at his father as if he could not believe his ears.

The Marquis gave him a wry smile. 'Come, is it *so* odd a request?'

'*Yes*, sir,' said the boy frankly before he could stop himself. 'I—I mean——'

He broke off and Salmesbury looked at the chaplain. 'By your leave, Eastleigh. Perhaps you would be so good as to give us the room to ourselves a moment. There is—something I wish to—to discuss with—with my son.'

'Of course, my lord, of course,' said the cleric hastily, and, concealing his astonishment, he bowed himself out of the room.

When he had gone, the Marquis hesitated for a moment, hardly knowing how to begin. The child remained by the desk, his big eyes, still registering suspicion and doubt, never leaving his father's face. Salmesbury could not meet that blue gaze, so reminiscent of poor Meg's innocent sweetness. He felt as if he were on the rack, and longed to leave the room so that he need not look upon it. Instead, he moved to the window and gazed down at the view of the ornamental garden some way below.

'I have met a friend of yours, Wystan,' he said.

The boy eyed him, fresh doubts entering his mind. *What* friend? Was his secret blown?

'Yes, sir?' he said, the doubt in his voice.

The Marquis turned. 'Yes. A lady.'

Relief blanked the boy's mind a moment. Then he realised some response was required of him.

'L-lady, sir?' he stammered.

Salmesbury smiled at his obvious amazement, real amusement making him far more natural. 'You think I am mad, I dare say.'

'Oh, no, sir,' the boy said automatically, but his frank eyes belied him. He took courage. 'What lady, sir?'

'The lady who saved you from the scaffold! Or rather, from a very unjust punishment.'

The boy's eyes widened. 'Oh, *her*.'

'Yes. Her name is Miss Lambourn and she is staying at Tunbridge Wells.'

Braxted came away from the desk at last and ventured to approach a step or two. 'Did you see her there?'

'I did,' replied the Marquis. 'She asked to be remembered to you.'

The boy grinned suddenly. 'I 'member her very well. She was kind.'

'Very. She—she asked after you, also. Unfortunately, Wystan——' Salmesbury looked away briefly and then forced his dark gaze back to the child's '—unfortunately, I could not tell her how you were, for I had not seen you from that day to this.'

Braxted did not speak, but his lip trembled a little, though his gaze remained steady on the sombre one above him.

'I—had not realised,' continued the Marquis with difficulty, 'how ill-acquainted we have become.' He threw up a hand as the boy winced. 'Oh, it is not your fault, Wystan. The blame is entirely mine. But I—I would like, if you will let me, to remedy this.'

He paused, but the child did not speak. He was flushing, and he swallowed once or twice. With a pain at his heart, Salmesbury realised that he was desperately trying to stop himself from bursting into sobs. He put out his hand, and his voice was gentle.

'Will you help me, Braxted?'

The boy nodded, biting his lip, and, as the tears spilled from his eyes, he reached out to take his father's hand.

* * *

'It is part of the war effort, ma'am,' Mr Tyson earnestly informed Lady Crossens. The master of ceremonies was fervently seeking support amongst the well-to-do patrons for a day of diversions to be held on Tunbridge Wells Common on the coming Saturday.

'We have had these troops quartered in Waterdown Forest, waiting to be sent off to France, and they have eaten the locals out of house and home.'

'Indeed? And do you imagine we are able to make good these depredations?' demanded her ladyship, raising her brows.

'No indeed, ma'am. It is rather for morale, you understand, that the people may see that their sacrifices have not gone unrecognised, and that the officers and men are engaged in a worthy cause against a common enemy.'

'Yes, yes, there is no need to lecture *us*, Tyson,' said Lady Crossens testily.

Richard Tyson bowed, and said with the utmost urbanity, 'Naturally you are quite conversant with these matters, ma'am, and will understand that we are also anxious to promote the interests of those few *émigrés* who have come among us.'

This her ladyship could appreciate, for the steady trickle of those unfortunates escaping from the Terror over the last few years was known to all the world.

'Poor benighted wretches!' she said, shaking her head. 'They arrive destitute and are thrown wholly upon our charity.'

'Quite so, ma'am. It is hoped that we may be able to alleviate their lot a little.'

'Very well. How are we to assist?'

The expected aid was, of course, pecuniary, for it was necessary to supply a number of prizes that might be won in the various races and raffles, the proceeds of which would be used for the fund to help the French refugees. But the master of ceremonies thought it would be a graceful gesture if some of the gentry would condescend to lend the occasion the cachet of their presence.

'You may count upon me, Mr Tyson,' said Verity at once. 'It sounds a delightfully entertaining manner of spending the day.'

'Most enjoyable, Miss Lambourn.' He glanced doubtfully at Lady Crossens. 'If, that is, her ladyship permits?'

'Oh, you will consent, dear ma'am, will you not?'

Lady Crossens frowned. 'You will not go unescorted, child!'

'Oh, stuff, ma'am! I dare say Dogget will be pleased to escort me, if you must have it. I am sure he will want to attend.'

Her ladyship could not like the idea of her protégée wandering among a gathering of common people accompanied only by a groom, but once she was assured that several of the gentlemen residents would be present she did not withhold her consent.

Verity, learning from Mr Tyson—who took care to inform her of it only when her patroness was out of earshot—that there were additionally expected to be in evidence stalls of various kinds, together with jugglers and acrobats and all the usual adjuncts of a fair, found herself looking forward to the treat in anticipation of no common degree of enjoyment. It would serve admirably, she decided, to turn her thoughts from the Marquis, and his ubiquitous assistant, Mr Haverigg.

Not that the latter's conspicuous absence from the Wells was of any interest to her. Oh, no. But it was odd that he had not been near the place since that unfortunate accident at the library almost a week ago. She could not help wondering whether he had been hurt more severely than he had thought. It would be comforting to see him again. Only to be certain, of course, that he was quite well. How could she forgive herself if he had been injured all through her carelessness? Useless, she supposed, to think that he might attend these diversions. Not even to accompany the Marquis's children. Gracious, no! There was no hope of that.

'Shall we go out into the garden today? It is close in here.'

Young Lord Braxted nodded. This was the third morning during the past week on which his father had taken time out from the business that occupied his secretary and himself for the better part of his time, and sought out his son, and Wystan was beginning to relax a little. So far there was not much pleasure to be gained in the rather stilted conversation between them, but the look he had hitherto dreaded, that bleak, white-faced look that had scorched him out of those vivid black eyes, had been absent from the man's face. The boy was still wary, for, although he did not remember his father ever being this way before, there was no saying how long such an unprecedented mood would last.

For the Marquis, the sessions were nothing short of torture. All the time he was with the boy, he was unable to forget the vision of Margaret's face, unable to drive out the haunting memories. He could only hope that familiarity would lessen the sensation. He had not yet subjected himself to the added torment of approaching little Margaret, though he promised himself to do so as soon as he could meet his son on comfortable terms.

They left the schoolroom, and Salmesbury very quickly found a fresh source of discomfiture as Braxted had to make an obvious effort to adapt his youthful bounding energy to his father's halting pace. Everything, it seemed, conspired against the closeness he was trying to establish. His limping progress was a fresh arrow that soon became so deep an irritant that he must express it.

As they slowly traversed the long gallery towards the grand staircase, he muttered fretfully, 'I am a poor hand at this! Perhaps we should have stayed in the schoolroom!'

Braxted was silent, looking at the injured leg. At last he ventured a glance up at his father's face.

'Does it hurt you?'

A short laugh was surprised out of Salmesbury. He looked down and recognised in the boy's face only the academic interest of childhood. There was no sympathy there. It was oddly comforting.

'Like the devil sometimes!' he answered with a rather twisted smile.

In fact the accident had smashed the bone of his thigh and thrown it slightly out of kilter with his hip. Although the surgeons had saved the leg, the bone had knit unevenly and he could no longer move his leg forward without an awkward manipulation of the hip. He was therefore unbalanced on his feet and any undue exertion or move put a strain on both the limb and the hip above it.

Braxted was examining the leg and the cane that aided his father as he walked, with the detached look of one who merely desires information.

'Will it get better?'

'I don't know,' Salmesbury answered truthfully. 'Probably not in the long term, the doctors tell me.'

'If it gets worse, will they cut it off?'

'My God, I hope not!'

'They would if it got gangrene in it,' said the child prosaically.

'It is more likely to lead to gout.'

'Mr Eastleigh calls that the drinking man's disease.'

'Very true,' agreed the Marquis solemnly. 'I had better not overindulge in the port, had I?'

'I never heard that you drunked,' Braxted announced unconcernedly. 'So I dare say it will be gangrene, after all.'

'I thank you,' said his father wryly. 'Perhaps you would care to prophesy a few more disasters for me!'

The child looked up, grinning suddenly. 'Oh, no, I think one leg is enough for any man!'

There was an answering twinkle in Salmesbury's eye. 'I cannot agree with you. I had by far rather keep the two!'

The boy burst into laughter, and for the first time in many months a little of the pressure lifted from about Salmesbury's heart.

When they eventually reached the gardens, however, talking together with much less constraint, the Marquis was brought up short by a very odd sight indeed.

'What in the world——?' he uttered, staring.

Braxted followed the direction of his gaze across to the outskirts of the park where the first few trees broke up the smooth lawns that rolled before them. Strung between two trees some yards apart was a long rope. Attached to this by a pair of leading strings was the Lady Margaret Haverigg, chasing between the two trees at her stumbling run, while some distance off her nursemaid stood, unconcernedly chatting to a gardener who was leaning on his rake, puffing at a clay pipe.

'That's how Kittle keeps her now,' explained Braxted. 'Ever since Peggy ran off into the woods that day.'

'Does she indeed?' demanded the Marquis wrath-fully. 'We'll soon see about this!'

He set off at once, limping as fast as he was able, oblivious to the dull ache that was at once set up in his hip.

'Peggy don't mind it,' the boy said, keeping pace beside him.

'Well, I do! Do you think I will have my daughter tied up as one would a dog? Outrageous!'

'Kittle says she may guard her better this way.'

'Oh indeed? Pray, is *that* how she guards the child, ignoring her while she gossips with a fellow servant? The woman is not even looking at her!'

In fact the nurse was now looking in their direction with, as they were able to observe as they came nearer, a not unnatural trepidation. Before they could reach the place, the gardener had gone off about his business and Kittle was rapidly closing the distance between herself and her charge. Peggy, however, having caught sight of her brother, had set up a delighted squeaking.

'Wissen! Wissen!' she shrilled, straining against her leash.

Braxted abruptly broke into a run. Just as the nurse came up, he reached the little girl, whose arms were stretched out ready to clutch him as he bent over her, laughing.

'Are you a dog, Peggy?' he cried gaily. 'Woof! Woof!'

'Oof! Oof!' she echoed.

'Peggy's a do-og! Peggy's a do-og!' chanted her brother.

'Peddy a do-yod! Peddy a do-yod!' mimicked the infant, without the smallest understanding of what he meant.

At any other time, Kittle would have scolded such impertinence in Master Wystan in no uncertain terms.

But her attention was all on the approaching Marquis, and she scarcely heard the squeals and giggles as Braxted threw himself to the ground and began to play with his sister, tickling her and teasing her with his new chant.

Kittle was a motherly-looking woman of some thirty years of age, whose eyes dilated nervously as she watched the approach of her employer.

'What, may I ask, is the meaning of this—this *bestial* usage of her ladyship?' demanded the Marquis in a voice of ominous quiet.

'M-my l-lord?' faltered the woman.

'And do not try to foist your feeble excuses of *guarding* the child on to me. You may have fooled Braxted, but you do not pull the wool over my eyes.'

'Oh, your lordship does not understand,' began Kittle in a whining tone. 'I only——'

'I understand well enough,' interrupted Salmesbury coldly. 'Your desire is to escape an irksome duty because Lady Margaret is now old enough to use her legs, though I doubt she will run you off your feet!'

'My lord, I did it for the child's good, I swear it!'

'Be silent!' ordered the Marquis, his black eyes snapping. 'Do you take me for a fool? Even if I did not already know that Braxted was obliged to perform your part because you were too busy gossiping that other time, I should not now doubt the evidence of my own eyes. Go to the house at once!'

Dissolving into tears, the nurse hesitated. She glanced over to where Peggy was bouncing on her brother's chest, although Braxted, even as he cheerfully endured this indignity, had half an ear cocked to what was going on between the two adults.

'But—but Miss Peggy. . .' ventured the nurse. 'I mean, Lady Margaret—shan't I——?'

'You may leave her to me,' Salmesbury said, his face

softening as he too looked over to see the children so merry together. Then he recalled his injury. He could never manage Peggy alone. He called after the nurse who had started disconsolately off.

'Send Hoff to me, if you please. Then go and see Inskip and await me there.'

Braxted, meanwhile, had risen and untied the leading strings to release his sister, and he now took her by the hand and led her over to their father.

'Do you mean to turn her off, sir?' he asked.

'Certainly,' Salmesbury said, but his eyes were on Peggy's pretty baby face with the yellow curls escaping from under her lace cap, and the big blue eyes looking up at him in open curiosity. He doubted very much whether the infant was aware of his identity.

'Hello, Peggy,' he said gently.

The little girl stuck a finger in her mouth and edged closer to her brother, but her eyes never left the face so far above her.

'Wissen,' she muttered, and, when her brother did not respond, she pushed at him, quite violently, saying crossly. '*Wissen*! Peddy want to pay!'

Wystan had been looking thoughtfully after the retreating nurse, but another little fist hitting at his chest brought the boy's head round.

'Stop it, Peggy!'

'Peddy want to pay!'

'Not now,' said the boy, his eyes going to his father's face where he discovered an amused smile.

'An insistent young lady, your sister,' said the Marquis, as another demanding 'Wissen', accompanied by a buffet, escaped the child's lips.

Braxted grinned. 'She's shockingly stubborn.' Then he frowned, casting another quick glance at the disappearing figure of Kittle. 'And that's why——'

A puzzled look appeared in Salmesbury's eyes as he broke off. 'What is it, Wystan?'

The boy looked at him doubtfully.

'Come, I shan't bite! What is it you wish to tell me?'

'Well, sir, it's Kittle. Turning her off, I mean,' he said in a burst of candour. 'I think you'll catch cold at it, that's all!'

'How so?'

'It's Peggy, see. She's all right now 'cause I'm here,' explained the child. 'But if Kittle don't come back, or—or she's not there when Peggy goes back to the nursery. . .'

He left the sentence unfinished, but the implication was clear enough. The Marquis cast his now frowning eyes over to where the infant had left off plaguing her brother in favour of investigating a butterfly which had fluttered down on to a nearby patch of wild flowers.

'She is so fond of Kittle?' he asked, still watching the little girl.

'There's no one else, see,' Braxted said.

Though he spoke in a matter-of-fact way, the words sent a sliver of pain into Salmesbury's chest. Here was yet another instance of his neglect! If he could not give his daughter a mother, he should at least have ensured that the substitute was worthy. He sighed heavily. There was no end to his self-inflicted punishment!

He noticed Braxted watching him curiously and forced a smile to his lips. 'Come, do you collect Peggy and we will start for the house. I will have to think this over.'

The butterfly having flown out of reach, Lady Margaret made no objection to being removed from its vicinity, but trotted happily at her brother's side, able, even with her unsteady gait, to keep pace with their much slower father.

By this time the unaccustomed exertion had begun

to tell on the Marquis, and he was obliged, after crossing the lawn, to sink down on the low stone wall that ran up to the ornate double stairway which marked the entrance to the house.

'I am sorry, children, but I must rest awhile,' he said faintly, and immediately came under the scrutiny of his son's intelligent gaze.

'Are you very bad? Shall I fetch Inskip to you?'

'No, no. Hoff will be here presently,' Salmesbury said, and managed a self-deprecatory smile. 'I had meant him to carry Peggy, you know, but perhaps he will after all have to play nursemaid to me!'

'Oh, I can carry Peggy piggy-back,' Braxted said offhandedly. 'Hoff may help you, by all means.'

'Let us hope he is not obliged to carry *me* piggy-back!'

Braxted found this idea so exquisitely humorous that it was some time before he could speak. His laughter was infectious and Peggy soon joined in, shrieking with mirth.

But even while the Marquis smiled in sympathy, images crossed his mind of the many occasions when his faithful groom had in fact borne his weight, after he had collapsed in exhaustion in those early attempts to get back upon his feet that Hoff had himself bullied him into making. But for Hoff, he would probably be bedridden to this day, for he had been able to find no incentive in himself at that time for resuming his life, and no representations by his doctors or certain members of his family had served to induce him to throw off the invalid. Only Hoff, who had guided his first steps when, as an infant not much older than Peggy was now, he had tottered into the stables to look at the horses, had been able to persuade him to learn to walk all over again. Hoff, who was, he knew, as successful at pacifying the daughter as he had been the father. His eyes were on the little girl.

'Do you think she will come to me?' he asked Braxted suddenly.

The boy was still chuckling, and in his present mood he did not hesitate, but lifted his sister and handed her up to the man sitting on the wall.

Peggy's own squeals were instantly quenched as she gazed uncertainly at the face of the man who held her on his knee.

'Peggy, do you know who I am?' the Marquis asked quietly.

Watching with interest, the young boy poked at his father's arm. 'Who's this, Peggy? Who is it? Who?'

The infant looked from one to the other, a little pink tongue travelling uncertainly about her lips. One tiny finger pointed at the man and she looked to her brother for guidance.

'Oo dis?'

Braxted poked again. 'It's Papa, Peggy. *Papa.*'

The word on his lips warmed Salmesbury's heart, and he cradled the infant a little closer. She was looking at him again, savouring this new identity, as if she was not quite sure of its significance.

'Oo dis?' she asked, pointing again.

'I told you,' her brother said impatiently. 'This is Papa. *Papa*, Peggy.'

The lesson had gone home. Her little finger jerked forward and prodded the Marquis in the chest. She said it with confidence.

'Papa. Papa.'

Salmesbury could not speak.

CHAPTER FIVE

'IT WILL not do, Inskip!'

The gentleman addressed, who had served as secretary to the most unexacting master anyone could
wish for since the Marquis came into his inheritance
just after the birth of his son, nodded his head.

'I agree, my lord. But it is difficult.'

Salmesbury frowned up at him from the huge desk
that dominated one end of the saloon that served as his
office. His secretary had a smaller desk on the other
side of the room, but in practice he rarely used it. For
since the accident, it was he who generally attended to
the administrative details of the business of the estate.
His master, once he had recovered enough to be
capable of participating, preferred to spend long hours
driving around, ostensibly visiting tenants and examining areas which were in need of repair or had been
complained of. Although Inskip suspected—not without some justification—that Salmesbury could the
more readily brood in isolation aboard his phaeton
without incurring criticism from his long-suffering well-
wishers, Hoff in particular.

Thus Inskip was invariably to be found on the other
side of the Marquis's desk where all the accoutrements
of the job were conveniently to hand. He had long
fallen into the way of making decisions without refer-
ring them, so that his master's access of sudden interest
in the children, and more particularly in the vagaries of
Lady Margaret's nurse, had taken him by surprise. His
faculties were for the moment dulled.

'It is difficult to know what to do, I mean,' he added apologetically, noting his employer's frown.

'Well, I know what to do,' the Marquis informed him with decision. 'She must be got rid of.'

'Yes, I see that, my lord,' agreed Inskip. 'But as you are no doubt aware, her ladyship will not tolerate the nurse's absence. Already, I am informed, she has—er—made it known that Kittle was missed when she returned to the nursery.'

The Marquis smiled. 'My dear Inskip, don't be shy! You may as well say she kicked up the devil of a dust and be done with it!'

The secretary grinned. 'Quite so, sir.'

'My hand may have been forced temporarily, for obviously I had to let her remain for the present. Nevertheless, after what I saw yesterday, she will have to go. Good God, I could not reconcile it with my conscience to leave Peggy in the charge of such a woman!'

He saw an odd look in his secretary's face, and had no difficulty in interpreting it. 'Yes, yes, I know, Inskip. I should have done something before this. And so I would have, had I known of it! But that is in the past, and I do not mean to allow myself to become ignorant of these things again.'

Inskip met his eyes. 'I am glad of it, my lord. We have missed you sorely.'

'Thank you,' Salmesbury said simply, and there was no need for more words between them on the subject.

The secretary paced a moment or two while his employer drew absently on a sheet of paper, his mind busy.

'I wonder, my lord,' Inskip said suddenly, 'if we could try a little subterfuge.'

'By all means, if you think it will answer.'

'Say that we employ a *second* nursemaid—at least so

we shall inform the world at large—and allow Lady Margaret time to become used to her.'

Salmesbury sat up eagerly. 'The very thing! Once Peggy accepts her, we may give Kittle notice and the change will be less drastic. An excellent idea!'

'It may not work,' cautioned the secretary. 'Children take odd fancies to people, and it may be——'

'Odd fancies indeed!' scoffed his lordship. 'Nonsense, Inskip! One nurse is much like another. It is all a matter of whom one is used to.' He saw that Inskip was eyeing him uncertainly and a bitter smile twisted his lips. 'You would wish to tell me that Kittle stands to Peggy in place of her mother, I dare say. But I cannot agree. Recollect, Inskip, that persons of our order are in general in the company of servants. Why, I scarce saw my own mother above a half dozen times in a month, I dare say.'

'But she was *there*, sir,' said the secretary with meaning.

The black eyes gazed at him, pain in their depths. Salmesbury's voice was very quiet. 'I can do nothing about that, Inskip.'

The secretary disagreed, but he did not say so. If the Marquis would only go out into the world, he felt, it would not be long before some young lady captured his interest. But he sighed inwardly, thinking how unlikely it was that his employer would expose himself as a cripple before the public eye. He was destined to be surprised.

After a moment the Marquis spoke again, his tone determinedly cheerful. 'Now we have that settled, I must have your help on another matter. It is Wystan's birthday in a couple of days and I would like, if possible, to think of something to do. Something different, unusual.' He looked hopefully at his secretary. 'Come now, Inskip, you are such a clever fellow. I am sure you can think of some suitable entertainment.'

Inskip smiled. 'Well, sir, an idea does spring to mind. Lord Braxted himself mentioned it to me, though where he had his information I am at a loss to imagine.'

'Good God, don't sound so mysterious, man! Out with it!'

'It seems there is to be one of these—er—diversions on Saturday.'

The Marquis covered his eyes with one hand and groaned. 'God help me! You don't mean one of those appalling occasions where old men puff tobacco for a quart of gin and young women engage in a donkey race?'

'Exactly so, my lord,' confirmed Inskip, grinning. 'It is to be held on Tunbridge Wells Common in honour of the soldiers who have gone off to France.'

'Tunbridge Wells!' echoed his lordship, and experienced an abrupt jolt in his chest as the image of bright hazel eyes and a friendly smile surrounded by black curls leap into his mind.

'Master Wystan—I mean, his lordship—did speak rather wistfully of a desire to attend the event,' offered Inskip in an apologetic tone. 'It seems there is expected to be quite the atmosphere of a fair. Lord Braxted expressed a strong wish to see a—a bearded lady who is to appear, and——'

'A bearded lady! Good God!'

'Yes, sir. And an enormously fat pig is promised. However,' he added, as a look of horror passed over his employer's face, 'I did venture to point out to his lordship that it was unlikely that——'

'No, no,' interrupted the Marquis. 'If he has set his heart on it, how cruel it would be to fob him off with some other amusement that he would not like half as well, I dare say. Besides, it will serve admirably for a birthday treat. We may celebrate here on Friday, the day itself, and then make an expedition of it to these diversions.' He nodded, briskly determined. 'Yes, we shall go. We shall take Peggy and Kittle, too. And you and Eastleigh may accompany us.'

'Well, if your lordship does not mind,' Inskip said hastily, 'I have a great deal of business on hand.'

The Marquis smiled. 'But I do mind, Inskip. And if you imagine that I will attend this dreadful event without your support, you were never more mistaken. Moreover, it was your idea, my friend. On your own head be it!'

Saturday dawned fair and bright, much to the Marquis's chagrin. He had half hoped for rain, which would have afforded a legitimate excuse to cry off the promised treat. But no such fortune occurred, and the whole party set off just after ten so as to be there in good time for the asses' race which was scheduled to begin at twelve. Inskip having provided himself with a programme of events, they were able to plan the day to encompass all those that Braxted particularly wished to witness.

The Marquis groaned in spirit when they arrived at the Common to find an enormous crowd of persons wandering about in their holiday best.

'For the Lord's sake, let us keep together,' he said in a tone that already sounded harassed.

'I think, my lord, it will be as well to appoint a place of rendezvous at which we might seek each other out should we become separated,' suggested Inskip.

'Yes, indeed,' agreed Mr Eastleigh. 'At my advanced years, you know, one cannot be racing about hunting for persons in a crowd. And I dare say you, my lord, would not wish. . .'

He left the sentence delicately unfinished, but the

Marquis laughed. 'Very true, Eastleigh. But Hoff will stick with me to succour me if I should be overcome by fatigue.'

'That I will, me lord,' said the groom grimly, who had joined the party on his own insistence for no other purpose.

A meeting place was appointed, and it was agreed that anyone who became lost should proceed to that point on the hour and wait there to be rescued.

'The pig, sir!' Braxted piped up, impatient of the delay, and becoming excited by the clamour and bright cloth awnings and ribbon-decked poles he could see dotted about. 'You said I might see the fat pig!'

'So I did.' The Marquis looked about rather hopelessly, daunted by the press of persons. 'Now, where in the world is the wretched creature to be found?'

Mr Eastleigh tutted, equally at a loss, and Inskip fell to studying his programme, hopeful that the celebrated pig's whereabouts might be mentioned therein. It was Hoff who saved the day.

'Never you fret yourself, me lord. Nor you neither, Master Wystan!'

With that, he let out an ear-piercing whistle and an urchin materialised out of the crowd.

'It's me sister's boy, me lord. Here, Tommy!' he called, pulling forward the lad, who came shyly, twisting his cap in his hands. 'Lives here, he does. I've arst him to find out where everything is so he might lead us there, me lord.'

'What admirable foresight, Hoff! And thank God! Well, then, young Tommy, lead on!'

It was therefore with surprising ease that the Marquis's party made their way through the throng, although their progress, hampered by the necessity of shouldering a pathway through the crowds—a task taken on by Hoff and Inskip—was necessarily slow.

This was to his lordship's advantage, and Salmesbury and his children, with Peggy carried in the nurse's arms, were able to move in a fairly leisurely way.

The little group attracted some attention as they passed through, for the quality of the Marquis's garb and that of his son was marked, although both wore countrified frock-coats and breeches of quiet hue. Added to that were Mr Eastleigh's clerical black, Inskip's neatness and Hoff's livery. Such an array could hardly fail to draw interest. But such was the festive mood of the party that none of them even noticed.

They caught a glimpse of the course on which the races were to take place, which had been marked out by the beribboned poles Braxted had seen, and there was plenty to look at on the way: stalls with sweetmeats and toys for sale, vendors with trays wandering through the crowd, and several tents in which were advertised other freakish objects to be gawped at.

But very soon they found themselves in the presence of the fat pig, which was indeed a revolting creature, so large as to have difficulty shunting about its make-shift sty. This did not prevent it, much to Braxted's delight, from rustling up to push its eager snout over the poles in search of further sustenance.

'It's so *fat*!' Wystan uttered in unaffected glee, and began to chant. 'Greedy greedy pi-ig! Greedy greedy pi-ig!'

Up piped the echo almost immediately.

'Geedy geedy pi-id! Geedy geedy pi-id!' sang Lady Margaret, making the assembled company laugh.

'Quite so, Peggy,' the Marquis said, grinning. He looked with revulsion upon the grotesque animal and added, 'That is quite the most disgusting sight I ever remember to have seen!'

'For once, sir,' said a new voice at his elbow, 'I find myself in entire agreement with you!'

Turning his head quickly, Salmesbury found himself looking straight into the clear hazel eyes of Miss Verity Lambourn.

'Good God!' he ejaculated. 'I had not thought to run into you as easily as this!'

He had spoken without thinking, surprised by her sudden appearance into forgetting his company. As a twinkle appeared in the bright gaze before him, his heart gave the oddest leap, and a sensation of warmth struck him at the sound of her voice.

'You will at least do me the justice to own that I refrained from *running into* you on this occasion!'

He smiled, conscious for the moment only of her presence. 'I do, ma'am, and must profess myself astonished at your forbearance!'

'Oh, that is easily explained,' Verity laughed, 'for you have brought my little friends with you.'

She turned to hold out her hand to Wystan, whose attention had been diverted from the pig as he recognised her voice. She was, coincidentally, attired in the same forest-green greatcoat dress she had been wearing when they met before, and she was thus more familiar to him than she might otherwise have been.

'Lord Braxted, how do you do? Do you remember me?'

Wystan grasped her hand eagerly. ''Course I do! You saved me from hi——' He broke off with a guilty look up at Salmesbury, and added adroitly, 'From the gypsies. This is a capital pig, I think. Don't you like it?'

'It is perfectly horrid, Lord Braxted,' Verity said frankly, prudently ignoring his slip, 'but I can see you like it extremely.'

'I should say I do! But you mustn't call me Lord Braxted, you know. I'm Wystan.'

'Now that is very friendly of you, Wystan. My name is Verity, you must know. Verity Lambourn.'

Braxted's quick glance went this time to his tutor Eastleigh, by whose precepts he was wont to conduct himself, and he said uncertainly, 'Yes, but I can't call you that. It—it wouldn't be polite.'

'Oh, stuff! If I do not care for that, I am sure you need not.' She smiled mischievously at Salmesbury, having missed the look at the clerical tutor. 'And your mentor will bear with us, I believe. After all he has undergone at my hands, I am sure it is only what he would expect!'

The Marquis had by now not only recollected the presence of other people, but was stricken all at once with the fear that someone in his retinue might inadvertently betray him. But he responded to her rallying tone with admirable sang-froid.

'One becomes inured to unconventionality in your society, certainly, ma'am.'

Verity chuckled. 'How unhandsome!'

The gleam appeared in his eye. 'I have never aspired to be an Adonis, ma'am, but it is hardly kind in you to tell me so.'

'I did not mean that at all, you wretch!'

'Unkinder still.'

He smiled as she bubbled over, but, catching a grin on his secretary's face out of the corner of his eye, he was again brought back to the danger attendant upon this meeting. It naturally did not occur to him to make known the members of his entourage to Miss Lambourn, but the remembrance of their presence made him suddenly aware of her solitary state and he frowned as he glanced about her.

'I trust, Miss Lambourn, that this odd streak of eccentricity of yours has not led you to visit this place alone.'

Verity's laughter was quenched. A trifle frostily, she answered, 'Not at all.' She indicated a burly man a few paces behind her whose face was vaguely familiar to the Marquis. 'Dogget is looking after me. He is Lady Crossens' groom, you must know.'

The lessening of warmth in her voice was not lost on Salmesbury. The black eyes looked an apology, though the suspect gleam was back in them. He moved a pace closer and spoke in a lowered tone meant for her ears alone.

'I do seem to have an unhappy knack of touching on precisely those matters which you justly believe to be no concern of mine, do I not?'

At once the colour stole into her cheeks. 'Oh, n-no! You are v-very right. My patroness was most insistent that I have an escort.'

Then before he could say any more, she quickly turned her eyes on the infant, still held in her nurse's arms. 'And here is little Peggy. Do *you* like the fat pig, too, Peggy?'

Lady Margaret eyed her a moment. Then her finger shot out, pointing at the animal. 'Pid.'

'Yes, it is a pig,' agreed Verity. 'A very fat one, too. Do you like it?'

'Peddy no like Pid. Pid geedy!' the little girl confided. 'Wissen no like pid.'

'Yes, I do!' argued her brother hotly. 'Wissen like pig very much!'

'No!' shouted Peggy. 'No like pid.'

'That will do!' intervened the Marquis as Braxted opened his mouth to retort.

'I should think so!' Verity put in with a merry laugh, as the two children glared at each other. 'I hope you do not mean to quarrel over the bearded lady, too.'

'Have you seen her?' demanded Braxted, diverted at once.

'Oh, yes, and I am sorry to say she is sadly disappointing. I was much more taken with the sword swallower.'

'Sword swallower!' echoed Braxted, eyes sparkling. 'Where is he? Oh, may I see him?'

'I am sure you may,' Verity said, smiling at his enthusiasm. 'There is a fire eater as well. Would you like me to show you?'

'Oh, yes, if you please!'

Miss Lambourn looked to Salmesbury for permission. 'May Wystan come with me? I will take every care of him, I promise.'

'I have no doubt of that, and I have only to thank you,' said the Marquis at once, almost glad of the excuse to get rid of her, for every moment the peril of discovery loomed large.

Not that he wanted Miss Lambourn to remain in ignorance of his identity, but he would choose to make the disclosure in private so that he might have an opportunity to explain himself. He hardly recalled his decision to keep away from Tunbridge Wells in order to avoid her company and so spare them both embarrassment. He only knew now that he must tell her the truth at the first opportunity, for it had become, in some inexplicable fashion, intolerable to him that she should hold a false impression of him.

Advising Miss Lambourn quickly of the rendezvous they had all agreed, and appointing a time for a reunion, he said he would himself repair to the racecourse to watch the coming events, and the party separated.

It was some time before Verity was able to drag young Lord Braxted away from the performances of the man who swallowed swords and his colleague who put out burning torches in his mouth. He was in such spirits that he seemed almost a different boy from the child she had met on the road. Then he had seemed too serious for his age, behaving in a manner worthy of an adult. Today he was far more juvenile, and consequently much more approachable and friendly.

He was finally induced to come away by a timely reminder from Dogget to Miss Lambourn that they would miss the donkey race if they did not hurry.

'Oh, no! I wanted *partickerly* to see that!' groaned Wystan.

'Then let us make haste,' Verity advised.

The boy took her at her word, and, grabbing her hand, rushed her through the crowd as he made for one of the beribboned poles, so that she arrived flushed and out of breath by the edge of the makeshift racecourse.

'Gracious, Wystan! Do you wish me to expire on the spot?' she protested, laughing.

'Pooh!' scoffed the boy. '*You* have not a game leg!'

She knew not how to reply to this oblique reference to poor Mr Haverigg's disability, for, while she felt the callous remark deserved rebuke, she was loath to jeopardise the good relationship she had established with Braxted. Fortunately, he was far too interested in what was going forward to notice the lack of response.

It was not so for Verity, who, reminded of the man once more, found it hard to shake him out of her thoughts. She had seen him with the children quite by chance as she was passing the booth, and at sight of the slight figure with its supporting cane, her pulses had quickened—with shock, naturally!—and she had moved to speak to him almost without volition. He had answered her in so friendly a way that she had found herself relaxing at once. She was delighted to see the children, too, but she was conscious of a wish that she might find a further opportunity to converse with Mr Haverigg.

There was the usual delay to the start of the asses' race, and a good deal to provoke hilarity among the onlookers. They greeted with gleeful jeers and catcalls the attempts of the would-be jockeys—not in fact females but lusty young teenage village lads—to mount, and the recalcitrance of the beasts, who proved either stubbornly static or so precipitate that their riders were unable to get them neatly arranged at the starting line.

Verity, deriving more amusement from Wystan's unaffected delight than from the antics of the entrants, noticed his hand go up in a surreptitious wave. A little surprised, she followed the direction of his gaze and noticed a small boy, dressed in near rags, grinning and signalling.

'Who is that?' she asked, nudging Braxted.

He looked up and away again, shrugging. 'No one. At least, no one I know.'

Verity saw him glance across at the boy, who had obviously taken in the situation and had averted his eyes.

'Wystan,' she said seriously, 'it is not becoming to disown one's friends. Particularly if they are of humbler station than yourself. That is to appear insufferably high in the instep!'

Braxted reddened and shuffled his feet, looking at the ground.

'Who is he, Wystan?' she asked again.

'Jed,' the boy answered in a low tone. 'He's—he's a climbing boy.'

'Well, that is not his fault. How did you meet him?'

'Fell down the chimbley in my chamber one day,' explained Wystan, gaining the courage to look up at her. The blue eyes pleaded. 'You—you won't split on me, will you?'

'Do you take me for a talebearer?' Verity demanded

indignantly. 'Of course I shall not. But I wish you will call Jed over. Only think how badly he must feel if he thinks you are ashamed to speak to him in public!'

'I thought if they knew of it, they would forbid him to come to the Park,' Wystan confessed frankly, 'and then I should have no friends at all!'

'He comes there to see you?'

Braxted nodded with enthusiasm. 'They think he is cleaning the chimbleys. And 'course he *is*,' he added hastily, '*some* of the time. But we go birds'-nesting in the woods and—and such things as that.'

'How splendid!' Verity said encouragingly, thinking hard thoughts meanwhile of that horrid Marquis who was so busy mourning that he neglected to provide his son with suitable companions for his age.

But no one was more surprised than Jed when his friend signalled to him to join them. He looked furtively about him as if seeking the custodians of his friend's person, and Braxted had to beckon furiously before he would cross the race track to join them. Verity welcomed him with a friendly smile and Wystan performed the introductions.

'Didn't think as how you'd make 'em bring you, Wys,' whispered the urchin in some surprise. 'How'd you manage it?'

Braxted grinned. 'I told Inskip and he fixed it. It's my birthday treat, see. Mind, I never thought *he* would let me!'

'Nor me,' said his friend, awed. 'Ain't you glad I tipped you the wink?'

'Of course I am. It's a capital go!'

Verity overheard this exchange with a swelling of indignation. If she could but have an opportunity to confront this *he* herself! For she had no doubt Wystan meant the Marquis.

She was diverted then by the beginning of the race.

Both boys became so excited, jumping up and down and shrieking imprecations at their chosen donkeys, that Jed completely lost his initial shyness of his exalted company in heated debate with his friend over the outcome when both their favoured mounts lost.

Verity bought them both toffee apples from a passing vendor, and was just congratulating herself on the success of her tactics when a remark of Jed's caught her attention.

'Ain't that your sister Peggy, Wys?'

'Where?' demanded Wystan, fright taking hold of him. In spite of Verity's wisdom, he still had doubts of his various mentors' possible reactions to this unsuitable friendship.

Jed pointed. 'There. With that there Kittle. Don't go up in the air,' he advised sapiently. 'Them nobs o'yourn ain't with her.'

'Is that the same nurse?' Verity asked in disapproval as she saw that the infant was drooping in the woman's arms. 'I cannot think she is very good at her job.'

Jed let out a crack of rude laughter. 'That she ain't! More like a kennel-keeper.'

Seeing Miss Lambourn's frown, Braxted explained about Kittle tying the little girl up. 'There was talk of turning her off,' he added, 'but Peggy screamed the place down when she wasn't there and they had to let her back.'

'Oh, dear.' Verity watched the child, dark thoughts again occupying her mind against the Marquis. The poor infant was exhausted! She was toying with the notion of going over and inviting the nurse to bring the little girl to rest at her lodgings, when Jed again drew her attention.

'Beats me why Kittle should be jawing with that there Sam Shottle.'

'Who is Sam Shottle?' demanded Braxted, noting for

the first time the thickset man in rough country clothes, who appeared to be arguing with the nurse.

'He's a bad 'un, is Sam Shottle,' Jed told them, his tone disparaging.

'A bad 'un!' echoed Wystan, round-eyed. 'Why, what has he done?'

'Ah! What ain't he done, more like. Why, he beginned by thievin' and poachin' when he was no more'n a lad like me. Now he says as how he got grander plans nor that. Reckons to make his fortune, he says. Huh! Me, I reckons he'll end in Botany Bay, if he ain't put to bed with a shovel!'

'Do you mean he could die?'

'By the rope, the road he's goin',' confirmed Jed.

'How in the world does Kittle come to be acquainted with such a man?' Verity asked, quite appalled.

'Ah!' nodded Jed. 'That's what I'm arstin' meself.' He grinned suddenly. 'And I reckons as how they be sweethearts, Wys.'

'Surely not!' Verity protested, shocked.

'How come he goes for to fondle her rump, then?' demanded Jed with a complete lack of self-consciousness.

Verity was obliged to control a reprehensible desire to giggle, and, as she saw that Braxted was interestedly studying the nurse and her companion, she devoutly hoped that he did not understand the significance that was clear to his more worldly-wise friend.

'Wystan, I think you should call to Kittle, and then we must go and find the meeting place. I am sure we are late.'

At this, Jed circumspectly withdrew, having even less dependence on the magnanimity of the 'nobs' surrounding his friend than even Wystan himself.

'Kittle! Kittle, I say!' called out Braxted.

The nurse turned her head and Verity was hardly

surprised to see the look of consternation that spread across it. No doubt she had thought herself unobserved. What did surprise her was that the man Shottle, instead of effacing himself, seemed rather to relish this sight of the boy.

He had an unprepossessing face, with heavy jowls and a nose that looked to have once suffered a breakage. A pair of keen eyes passed over Braxted, dwelling on his face until his companion said something to him in a low tone. He nodded and, as it seemed to Verity, reluctantly removed his gaze from the boy. A word to the nurse, and he had turned and made off through the crowd.

Kittle came towards them, an anxious look on her face. Whatever she had been about to say was forestalled by Braxted, however.

'Miss Lambourn thinks you should come with us now.' Then he turned to Dogget, who had been behind them the whole time. 'Do you know where the coach office is? We are to meet there.'

The groom nodded, and his relief was visible, at least to Verity. 'This way, sir.'

As they wended a path through the crowd, which was beginning to thin as a number of people made for the alehouses, Verity found her mind dwelling on all the things she wished to say to Mr Haverigg about his precious Marquis, and she had only half an ear to spare for Wystan's chatter. But, when the boy stopped in his tracks and urgently grasped her arm, she jerked into full awareness.

'What is it?'

'That man!' whispered the boy urgently, and there was fear in his voice. 'It's that gypsy!'

CHAPTER SIX

'WHAT? Where?'

But even as she asked, Verity's darting eyes found the figure of the man whose appearance had precipitated her into her adventure and acquaintance with the inhabitants of Braxted Park.

'Gracious heaven, I believe you are right!' she uttered, her voice pitched low.

The handsome gypsy was standing by a stall, idly glancing at the wares set out there: a collection of scarves, together with cheap rings, fans and necklaces. At once Verity thought of the gypsy dancing girl she had visualised, and saw in her mind's eye this man fastening a gold chain about her bare neck and placing his lips to the back of it. Involuntarily she shivered, as if she were the recipient of that intimate caress, and, as in her imagination the lady turned to look at her lover, she knew that his face was not that of the gypsy.

'They are camped on our land, you know,' Braxted told her as they moved on.

'Indeed?' she said absently, still shaken by the strange vision that had entered her mind. Whose face was it? Her eyes were still on the gypsy and, as if he felt her gaze, he suddenly turned, looking straight at the boy. She felt Braxted close into her, and groped for his hand.

'Don't be afraid!' she whispered.

'Oh, no!' he whispered back, but his hand clung tightly to hers. When they were safely past, he added, 'I wonder if I should ask my father to turn them off.'

'Turn them off!' repeated Verity in a shocked tone.

'No, no, Wystan. That would be shockingly cruel!
Why, they have done nothing.'

'Gypsies are dangerous,' Wystan said obstinately.

'Stuff! I am sure they would not think of harming
you.'

'Why did you stop that day, then? For you thinked
he meant us harm. You know you did!'

'Yes, that is true. But it was because, like you, I
reacted to an unnatural prejudice,' Verity explained.
'It was wrong of me. Very wrong. But that is just the
difficulty, you see. Gypsies have such a shocking repu-
tation that we are all stupidly afraid of them, when I
dare say all they wish is to be left in peace to enjoy
their lives just as you or I.'

Wystan digested this in silence for a moment or two.
'Very well, then, I shall say nothing—yet. But I 'spect
they're poaching our woods. Jed says there are any
number of them here at the fair, picking pockets, I'd
wager!'

Verity was about to deny this assertion with some
heat when they were interrupted by Salmesbury's
voice.

'There you are at last! I had begun to imagine you
had all been spirited away by the gypsies.'

This was so apposite that both Miss Lambourn and
Braxted burst into laughter.

'I am glad you are so merry,' said the Marquis,
smiling, 'but I must ask you, Wystan, to go with
Eastleigh. You, too, Kittle. Inskip has procured a
nuncheon and it is awaiting you.'

'What about you?' asked the boy, poised to run to
where he perceived his tutor waiting a few yards off.

'I have eaten. Go on. I want to talk to Miss
Lambourn.' He saw a suspicious frown come into his
son's eyes and added gently, 'To thank her, you know.'

Braxted flushed. 'Oh, yes, of course. Thank you,

Miss—I mean, Verity. It was capital! Will I see you again?'

'I hope you may——' Verity began, but was cut off.

'Certainly you will see Miss Lambourn again. Now be off with you!'

'Well, really, Mr Haverigg!' protested Verity as the boy scampered off.

But 'Mr Haverigg' was not attending. He was addressing her groom. 'You need not fear to leave Miss Lambourn to my escort. I promise I shall return here with her within the hour.'

Dogget, looking extremely worried, turned to Verity for guidance. As she had a strong wish to talk to Mr Haverigg privately, she endorsed this view.

'Oh, yes, Dogget. I am sure you need refreshment. Do you go and find some and meet me here in a little while.'

Thus adjured, there was nothing for the groom to do but take himself off. The Marquis turned to Verity.

'Let us remove from here, Miss Lambourn. There is something I particularly wish to say to you.'

'Oh, yes, and I wish particularly to talk to you, Mr Haverigg,' Verity said eagerly, turning to stroll beside him.

He had met them across the road from the coach office and now began to lead her away from the centre of things to the outer areas where the Common stretched away, and where those pleasure-seekers who did not come for the alehouses were sparsely dotted about, seated on the grass, enjoying their own impromptu picnics. So anxious was Verity to talk to him that she did not see Sir John Frinton wave to her, and so did not notice the old man's eyes following them as they walked away together.

'Miss Lambourn,' began the Marquis, about to tell

her that he was not in fact Mr Haverigg, 'I hardly know how to say this, but——'

'Oh, Mr Haverigg, I beg you will not trouble yourself!' chimed in Verity at once. 'You are going to disclose to me the shocking tidings about the Marquis, are you not? But there is no need. I have heard the terrible story of the accident that killed his wife and I am heartily sorry for it! Indeed, that is why I wanted to talk to you, for I am sure you, in your situation, must have some influence.'

'Miss Lambourn, you mistake my situation,' he said desperately. 'I am not——'

'No, no, do not say it!' she interrupted. 'If you are not a relative of some sort, you must be in his employ. But I am not blind, sir! You are treated with a deference accorded to no servant and even Wystan answers to you. You cannot tell me you have no power to change things.'

'I have indeed,' agreed poor Salmesbury, trying to stem the flow, 'but the fact is I——'

'Then, Mr Haverigg, you *must* do something to persuade that dreadful man that his attitude is grossly mistaken!'

Utterly confounded, Salmesbury could say nothing for a moment. Good God, he must speak now! Tell her that he was 'that dreadful man'. But his tongue refused to obey his command, and after the briefest of pauses Miss Lambourn had resumed speaking.

'You see, Mr Haverigg,' she was saying in a tone both persuasive and passionate, 'I *know* how it must have been for him, indeed I do! I, too, have suffered such a loss. More than one. And I do understand. But to become a hermit, to forswear the world, and leave those poor little children to the indifferent care of *servants*! Oh, it is too bad of him!'

It was too much. Salmesbury stopped walking and

turned to her, his face pale and set. 'Forgive me, Miss Lambourn, but you do *not* understand. Oh, yes, it is just as you say. Shockingly self-indulgent! And believe me I—that is, the—the Marquis—is only too well aware of it. But what you do not know—how should you, indeed?—is that the accident was caused by the Marquis himself. It was *his fault!*'

He stopped and the distress in his black eyes pierced Verity to the heart. Her own eyes filled.

'Oh, poor man!' she uttered brokenly. 'Poor, tormented man!'

They gazed into each other's eyes for a long moment, in an empathy too deep for words. Until a raucous voice shattered the intimacy.

'Cross the gypsy's palm wi' silver?'

Verity blinked, stepped back hurriedly and turned to see an old crone, swathed in shawls of bright patterns with large hoops in her ears, standing close beside her and grinning toothlessly up at her out of a wizened face.

'Cross the gypsy's palm wi' silver?' she offered again in a cracked voice thick with a west-country accent. She reached up to take Verity's mittened hand. 'Tell yer fortune, dearie?'

'Oh, no!' Miss Lambourn said, trying to retrieve her hand. 'No, thank you.'

The gypsy kept hold of her hand and looked closer into her face. Her own features lost their smile. 'Tears, dearie? Let old Mairenni seek out reason in yer hand.'

The Marquis, jerked out of the mood he had himself evoked, was about to order the gypsy to leave them alone when he changed his mind. Here was an opportunity to dispel the tension, and perhaps amuse Miss Lambourn and so bring the smile back into her eyes. At this moment, revealing his identity was quite impossible.

'Why not, Miss Lambourn?' he said encouragingly, digging a hand into his pocket.

'Oh, I could not,' Verity protested, but the gypsy was already turning her hand, looking at its shape, and she began to be intrigued.

'It is a holiday, Miss Lambourn,' Salmesbury said, slipping a silver coin into the old woman's ready palm. 'To partake of such amusements is positively *de rigueur*!'

'Off with the glove, dearie,' ordered Mairenni, tugging herself at the mitten and exposing Verity's hand.

She studied the palm in silence for a moment and Verity waited, succumbing to the age-old curiosity of every young lady to know what was to befall her. But when the old crone glanced up at her, she saw trouble in the woman's face.

'What is it?' she asked, seized by an apprehensive chill.

'No wonder ye weep!' said old Mairenni. 'Many a sorrow have ye weathered, dearie, only to encounter more.'

'Gracious, don't say so!' exclaimed Verity.

'Worry not, child, worry not!' chided Mairenni, clicking her tongue. 'For though, t'be sure, there be many tears to shed, there be smiles to come hereafter.'

'I am glad,' put in the Marquis with an attempt at lightness. 'I had begun to think I had done you an ill turn!'

Verity chuckled, but Mairenni's sharp old eyes sought and held Salmesbury's black ones.

'So ye have, sir, so ye have,' she cackled. 'But not fer crossing my palm!'

'What in the world do you mean?' demanded Verity, looking from one to the other.

'Gentleman know,' said Mairenni, and winked at the Marquis.

'Do you?'

He smiled, but with an effort. 'Possibly. We will talk of it later.'

'Very well, then, is that all you have to tell me?' Verity asked.

'And what d'ye want more?' asked the old woman, eyes glinting. 'Shall I see fer ye a handsome stranger to wed ye and a quiverful o' brats, eh?'

'No, but——'

'Aye, but ye shall have 'em. Ye shall have 'em all! And beyond that, dearie, ye shall have you'm heart's desire, fer that ain't it. Only it happens you'm mistaken, and one fine day that wild imagination o'yourn that fires yer mind with visions shall find a home. But by then ye'll have found it out, for the heart be its own mistress, dearie, and, looking fer you'm heart's desire, ye'll find ye have it in yer hands.'

Verity stared at her, quite dumbfounded. But Salmesbury laughed out loud.

'You speak in riddles, old woman! Miss Lambourn, if you are able to make head or tail of all that, I wish you joy of it!'

The crone cackled and gave him a knowing grin. 'She'll have joy, sir. . .at the last.' Then she handed Verity her mitten and went off in search of further custom.

Verity looked at Salmesbury. 'That was uncanny.'

'Did she hit on a truth, then?' asked the Marquis with a faint smile.

'What she spoke of as my heart's desire,' Verity said slowly. 'She certainly seems to have known how I use my leisure time. And I *do* dream of——' She broke off. 'Oh, well, it must all be nonsense, I suppose.'

'My dear Miss Lambourn, how could you possibly tell? She said nothing to the purpose, and what she did say could be applied to any set of circumstances you care to name. I beg you will not take it seriously.'

'Of course not. Upon my word, if I did, I should be in a fever of anxiety about these sorrows which she says are gathering about my head!'

'Let us hope she is mistaken. Indeed, I am sure she is. I cannot suppose, Miss Lambourn, that anyone of sensibility would wittingly give you any cause for sorrow.'

Something in his voice arrested her, and as she looked at him there was more than a smile in the back of his eyes and her pulse did a little dance.

'Oh, Mr Haverigg!' she sighed unvoluntarily.

His face changed and the smile left it. His voice sharpened. 'They might, however, give you cause for anger.'

She flushed a little and drew back. 'You mean I am quick-tempered, I dare say. Alas, I know it!'

He shook his head. 'I did not mean that. Miss Lambourn, it is quite time that I——'

'*Salmesbury*!'

The shout came from his left. In instinctive reaction he turned his head, and realised that she did, too. A dapper young gentleman with a pleasant face, all smiles, was waving a beaver hat in the air.

'Salmesbury, you sly dog!' he called as he approached. 'Went to visit you at Braxted, like the good cousin I am, only to be told you'd slipped your leash and gone off raking! Here's a new come-out, old fellow. What do you mean by it, eh?'

There was an ominous silence. Seeming to become aware of tension, and catching the Marquis's glance, the new arrival saw that the young lady was staring at his cousin with dilating eyes, her colour fluctuating.

'How *could* you?' she got out in a barely audible voice. 'Oh, how could you deceive me so?'

'Have I,' asked the unfortunate newcomer, 'said anything in any way out of place?'

'No, of course not,' answered the Marquis automatically. 'Miss Lambourn——'

Verity, her lip trembling, and tears pricking at her eyes, shook her head.

'The gypsy was right, *my lord*!' she threw at him huskily, and, turning, she fled from him to seek refuge in her lodgings, her happy day in ruins.

Salmesbury stood where she had left him, his pale features quite ghostlike.

His cousin touched his arm. 'I'm so sorry, old fellow, I seem to have blundered. Though I've not a notion what is going on!'

The Marquis clasped the hand on his arm and gripped it, dredging up a weak smile. 'Quainton, it is not your fault. It is I who have blundered. I meant to tell her the truth, but I allowed myself to be distracted and. . .however, it can't be helped. I dare say it would have provoked the same reaction if I had told her myself.'

Mr Leonard Quainton tutted sympathetically. 'Poor fellow! You never seem to have any luck!'

Salmesbury managed a laugh. 'Oh, it is not as bad as that! Besides I do have luck. Meeting Miss Lambourn has been the greatest piece of good fortune to befall me in many a long day. Thanks to her, I have begun to make some very necessary and long overdue alterations in my way of life.'

'I can see that!' agreed his cousin bracingly. 'To see you at a fair of all things! You could have knocked me down with a feather when Cradoc told me where to find you. Didn't believe it, in fact. Said I'd come and see for myself. And here you are, large as life!' He pressed his cousin's shoulder. 'I'm devilish glad to see you out like this, old fellow.'

The Marquis smiled, in genuine amusement this time. 'I should think you might be! After all, you have been plaguing me to come out of hiding for months.'

'Yes, and a fat lot you did about it!' retorted Quainton. 'Who is this Miss Lambourn, that she succeeds where we have all failed?'

A shadow clouded the Marquis's smile. 'She is heaven's messenger, and I cannot *bear* it if she is to harbour this ill opinion of me!' He turned to his cousin and grasped his hand. 'You must help me, Leo!'

'Anything in my power, old fellow. My mistake. Only too happy to help to set it to rights.'

Mr Haverigg—the Marquis! Oh, it was too mortifying!

Pacing the carpet in the small parlour of Lady Crossens' lodgings, Verity clasped and unclasped her mittened hands. The tears she had been obliged to keep back as she hurried across the green had given place to justifiable anger. Her thoughts had been so much occupied that she had passed by Dogget, anxiously awaiting her return, without even seeing him.

'Miss! Miss!' he called out, and then had to chase after her and forcibly put himself in her way. 'Are you all right, miss?' he asked in quick concern, noting her distress. 'Shall I fetch you to her ladyship?'

'No, no, Dogget, I am perfectly well,' she lied hastily. 'I am—I am a little fatigued and so I will go home. Thank you for your escort.'

But Dogget, knowing his mistress would expect it of him, insisted on seeing her to the door of her lodgings. He determined to wait outside also, for with miss in one of her odd moods there was no saying but she might not dash out again at any moment and run off the Lord alone knew where!

Miss Lambourn's mood was decidedly odd. While she raged at the deceit that had been practised upon

her, she was haunted by the memory of that tragic look
in the black eyes when he told her that it was his fault
that his wife was dead.

His wife. *His* children! Everything began to fall into
place at once. She had *told* him that she did not think
he could be the father. She had expressly stated her
opinion of him—as the Marquis. How could the poor
man have revealed himself after that? What a wretch
she was! To say such wounding things! Though to be
sure she had no notion then that she could hurt him.

Fool that she was! Papa would say that she merely
quibbled. Could she not have found out, made certain?
Remembering now the way he had behaved, the reaction of his servants, she thought how blind she had
been not to guess at once. But no! She was shackled to
her prejudice of what a Marquis *should* be! And so she
refused to believe that so insignificant, so mild a man
could occupy such a place.

The image of him came into her mind and she
realised at once that of course he was not insignificant
at all. He had a power, a presence that made one
notice him. It was not merely his title that commanded
the respect of his people. Nor was he mild. She smiled
at her own simplicity. What an epithet for a man of
such inner fire! He was far from mild, in spite of that
quiet manner of speech, that pale face and the limp he
carried with becoming dignity.

'Oh, dear God!' muttered Verity aloud suddenly.
'He was injured in the accident! Oh, Mr Haverigg!'

Tears rose to her eyes again and she dashed them
away as she realised what she had said.

'Fool. He is *not* Mr Haverigg. He is the Marquis of
Salmesbury,' she told herself savagely, 'and the sooner
you realise that Miss Verity Lambourn and the Marquis
of Salmesbury are poles apart, the better it will be for
you!'

After which, she collected the second volume of *The Adventures of Peregrine Pickle* and retired to a comfortable armchair, where she sat with the book open in front of her, her eyes gazing unseeingly into the middle distance, and thought about the Marquis without cessation until the return of Lady Crossens obliged her to assume a cheerful aspect she was far from feeling.

'There you are, child!' said her ladyship, walking into the parlour. 'Dogget tells me you left the diversions somewhat precipitately. Are you unwell?'

'Oh, no,' Verity said at once, blushing a little. 'It was—I—oh, I was overcome by the press of people, ma'am, that is all.'

'I am not surprised. We have been positively deafened by the appalling din!' Lady Crossens complained. She animadverted somewhat bitterly for a moment or two against the unwisdom of persons who saw fit to ruin the peace of visitors by allowing the mob to cause a riot and rumpus at their very doors.

Miss Lambourn could not allow this to pass. 'Dear ma'am, you surely cannot begrudge them one day of rational enjoyment! Besides, it *was* extremely pleasant until——'

She broke off, flushing, and Lady Crossens looked at her rather hard. She had noticed of late a tendency in her young charge to go off into daydreams when she thought no one was observing her. Indeed, Grace Lambourn had warned her to expect this. But her ladyship was not a fool, and she was certain there was something behind Verity's odd silences. If she had not been upset today, Lady Crossens was no judge of the matter! Even if her faithful groom had not reported the threatening tears he had observed.

'What ails you, child?' she asked with unwonted gentleness.

At once there was a pricking in Verity's eyes and she averted her face. 'If you please, ma'am, I—I would rather not talk of it.'

There was a moment of silence, and then her ladyship said with sudden energy, 'I declare, I am famished! Where is that woman with the dinner?' She crossed to the bell and tugged at it. 'Tell her to serve as soon as she can, Verity. I will be in my room. Do not forget there is the special ball tonight. After all, if the villagers may disport themselves on the Common, I am sure we may do likewise at the Assembly Rooms!'

Miss Lambourn had little heart for the event, but she could not refuse to attend. Since it was a special occasion, she arrayed herself in her best evening gown of primrose silk, open from the waist over a petticoat of pale yellow gauze worked with gold thread. From the lace tucker about her low *décolletage*, the swell of her bosom peeped, and her dark curls had been coaxed into ringlets and tamed into a chignon at the back. Not surprisingly, this charming picture drew a great many jaded male eyes.

In keeping with the mood of the day, Mr Tyson had decided that all formality would be dispensed with, the company taking their partners for a succession of country dances without any preliminary arrangement or introduction. Since everyone in Tunbridge Wells was already acquainted, this relaxing of the rules might have been thought superfluous. But it did, as Verity soon found out, mean that gentlemen might mingle freely to solicit the ladies of their choice rather than politely standing up with the members of their immediate circle.

Miss Lambourn consequently found herself going down the dance with a variety of elderly gentlemen, who had until now been content to leave a clear field to Sir John Frinton. She was in the middle of a particularly trying ordeal, involving the energetic gyrations of the old nabob, Martin Yorke, who was wheezing a tale of his dancing prowess in the old days in India, and treading on his partner's toes the while, when she became aware that a good deal of attention was being directed towards the entrance, where Richard Tyson was bowing deeply and ushering in some new arrivals.

As he moved aside and her view cleared, Verity missed her step and almost stumbled. Two gentlemen stood revealed, in whom, in spite of the unexpected elegance of their attire, she had no difficulty in recognising the Marquis of Salmesbury and the young man whose revelation had plunged her into gloom.

It quickly became obvious that 'Mr Haverigg' had abandoned any attempt to maintain that identity. In the fans raised to cover mouths, and the cupping of hands against ears, Verity recognised the passing on of a juicy titbit of gossip. For as each fan lifted, two pairs of eyes cast significant glances over to the slowly moving procession as Mr Tyson performed those introductions he considered essential. But Sir John Frinton walked up to the Marquis unannounced and greeted him as an old acquaintance.

With a sinking heart, Verity realised that the erstwhile 'insignificant' man had leapt into the role of guest of honour merely by virtue of his rank. She shrank into herself, cravenly hoping that he would not attempt to single her out. For that must give rise to the sort of tattling that would embarrass not only herself, but also her kind patroness.

Judging by his previous form, however, Verity could place no dependence on the gentleman's discretion. Even as she thought this, keeping a surreptitious eye upon the pair the while, she saw the second man glance over in her direction and nudge his companion.

Quickly looking away, Verity was glad to find the dance ending, hoping that she might disappear into the crowd as the dancers left the floor. She was deposited at Lady Crossens' side, and pounced upon immediately by Mrs Polegate.

'My dear, do you know who has just come in? I declare, I am all of a twitter! Salmesbury, of all people! He is exciting no little attention, I can tell you. What in the world should bring him here?'

Miss Lambourn did not enlighten her, but she could not prevent a faint flush from creeping into her cheek and was aware of Lady Crossens' penetrating eyes upon her. Her ladyship, however, merely scoffed.

'Pish, Maria! Why should he not come here? If he has decided to show his face in society again, what better than a gathering such as this to give him a little confidence?'

'Oh, yes, poor man!' sighed the widow at once. 'I dare say he is quite unused to be stared at.'

'Well, he is certainly getting a deal of practice in enduring that!' Verity said tartly, pointedly placing herself so that she presented her back in case those black eyes should be seeking her out. Heavens, nothing could be worse than to have him attempt to speak to her in this assembly! Though she had to make a valiant effort to suppress a growing feeling of pleasure that he had come at all. The thought flitted across her mind that she had not realised how very attractive he was. Whether it was the silvered blue brocaded coat with the buff satin breeches, or the powdered hair, that enhanced his appearance, she could not have said. But he seemed so much less pale that the black eyes were more dominating than ever.

Mrs Polegate's speculation and exclamations continued unabated and Verity was glad when the musicians struck up, for she was sure to be solicited for a dance. Indeed, she could see Richard Cumberland bearing down on her, but, before he could reach her, a voice spoke at her side.

'Miss Lambourn, may I have the pleasure?'

Even as she turned, Verity recognised the voice, but a ripple of shock went through her just the same. Salmesbury's companion stood bowing before her, his dark coat and breeches lending him an elegance belied by a cheery, chubby-cheeked countenance.

'Oh!' she uttered foolishly, all coherent thought suspended.

By the time she was able to think again, she found that her hand was tucked into the gentleman's arm and he was leading her into one of the sets then forming.

'May I make myself known to you, Miss Lambourn? Leonard Quainton. Salmesbury's cousin, you know.'

'Have you a title?' Verity asked abruptly, and her voice shook. 'I mean, I should not l-like to make another s-stupid blunder!'

Mr Quainton reddened. 'Must beg you to forgive me, ma'am. Stupid sort of thing to do. Had no idea, you see. That you didn't know him, I mean. But no. No title. I'm not a Haverigg, you understand. Cousin on his mother's side.'

'Oh, I see,' Verity managed, though she was hard put to it to speak at all sensibly. 'But please don't apologise. It—it was not your fault, Mr Quainton.'

'So Salmesbury says,' uttered Mr Quainton gloomily. 'But I set the cat among the pigeons, nevertheless.'

'Please, don't let us speak of it,' begged Verity.

'Must speak of it!' protested the gentleman. 'Pledged my word, you understand.'

They were separated at this moment by the movement of the dance, and Verity went with her head in a whirl, and a rush of gratification in her bosom. He *had* come for her! He had braved the world again, exposed

himself to the minefield of Wellsian gossip, just so that
he might mend the breach. At least, so she must
suppose. Surely this Mr Quainton had come to her in
the guise of peacemaker, had he not?

So it proved. 'Miss Lambourn,' he began at once, as
soon as they were together again, 'Salmesbury begs
only the favour of a word, that he might explain
himself.'

'Oh, no, there is nothing he need explain,' Verity
assured him quickly.

'Good God, yes, he must, ma'am! Even I can see
that.'

Verity gazed at him and her cheeks burned. 'Has
he—has he told you *everything*?'

'Pretty well, I think,' Quainton said earnestly,
anxious to convey his understanding.

'Oh, gracious heaven!' Verity uttered, appalled.
'About—about the library, and—and the boxes?'

'Ha! Ha! Yes, indeed, ma'am. And didn't I roast
him heartily! Never thought to see the old fellow caught
up in such a chapter of accidents!'

His bright laughter was not shared by his partner,
and under that wide, clear gaze he coloured a little,
and coughed in embarrassment.

'Tell me,' Verity said coolly, 'does his lordship find
it as amusing as you do?'

'Good God, no! Poor fellow is quite cut up. Vows
he will set all to rights with you before he comes down
to Brighton.'

A cold hand seemed to grip Verity's heart. 'He is
going to Brighton?'

'Well, hasn't exactly agreed to it. But I'm hoping to
persuade him. Best thing for him, you understand.
And while he has a mind to venture out of his hidey-
hole, seems to me I'd best strike while the iron's hot.
Get him used to it again, you understand.'

'Yes, I dare say you are right,' Verity said automatically, struggling with an inexplicable desire to burst into tears.

'I am,' agreed Quainton confidently. 'Don't want him bolting for cover again the minute you go off. Tells me it's all due to you he's come out of his shell at all.'

'I fear he flatters me, Mr Quainton,' Verity said, with an attempt at lightness.

'No, no. Sticks to it buckle and thong—if it hadn't been for you——'

'Then I am happy to have been of service,' Verity interrupted, unable to bear any more. 'I beg you will tell his lordship that I understand everything and that no explanation is due to me of any kind.'

'But he wants to talk to you himself,' protested Quainton, dismayed.

'Believe me, it is quite unnecessary that he should do so, sir. I think you should certainly put forth your best endeavours to persuade him to accompany you to Brighton.'

There was time for no more, for the dance was coming to an end and they were obliged to abandon conversation as the dancers began the *grande ronde* that completed it.

Afterwards Verity hurried across the floor with her mind all chaos, lending only half an ear to Mr Quainton's continued protests. The news that the Marquis was to be spirited away to Brighton—having first made 'all right' with her, so he had said!—had dealt her an unaccountably heavy blow. She had never known him as the Marquis. To meet him now in this guise, as if they were strangers, before all these avid Wellsian eyes, must be unendurable. Better she should remember him only as the 'Mr Haverigg' with whom she had enjoyed a brief acquaintance through the adventures of a pair of adorable children. Better never to see any of them again!

Yet here was Mr Quainton asking of her, as if it were a small favour, to face that fearsome ordeal! She *could* not do it.

'I say, Miss Lambourn, won't you at least speak to Salmesbury?'

'Pray say no more, sir,' Verity begged, and turning at her patroness' side, she resolutely held out her hand. 'Thank you for the dance, Mr Quainton. Goodnight.'

The discomfited intermediary had nothing to do but to make his farewells and return disconsolate to relay the ineffectual result of his mission to his principal. Miss Lambourn, who would have liked to run away to her lodgings to indulge in a hearty bout of tears, was denied this solace. For Mr Cumberland had waited for her return, jealously determined not to be ousted a second time.

As she took to the floor again on this gentleman's arm, she had the doubtful satisfaction of seeing my lord of Salmesbury limp out of the room set aside for dancing and into the cardroom where, apparently, he remained for the rest of the evening. Although Mr Quainton was to be seen dancing several times with other ladies, he did not again approach Miss Lambourn.

A restless night brought Sunday, and the opportunity to pray for help in a matter that was fast becoming an obsession. Dear Lord, if I am never to see him again, please help me to bear it! But she was no nearer to a reconciliation to this dismal prospect on the following morning when she was wakened early by the maid.

'What is it, Dawson?' she asked sleepily.

'Begging your pardon, miss, but her ladyship sent me to fetch you at once.' The maid simpered knowingly. 'There's a caller in the parlour, Miss. A *gennelman*.'

CHAPTER SEVEN

VERITY let out a small shriek and leapt from the bed.
'Oh, gracious heaven! Oh, no! Oh, Dawson, what shall
I do?'

'Seems to me you'd best get dressed, miss,' said the
maid practically. 'I've brought your hot water.'

Crossing to the table, she proceeded to pour water
from the jug into the basin. Then, as Verity began
hastily to wash, she chose from the meagre wardrobe,
with great presence of mind, a chemise gown of floral
chintz which she laid out on the bed.

Ten minutes later, her heart hammering and her legs
like jelly, Verity entered the parlour. The gentleman
rose from his chair by the window and moved into the
centre of the room. It was Mr Leonard Quainton.

'How do, Miss Lambourn?' he said pleasantly.

Verity was so much disappointed that it was a
moment or two before she could say a word. Fortunately Lady Crossens saved her the trouble.

'There you are at last, child! Bless me, how long it
has taken you! Here is Mr Quainton left with only an
old lady's chatter, when all the time he was hoping to
speak to you.'

'H-how do you do, sir?' Verity managed, holding
out a hand that trembled still. 'What a surprise!'

'Ah, well, you see, had to come early so as to catch
you before you got lost in the dissipations of Tunbridge
Wells! Ha! Ha!'

'Pray be seated again, sir,' Verity said politely,
herself taking a chair by Lady Crossens. 'What is it that
you want of me?'

'Ah, yes. Come to ask if you'd care to join a—a party of pleasure, ma'am. Going to High Rocks, you understand.'

'High Rocks?' she repeated stupidly, as if she had never heard of that famed place about which the Tunbridge Wells crowd were wont to rave. Her heart, which had lain like lead in her chest, suddenly came to life again, making speech difficult. She pulled herself together. 'Oh, yes, High Rocks. It is a—a notable site, I collect.'

'Then you've not seen it yet? Capital. Come with us, ma'am. Make a day of it.'

'Well. . .' Verity began, with a glance at her patroness.

'If you are looking to me,' said the lady at once, who had no notion of putting a bar in the way of her young friend becoming further acquainted with the first eligible male to come in her way, 'you may take it that you have my full permission.'

'But——'

'If you are thinking of a chaperon, my dear,' went on the old lady, 'I am sure you will find that Mr Quainton has provided for all that. How many are in your party, sir?'

'Oh—er—quite a number,' the gentlemen said, a little red about the gills. 'Several very respectable females, of course. I suppose there must be seven or eight of us.'

Verity was at a loss to know what to do. To accept, she knew, must put her in the position of deceiving Lady Crossens, who would not, she was sure, give her consent did she know the likely composition of this *party*. Mr Quainton's acquaintance at the Wells was next to non-existent, she knew, and as for the Marquis of Salmesbury—— Well, unless they had made friends on Saturday night, she had little doubt that the party would be found to contain one small boy and his entourage, and that the 'respectable females' would number among them a toddler in leading strings!

To refuse, however, would mean that she truly would never see the Marquis again. For surely, if she rejected his olive branch a second time, he would abandon any further attempt to make contact with her. She *should* so reject it. It was the only sensible course to pursue. But Verity was not feeling very sensible.

'Well, Miss Lambourn,' Quainton said, a trifle anxiously, 'can we count upon your joining us? Wish you would! I mean, very much hope you can see your way to——'

'Tush, sir!' broke in Lady Crossens irritably. 'Of course she will go with you. Come now, Verity. Go and get your breakfast—for allow you to go off with nothing inside you I will not!—and then fetch your pelisse and bonnet and be off with the pair of you!'

It was a relief to have the decision taken out of her hands, but as Verity moved to the little dining parlour she vowed secretly to confess all to her patroness at the earliest opportunity. When she sat to her meal, however, she found herself unable to swallow more than a few mouthfuls of coffee. Her nerves, already in shreds, were not improved when, as Quainton handed her up into the Marquis's phaeton, he spoke in a low tone so that the attendant groom should not hear.

'I dare say you have guessed that Salmesbury sent me. Said I made wretched work of it at the dance. Quite true. I bungled it shockingly. Must thank you, though. He would have had my head if I'd come back without you this morning!'

His words did much to lighten Verity's heart, but the presence of the groom prevented any further conversation on the subject. Verity put an oblique question. 'Where is the rest of your *party*, Mr Quainton?'

'Meeting them at High Rocks, ma'am.' He glanced at her, the picture of guilt. 'Not exactly a party, mind. Had to hoax the old lady, though.'

'I am aware of it,' Verity said repressively.

He looked relieved, and added, 'Set out early myself, so they should all be there by this time. Only a couple of miles, you understand.'

'Yes, so I believe.'

Apparently cheered by her mild response to his deception, Quainton kept up a steady flow of small talk on the short journey, the sort of thing that came easily to *habitués* of fashionable society. Miss Lambourn, though she bore little part in it herself, was grateful for it, for the stream of inanities kept her imagination from winging ahead to the forthcoming meeting, the thought of which was causing a profusion of butterflies to dance around her stomach.

But when the phaeton reached High Rocks and pulled up next to a carriage with a crest on the panel, such a commotion greeted their arrival that the first moments of meeting passed almost unnoticed.

Braxted, seeing the approach of the carriage, set up a shout. 'Here's Verity, sir! Verity! Verity!'

He began to run towards them, while behind him, a little voice echoed, 'Vetty! Vetty!'

Then little Lady Margaret, too, started forward, but, catching her foot on a protruding rock on the uneven surface, she fell headlong and began at once to wail.

Two females sprang to the rescue, scolding as nurses did, and Braxted dashed back to add his voice to the cacophony, explaining heatedly to his father, who had limped on to the scene, and Mr Eastleigh, tutting ineffectually, that he was not to blame.

'Can I help it if she follows me all over?' he demanded. 'Kittle had ought much better to keep her on a lead!'

'That will do!' said the Marquis. 'No one is blaming you.'

'No indeed,' corroborated the tutor. 'But, you know, Master Wystan, it is your part to have a little foresight where your sister is concerned.'

'But I wanted to greet Verity,' protested Wystan, causing the Marquis to turn at once towards the phaeton.

By this time Verity had already been handed down by Mr Quainton, and was walking towards the agitated group. For a moment there was pandemonium, as several voices greeted her at once, calling loudly over Peggy's wailing.

'Gracious, what a to-do!' she exclaimed, laughing, her nervousness forgotten. 'And here is Mr Quainton inviting me on a party of *pleasure*!'

Salmesbury grinned. 'Indeed, you might well be pardoned for climbing straight back into the carriage and demanding to be driven home!'

'Pooh!' chimed in Braxted. 'She ain't so poor-spirited, are you, Verity?'

'I trust not,' smiled Miss Lambourn, and moved forward to address the grizzling Lady Margaret, who was nestling in Kittle's arms. 'What happened, Peggy? Did you fall?'

Peggy, seeing a new face, ceased her lamentations to stare at it. Apparently she remembered it, for she pointed to the ground. 'Peddy faw down.'

'Oh, that was too bad!' Verity said sympathetically. 'But you're such a brave girl, I know. You won't cry any more, will you?'

Peggy considered this for a moment. Then a bright smile creased her face. 'Peddy no cwy. Peddy bave.'

'And so you are!' agreed Verity admiringly. 'And will you show me High Rocks? I have come to see them, you know.'

This was going too far, however, and Lady Margaret frowned. 'No sow. Peddy pay.'

'Very well, then, I shall ask Wystan to show me,' Verity said equably.

But Peggy would have none of this either. 'No! Wissen no sow you! Wissen sow Peddy.'

'He won't!' began Braxted loudly. 'Wissen no——'

'Come along,' intervened the Marquis quickly. 'We will all go. After all, there they are.'

He turned and pointed to the high cliff-like rocks that stood towering above them some distance away. It was enough for Braxted, who set off at once, calling to the rest to follow. The two nurses hurried along with Peggy, who was pointing after her brother and shrieking his name, and the rest of the adults followed more slowly.

Quite how it happened, Verity did not know, but, long before they reached the Rocks, she found herself strolling beside the Marquis, whose progress was necessarily slow, while the rest of the company had gone some way ahead.

When he judged them to be out of earshot of the rest of the party, Salmesbury left off discussing the merits of the Rocks they could see ahead, and abruptly stopped and turned to his companion.

'Miss Lambourn, now that we have a moment to ourselves, please allow me——'

'Oh, no, pray!' Verity begged quickly, stopping in her turn and showing him a face lit with such warmth that his breath caught. 'You must not say anything, sir! If I seemed to you—if I said anything to—oh, gracious heaven! What *can* I say? I have said *too much* too many times already!'

'Nonsense!' broke in the Marquis. 'It is I who——'

'No, no, no! I will not have you blame yourself! All the conclusions I drew—so *false*!—were of my own

doing. I had no right, no business saying *any* of the
unutterably cruel things I did say. Believe me, sir, if I
have a fault, it is a too over-active imagination which is
apt to lead me into——'

'If you have a fault, Miss Lambourn,' interrupted
Salmesbury firmly, 'it is that you will never permit a
fellow to edge in a word!'

Verity stared at him open-mouthed, taking in the
teasing gleam in his black eye and the twitch at the
corner of his mouth. Her own lips quivered irrepressi-
bly and she began to laugh.

'That is better!' he said, smiling. 'Now, if you will
allow me to speak?'

'You have the floor, sir,' Verity gurgled. 'Indeed,
you are very right. I am all too ready to——'

'*Miss Lambourn*!'

'I beg your pardon!' Verity said contritely, and
resolutely closed her lips, though her eyes danced.

'Miss Lambourn,' the Marquis repeated, in a much
gentler tone, 'let us by all means agree that there have
been faults on both sides. How could it be otherwise?
But your outspokenness—if it *is* a fault!—has been of
immense service to me, and I am far from subscribing
to your own critical view of it. But there can be no
excuse for my failing to enlighten you as to my real
identity at those accursed diversions, as I promise you
I had the intention of doing.'

'Had I only allowed you to edge in a word!' Verity
put in.

'Quite so!' he agreed, grinning. 'Or if you had only
deigned to notice me that night when you looked so
lovely and so—so *unnervingly* unapproachable in all
your finery.'

'*My* finery!' gasped Verity. 'Upon my word, sir, I
can scarcely believe my ears! There *you* were, so very
much the Marquis, so *elegant*! Gracious heaven, how

could I possibly have borne you to approach me after all the dreadful things I had said about you?'

'Don't, *don't*! You make me feel so badly.' The black eyes had grown serious again. He reached out to take one of her hands. 'I owe you so much, Miss Lambourn! Forgive me!'

Tears sprang to Verity's eyes as he bent his head and kissed her mittened fingers.

'There is nothing to forgive, sir,' she said huskily, and felt his fingers tighten briefly on hers before releasing them.

There was a brief pause. As Verity struggled to regain command over her voice, the black eyes looked into hers. He must perceive the tears there, she thought, but he remained tactfully silent. She became conscious then of what he had said and spoke suddenly.

'What do you mean by saying you owe me so much? You owe me nothing.'

He smiled and shook his head. 'You must allow me to be the judge of that.'

'I don't understand,' Verity said frowningly.

'I will explain it to you presently, but not today.'

Verity thrilled to the implication that they must meet again. Then perhaps he meant to stay at Braxted Park!

The Marquis gestured towards the Rocks with his cane. 'Shall we go on?' he suggested, and they turned together and began to stroll towards the others.

'Your cousin told me you are thinking of going to Brighton,' Verity ventured, hardly aware that she held her breath as she waited for his reply.

'Perhaps,' he said, his tone offhand. 'It depends. At present Brighton holds little attraction for me.'

Her heart leapt at his words and it was with difficulty that she refrained from asking on *what* his decision depended.

'I dare say,' she said carefully, 'that it would do you good to go among people of your own kind once more.'

'I don't know that,' he responded lightly. 'I was never very much a social animal, you know, even before——'

He broke off and Verity, conscious of awkwardness in this reminder of the dreadful past, rushed into the breach.

'No, I suppose merely because one is—is born to it, there is no guarantee that one will enjoy the social advantages of one's rank.'

'Precisely. In fact, although I would be the last to deny that it is very comfortable to enjoy these privileges, there are certain disadvantages.'

'Gracious, I should think so!' Verity agreed at once. 'I can think of nothing worse than to be obliged to keep up vast estates and employ hordes of servants. Had I my choice, I should like a quiet cottage, with perhaps a maid and a cat, where I might shut myself up for hours with my pen, and indulge in——'

It was her turn to break off, putting a hand to her mouth as if to force the words back in, and glancing up at her companion in consternation. He was looking puzzled.

'You intrigue me greatly, Miss Lambourn. Am I to understand that you *write*?'

'Oh, pray do not ask me!' she begged. 'I should not have said so much. I did not mean to do so.'

The Marquis had halted again and was staring at her. 'But Miss Lambourn, what is there to be ashamed of in that? Good God, you must be very clever!'

'Oh, I am not!' protested Verity, blushing. 'And as for being ashamed, it is no such thing! Only I am obliged to prevaricate a little, you see, because my parents would be quite shocked if they knew of my plans.'

'Nonsense! They must be proud and pleased,' argued his lordship.

'Oh, pray hush, sir! You do not know! My father is a clergyman, and, although he is the best and kindest of men, I cannot think he would regard with anything but horror the knowledge that one of his daughters plans to live by the writing of Gothic tales of adventure!'

'Live by it?' echoed the Marquis. 'I should think not indeed!'

Verity's eyes flashed. 'And pray why should I not? Because I am a female?'

'Well, partly, but——'

'Let me tell you, sir, that, if I had the good fortune to succeed in having a novel published, I would certainly consider myself entitled to live on the proceeds, in preference to depending on *marriage*, which I take it you imply to be my lot in life!'

'Miss Lambourn, I meant nothing of the sort. I assure you, this wrath is misplaced,' said poor Salmesbury. 'I had no idea of incurring your displeasure.'

'I beg your pardon,' Verity said stiffly, turning away from him. She breathed deeply once or twice to recover her temper, and turned back, speaking with an apologetic air. 'You see, sir, the case is that my mother has a positive bee in her bonnet on the subject of matrimony. I suppose it is because there are so many of us and she has always believed it her duty to see us all off. That is why I was sent here, of course. Though why she should suppose anything could come of it when both Prudence and Patience failed so dismally to procure husbands when they came here, I am at a loss to imagine!'

'Are you all named for the virtues?' asked Salmesbury, seizing on a change of subject that might divert her.

'Oh, yes, it is the greatest trial to all of us!' Verity

said instantly. 'You see, Mama is called Grace, so I suppose that is why they thought of it. They began with Faith, Hope and Charity and continued from there.'

'Good God!' exclaimed the Marquis, amused. 'How in the world did they find such names for—was it six sisters you said you had?'

'Oh, they managed far more than that. We lost so many of my sisters, you know, and they could never bring themselves to use a name of one of the dear ones who had died. So by the time I was born—and I was the seventh—they were hard put to it to find anything acceptable.'

'I think Verity a charming name,' commented his lordship with a smile.

'Oh, I do not mind it. It is my younger sisters who suffered most. Poor Mercy and little Peace are in despair! And when it came to *Temperance* and *Obedience*, who were the last, it was the outside of enough!'

The Marquis could not help laughing, 'I should say so!'

'Yes, but *most fortunately* both of them died, poor little dears.'

'Very understandable,' murmured Salmesbury, the gleam in his black eyes pronounced.

'Ah, but that was before either knew anything of the matter, so I don't feel they can have done so by *design*,' Verity said seriously.

The Marquis's lips twitched, but he managed to preserve his countenance. 'And have you no brothers at all?'

'Only the one,' Verity answered. 'He is the baby, and naturally everyone's favourite. He is spoilt to death and will doubtless grow up to be quite unbearable!'

'Do tell me! I am agog to know. Does his name accord with family tradition?'

'No, it does not!' Verity said with unexpected heat.

'Would you believe it? After saddling us girls with all
those terrible names, what did Mama and Papa do but
come up with something quite ordinary. After my
sisters and I had raided the Bible, too, and discovered
several quite unexceptionable *virtuous* names. But all
they could think of was "Henry". The most common-
place name in the world!'

There was a silence. Then Salmesbury said, a little
diffidently, 'Do you—er—dislike the name "Henry"?'

'Not precisely. For my father is Harry, which is
why——' She stopped and stared at him, struck with a
sudden thought. 'Oh, no! Don't say *you* are called
Henry?'

The Marquis nodded, ruefully grinning. 'I am deso-
lated to be obliged to confess it, but yes.' He bowed.
'Henry Wystan Haverigg, ma'am. Very much at your
service.'

'Oh, *no!*' cried Verity, and went off into a peal of
laughter, in which Henry Haverigg readily joined her.

Then they both became aware that someone was
calling to them.

'Sir! Sir! Verity!' Braxted came running up. 'Don't
you mean to come and see the Rocks? What are you
laughing at?'

'We have been discussing Christian names,' Verity
explained. She looked at the Marquis. 'And this, no
doubt, is Wystan Henry Haverigg?'

'That's right!' Braxted shouted, surprised. 'How did
you know?'

'Pure deduction, Wystan,' Salmesbury said. 'Miss
Lambourn is an extremely clever lady, you must know.'

The comfortable privacy was shattered for the day.
There was no rational conversation to be had with
every other sentence punctuated by Braxted's chatter
or Peggy's terse comments, delivered at the level of a
shriek. It warmed Verity's heart, however, to see the

children so joyous, their pleasure unalloyed by any
suppression of high spirits. For the Marquis forbore to
scold, rather smiling at their exuberance, and the rest
of his entourage took their tone from him.

Miss Lambourn had been interested to note the
presence of a second nurse, and found an opportunity
to make the woman's acquaintance. She chose a
moment when the gentlemen were engaged with
Braxted, who was pointing out the scars made by
previous visitors cutting into the stone of the great
rocks.

'How do you do?' she said in friendly fashion, smiling
at the woman. 'Kittle I have met, but you are new, I
believe?'

The nurse dropped a curtsy. 'Yes, ma'am, I'm the
junior. Bradshaw is the name.'

'And how do you like the position, Bradshaw?'

'Early days, ma'am,' said Bradshaw frankly.

She was a rather gaunt woman, a year or so younger
than her senior nurse, but there was intelligence and
kindness in her gaze, and Verity suspected that a warm
heart beat under the gruff exterior.

'I envy you the charge of little Peggy,' Verity said.
'She is a delightful child.'

Bradshaw's face softened. 'Yes, poor little mite! But
she's a handful, ma'am—except when her brother is
by. Adores the lad, she does.'

Verity nodded. 'And he her.'

'Small wonder, ma'am!' commented the nurse, a
trifle grimly.

The eyes of the two women met and a look of
understanding passed between them. Verity made no
reference to it, however. She could not be seen to
gossip with Henry Haverigg's servants. She smiled
warmly instead.

'I am glad you have come, Bradshaw. Take good care of the little one.'

There was time for no more, for Kittle came up with Peggy, her eyes going from one to the other in quick suspicion. It was evident, Verity thought, that there was some rivalry here.

She had also managed to acquaint herself with the cleric, Mr Eastleigh, and discovered him to be so sensible a man, and so warm in his praise of young Lord Braxted's potential, that she found herself thinking of both children with an easier mind. As if it was any of her business! she chided herself. But the conviction that it *was* her business—that *Henry* was her business!—could not be shaken off.

She thought Mr Eastleigh cast puzzled glances at his employer now and again as he exchanged laughing banter with his cousin, his children and herself, and guessed that the picture Henry was presenting of carefree domesticity was something new, and her heart swelled.

It seemed no time at all before the picnic, served by liveried attendants, had been disposed of, and the Lady Margaret's drooping eyelids signified the end of an enjoyable day. As the disposition of persons in the carriages was being discussed, it became apparent that Salmesbury had the intention of driving Miss Lambourn back to Tunbridge Wells. All at once, the difficulties of her position came home to Verity and she contrived to draw the Marquis a little aside.

'Pray, sir,' she begged in an undervoice, 'do not you trouble to escort me. I can very well go with the groom.'

'You will do nothing of the kind!' argued Salmesbury in a somewhat peremptory tone. 'Good God, how could you think I would treat you so shabbily?'

'No, no, you mistake me,' Verity told him urgently.

'I don't think that. It is only—oh, can you not see how such a course must give rise to gossip?'

The black eyes flashed in sudden anger. 'Are you afraid to be seen with me, ma'am?'

'Well, of course I am!' Verity responded frankly. 'Gracious heaven, what do you suppose people will say of me if it is reported that I left town with one gentleman and returned with quite another?'

'Oh!' said the Marquis blankly.

'Exactly.'

'Hell and the devil!' he swore, and then, recollecting himself, stiffly begged her pardon.

Verity brushed this aside with an impatient gesture. 'You must also realise that it would be quite ineligible for me to be seen with you, in any event, now that you are known in Tunbridge Wells.'

'Oh, indeed?' he returned ominously. 'May I ask why?'

'Well, what a stupid question! Because I am only a clergyman's daughter, and you are a Marquis, of course.'

'What in heaven's name has that to say to anything?'

'Everything! You must know what a hotbed of gossip is the Wells. It may be very well for you to ignore such whisperings, but I, let me tell you, am obliged to be more circumspect.'

Tight-lipped, he stared at her, the black eyes snapping. When he spoke, that intimidating ice was back in his voice. 'Does this mean that I am barred even from calling upon you?'

Verity met his challenging gaze bravely, but her own eyes were bleak. 'I think perhaps it does, yes,' she said, in a sad little voice that spoke volumes.

The anger vanished from his eyes and he caught her hand. 'Forgive me! I thought——' He lowered his voice to a murmur. 'I thought you were attempting to warn me off.'

'Oh, no!' Verity said quickly. 'It is only——'

'Say no more! I comprehend prefectly and I would not for the world embarrass you.' He smiled and pressed the hand he still held. 'Quainton shall take you home.' Abruptly his hand tightened on hers. 'My God, if I had not forgot!'

'What is it?' she asked, made a little anxious by his manner.

'Wait one moment!'

He limped quickly to his coach and leaned inside. As he came back towards her again, Verity saw that he held a package in his free hand.

'What in the world. . .?' she began.

'You cannot now refuse it,' he said, a gleam in his black eyes as he pressed the package into her hands. 'A memento, Miss Lambourn. Until we meet again.'

Verity looked up at him, a smile of mischief hovering on her lips. 'Not those wretched boxes?'

'The very same,' he said softly. 'And God bless them, say I, for they brought us closer!'

'Th-thank you,' Verity managed, her fingers around the package trembling while her eyes spoke her feelings more clearly than any words.

Henry read them, and grasped both her wrists. 'Verity! I can't speak my mind here, but I hope—I believe—— Oh, God, Miss Lambourn, I shall see you again very soon! I *must* see you. Somehow I shall contrive it.'

Then, before she had a chance to speak further, he released her, turned and was calling to his cousin. There was hardly time for a conventional farewell before the phaeton was bowling back along the road to the spa town, but, although Mr Quainton kept up his usual stream of small talk, Verity answered him quite

at random. She was not even listening. Her thoughts
were wholly occupied with that last disjointed speech
from Henry Haverigg, which argued much more than a
simple desire to see her again. Breathless against the
hammering of her heart, she heard his voice over and
over again. '*I can't speak my mind here. . . I must see
you.*' There had been a wealth of meaning in those
words. Might it be—did she dare to hope that he,
too——?

Afraid to put her thoughts into words, she found
instead as she turned the package over and over in her
hands that his name kept revolving in her mind. Henry,
Henry, Henry. But it was as Henry Haverigg she
thought of him, she realised with a start. Not as the
Marquis of Salmesbury. It had been Henry Haverigg
who had intruded into her life. That he was also a
Marquis, *the* Marquis, was almost incidental. Except,
of course, that he *was* the Marquis. That he lived in
some huge house, among who knew how many servants, in a vast estate, no doubt peopled by such
minions as her father was to Lady Crossens in the
village of Tetheridge.

An impossible vision of herself in such a milieu
presented itself to her mind, and was at once superim-
posed by a creature with a shadowed face who haunted
the heart and memory of the Marquis of Salmesbury.

But not Henry Haverigg! No, not Henry! she begged
silently. Only it was Henry Haverigg who was scarred
and lacerated by that vision. How could she, ordinary
Verity Lambourn, hope to oust it?

A profound depression settled on her spirits, and it
was with an effort that she roused herself to bid
farewell to Mr Leonard Quainton at the door of her
lodging. She found Lady Crossens chatting to Mrs
Polegate as both ladies partook of tea and cakes, and
was glad that she had had the forethought to dart into

her bedroom to take off her bonnet before entering the parlour. She did not want to be obliged to explain away the nest of boxes reposing in the package on her dressing-table.

'Oh, you are back,' remarked the latter unnecessarily, her eyes darting past Verity to the door as if she sought her escort there. 'Mr Quainton did not come up with you? What a pity! Not extremely wealthy, of course, but *most* eligible, as I have been at pains to assure dear Emilia.'

'Maria, be quiet!' snapped Lady Crossens, quite exasperated. 'Sit down, child, and have some tea. I will ring for another cup.'

'Oh, no, thank you, ma'am,' Verity said, sinking into a chair beside her. 'But what are you doing at home, ma'am?'

'Oh, she has not been out all day!' exclaimed the widow. 'Poor dear Emilia is not feeling at all the thing! I have been trying to persuade her to have the doctor, but——'

'Maria!' said Lady Crossens warningly.

But Verity turned horrified eyes on her patroness. 'Oh, ma'am! Why did you not tell me? I should not have left you alone!'

'Pho, child! What could you have done? Besides, Maria has been with me, the good creature.'

'Oh, yes, and we have enjoyed *such* a delightful cose,' chimed in Mrs Polegate.

'I am so glad you stayed with her, dear ma'am,' Verity said warmly. 'And how do *you* do?'

'Never mind me,' said the irrepressible widow impatiently. 'How was your day? Did you like High Rocks? Who was of the party?'

'She can only answer one question at a time, Maria,' said her ladyship drily.

'Oh, I know, but I am *so* eager to hear it all,'

fluttered her friend, fixing Verity with an eye alight with anticipation.

'It—it was a very pleasant day, ma'am,' Verity managed, though her cheeks were tinged with colour as she thought of all that had passed.

'And was the Marquis there?'

'Maria!'

'Yes, he was,' Verity admitted, wondering how she was to avoid revealing the actual composition of the party.

Fortunately, Mrs Polegate appeared to be quite satisfied with the presence of Salmesbury himself, confining her flood of questions to his appearance and demeanour, and his conversation.

'He—he is a very amiable man,' Verity said lamely. 'Quite unlike what I had been led to expect.'

The widow was disappointed. 'Was there no air of melancholy about him, then?'

'None that I could see,' said Verity truthfully.

'Pish! Would you have him wear his heart upon his sleeve, Maria? You may depend upon it that his breeding would preclude such a display of emotion. More to the point, did you find Mr Quainton agreeable, child?'

'Oh, yes, quite,' Verity said, with a marked lack of enthusiasm.

Lady Crossens looked at her rather hard, while Mrs Polegate broke into a sentimental diatribe about young persons falling in love on just such an outing as dear Miss Lambourn had enjoyed.

At length Verity managed to turn the subject back to her patroness's health, and was relieved to learn that the day's rest had very much improved it. She excused herself at last on the score of cleansing the dust from her person and dressing for dinner. But once alone and free to indulge her thoughts, she found her mind numb, so that she had difficulty even in recalling what had been said that day, though the pale features of Henry Haverigg with his gleaming black eyes swam in and out of her thoughts.

She discovered, over the next day or so, that her caution had been justified. Mrs Polegate's tongue was not the only one to wag. Sir John Frinton even went so far as to slyly twit her on her new conquest.

'Ah, me! The perennial fate of such an ancient *prétendant* as myself. Cast aside by the explosion of youth!'

'If you will pardon the liberty, sir, you talk a great deal of nonsense!'

Sir John laughed gently. 'But then I have had many years of practice.'

'That I do not doubt.'

'Nevertheless, I am not so sure that this young popinjay is the man destined to steal you from me.'

Verity's startled eyes flew to his. 'What—what do you mean?'

Sir John's lips quivered on that tantalising smile. 'Miss Lambourn, I am neither so blind nor so gullible as the majority of our dear neighbours.' He grinned as the dismay spread over her features. 'Fear not, my dear. I shall not betray you. In fact, you may command my services at any time, should circumstances so arrange themselves that you stand in need of help.'

'Th-thank you,' stuttered Verity, dazed. 'You are very good.'

'I am very *old*,' he contradicted with a wink, 'else I should not so imperil my own interests!'

Verity was obliged to laugh. But she found it increasingly harder to smile as the days wore on with no word and no sign of the Marquis of Salmesbury. Admiring the boxes of Tunbridge Ware in secret had become her solace, as she recalled how he had said they were a memento until they should meet again. But they were no substitute for his presence, and she began to believe that she had misunderstood his urgent words. Surely if he wanted so much to see her, and speak his mind—oh, Lord, what was it he wanted to say?—he would have found a way by now? It was almost four whole days since that hurried parting on Monday.

For the first time, she could see the date of the end of this adventure at Tunbridge Wells looming large, though it was still over a week away. For they were to start for Tetheridge in their fifth week to allow for Lady Crossens' slow method of travel. Her patroness was so clearly feeling the strain on her delicate health that there could be little hope that she might postpone their departure. Suppose the Marquis failed to contact her before that time? She would go away from here, never to see him again! This melancholy idea possessed her mind to such a degree that she found it hard indeed to concentrate on the action going forward on the stage when she accompanied her patroness to the theatre that night.

Mrs Baker's company were performing *The School for Scandal*, a piece which appeared to afford the rest of the Wellsian audience with food for much laughter. In Miss Lambourn's present mood, she found little to divert her in the antics of Lady Teazle and her companions. Besides, the crowded theatre was insufferably hot. She felt quite faint, and at last turned to murmur to Lady Crossens.

'The heat is intolerable, ma'am. Do you object to it if I walk in the corridor a little?'

The old lady, who was much enjoying the play, merely nodded her assent, and Verity slipped thankfully and unobtrusively out of the box. Closing the door softly behind her, she took a couple of paces forward, vigorously plying her fan, when a shadow loomed up before her and she almost screamed.

'Don't be alarmed, Miss Lambourn,' said a familiar voice quietly. 'It is only I.'

Wordlessly, she reached out, and the Marquis of Salmesbury took her hand in a strong clasp.

CHAPTER EIGHT

'I HAD not dared to hope I might catch you alone,' Henry said softly, drawing her a step or two closer to one of the wall-sconces so that a number of candles threw light over them both. 'I was going to wait for the first interval and waylay your party then.'

'But what are you doing here?' Verity asked foolishly, unaware that her fingers clung still to his.

'Can you ask? I had to see you!'

'But to meet in such a way!' Verity exclaimed, pulling away and tugging her hand free. 'If anyone were to see us!'

'Don't distress yourself. I shall not keep you above a moment.' His eyes travelled over her features. A smile lifted the corners of his mouth, and he whispered, 'Though I confess I should wish to do so—*forever*.'

'What?' Verity said faintly, unable to believe that she had heard him correctly.

'Never mind.' He spoke hastily, even a trifle curtly. 'This is hardly the time or the place to discuss such matters. Miss Lambourn, I must see you. Not like this. Openly, so that we may be free to talk. There is so much I want to say to you. I beg you, appoint a day when I may come to visit you, correctly and freely——'

'But I cannot!' she broke in. 'You must know what it is like here. Nothing—but *nothing* occurs in the town but everyone is instantly aware of it.'

'No one knew of our earlier meetings, however.'

'Yes, but you were not known then. I was questioned, believe me, but I turned it off. *Now*, however——'

'Very well, then,' he interrupted impatiently, 'you must come to me.'

'But, Mr Haverigg—I mean, my lord——'

'*Don't* call me that!' he ordered tersely. 'I am not "my lord" to you.' He seized one of her hands and held it tightly. 'Am I? *Am I*, Verity?'

Dumbly she shook her head, mesmerised by the force of those dynamic eyes.

He hissed in a breath, and his other hand let go his cane and took hold of her. As he drew her closer, the cane clattered to the floor, startling them both.

'Oh, take care!' Verity uttered as he let her go abruptly, cursing under his breath. She cast a furtive glance over her shoulder. 'I must go back.'

'Yes, yes, you will do so directly. Only help me to retrieve that accursed cane of mine.'

Quickly Verity bent and picked up the cane. She gave it to him and would have sped away, but he grasped her arm.

'A moment. You could come on another outing such as we had the other day, could you not?'

'I—I suppose that would be possible,' Verity said doubtfully, too anxious to think coherently.

'Very well. Tomorrow, then.'

'Tomorrow? No, I cannot! There is to be a cotillion ball in the afternoon, and——'

'Would that I could still dance!' the Marquis interrupted. 'Or that you preferred *my* company to so energetic a pastime.'

Verity shook her head vehemently. 'It is not that, indeed it isn't! I would like nothing better than to— but it would look so particular if I was absent, don't you see?'

He captured the hand with which she emphasised

her words and brought it to hold against his cheek for a moment.

'The only thing I see, Miss Verity Lambourn, is your clear, innocent orbs looking straight into my soul.'

Verity stared into the black depths of his eyes which glittered oddly in the gloom. Her heart skittered madly, and it was only at a distance that she heard his voice, matter-of-fact now.

'The next day is hopeless, of course, for a clergyman's daughter, so it will have to be Monday. How I will find the patience I do not know!'

'Monday?' she said vaguely.

'Our meeting.'

'Oh, yes.'

'Good. Monday it is. You will say Quainton has arranged it.'

'Quainton? Why did you not send him tonight?'

'He has gone to Brighton. That is why you did not hear from me sooner. I will send my coachman for you. At ten o'clock?'

'Ten o'clock,' she repeated.

He brought the hand he still held to his lips. 'Until then.'

Verity nodded and turned to go back into the box. She felt unreal still, as if she were in a dream. At the door, she stopped and quickly glanced back, afraid she had imagined the whole. But Henry Haverigg was there, standing under the light, still watching her. He raised a hand in farewell and she slipped back into the box in something of a daze.

From the chaos of her thoughts one thing grew clear. She would have to tell Lady Crossens the truth. The Marquis had said she should mention it as his cousin's scheme, but Verity knew she could no longer prevaricate. The situation had grown far too serious for that.

She made up her mind to confess the full story to her patroness before she slept that night.

'And you are telling me this is the very same man with whom you quarrelled that first day?' demanded Lady Crossens, her intent gaze under its lace nightcap fixed upon her protégée's face.

'Yes, ma'am,' Verity admitted, and looked away to examine with apparent interest the quilted coverlet on Lady Crossens' bed.

She had crept into her patroness's room after the maid had departed, to make her confession. The old lady had listened to the tale with admirable restraint, refraining alike from scolding or exclamatory comment. Indeed, it seemed to Verity, shamefacedly recounting it all, that Lady Crossens was not even disapproving. At the end, however, she expressed herself as having received a severe shock.

'What your poor dear father would have to say I shudder to think! As for your mama——'

Lady Crossens broke off and, to Verity's alarm, seemed at first to cackle in a gleeful way and then fall into a fit of choking.

'Dear ma'am, are you all right? May I do anything for you?' Verity offered anxiously, jumping off the edge of the bed where she had been sitting and starting towards her.

The old lady waved her away. 'I am perfectly well,' she answered from behind her hand. In a minute or two she seemed to recover and patted the coverlet. 'Sit down again, child. I have not finished with you yet.'

Verity obeyed, sighing deeply. 'I cannot blame you, ma'am, if you mean to give me a scold. Truly, I had no wish to deceive you.'

'Tush! How could you do so when you were yourself deceived?'

'He—the Marquis—did not mean it, either. Indeed, it was all my folly that caused him to prevaricate.'

'And I suppose it was due to your folly that he chose to hover secretly in the theatre corridor, instead of approaching you decently, like an honest man!' snapped Lady Crossens tartly.

'Yes, it was!' Verity answered, unexpectedly firing up. 'At least, it was *not* folly, for I knew how everyone must gossip and I begged him not to seek me out.'

'God grant me patience!' ejaculated Lady Crossens in exasperated tones. 'Folly? I think you have taken leave of your senses, child! After all, he is *only* a Marquis!'

Impervious to the heavy sarcasm of her patroness's tone, Verity defended herself vigorously. 'That is just the difficulty! If he were only plain Mr Haverigg, as I at first thought him, I could have borne it better.'

'*Borne* it? Borne what?'

'Oh, everything! The disorder of my mind, the—the misunderstandings, the tragic history behind him.'

Lady Crossens' eyes suddenly narrowed, her ill-temper arrested. Her wayward protégée, it appeared, was touched by something far other than a coronet. It was better, far better than she could have hoped. But the girl was altogether too nice in her notions. If care was not taken, the whole affair could yet come to nothing. She knew she was prone to be crotchety, for in truth she was tired and would be quite glad to get home to peace and quiet. But she must try not to allow her tetchiness to overcome her and alienate the girl! She stretched out a hand to grasp the one agitatedly fingering the pattern on the coverlet.

'Come, my child. What is done, is done. No use crying over spilt milk. Now tell me. What is the expedition he speaks of for Monday?'

'Hardly an expedition, ma'am,' Verity said more

calmly, grateful for her ladyship's change of mood.
'There was no time to arrange the details, but I imagine
it will be much the same as the other day, when we
were chaperoned not only by his children, but by the
nurses and Braxted's tutor, as well.'

'Hm. A trifle irregular, but I cannot think the
sternest critic could cavil at it,' judged the old lady,
who had no intention whatsoever of putting a spoke in
this wheel. 'I think you may go with a clear conscience.'

'Oh, yes, ma'am,' Verity agreed at once. 'I am not
afraid of anything—I know *he* would not behave other
than gentlemanly. It was only that I was obliged before
to deceive you for I knew how it would be, and I
allowed you to think——'

'Pish and tush! All that is behind us. No, no, you go
along on Monday and enjoy yourself. Now you had
best get to bed, for if you do not need your rest, I do.'

Verity dutifully went off, able, now that her patroness knew everything, to look forward with a singing
heart to a whole day in the company of Henry
Haverigg. Although how she would get through the
next two days she did not know. Had she been able to
see into Lady Crossens' mind, she might have been less
tranquil.

It was long before the old lady obtained the sleep
she needed, for her own heart was bursting with
triumph. How Grace would stare! A Marquis, no less!
Never, never had she thought to do so well by the
child. Not that she had had anything to do with it,
except to bring her here. But a Marquis! Gracious
heaven, but they were all, *all* of them, taken care of
now! For Verity, as Lady Salmesbury, would see to all
her sisters' husbands; would arrange her little brother's
education. Why, Salmesbury might stand patron even
to dear Harry himself. She could not have been more
delighted if the child had been her own flesh and blood.

Such an odd little creature to have secured such a fortune, too!

Here her ladyship's heady triumph suffered a check. An odd girl, indeed. Pray heaven she did not allow some idiotic scruple to stand in the way! What was more, if she had not gauged what that scruple might be, her name was not Emilia Crossens!

Whether or not her ladyship had correctly identified what might stand in the way of a potential union between Miss Verity Lambourn and himself, the Marquis had every intention of sweeping that particular obstacle out of his path. He had offered another such outing as the one to High Rocks, but in fact he had no idea of burdening himself with a party. He therefore arranged to pack into the carriage on Monday only the children and one of the nurses, and drive the vehicle himself.

Kittle, informed of the plan by Inskip, who told her one of them must be ready to accompany his lordship on Monday, immediately pulled rank over the new nurse and insisted on making the trip herself. Bradshaw, aware of her jealousy of her threatened position, made no objection, although she would have liked to meet Miss Lambourn again.

Salmesbury's coachman had been instructed to collect Miss Lambourn and bring her to the ruins of old Haverigg Hall, the medieval manor that had stood on the other side of the forest on a high hill overlooking the valley where the gypsies were at present encamped. Braxted, the Marquis knew, would love to scramble among the fallen stones, and Peggy would follow him, so that Verity and himself might enjoy a period of peaceful privacy. That this plan would make nonsense of the business of chaperonage did not bother Salmesbury in the least. What he had to say to Miss

Lambourn would, he hoped, obviate the need for a chaperon either now or at any future time.

The day began a little overcast, much to his lord-ship's consternation, and he determined that if it were to come on to rain he would simply transfer the engagement to the comfort of Braxted Place. But by the time the coach set Miss Lambourn down at the broken lodge gates of the old hall, where the Marquis was waiting to escort her, the sun had broken through the cloud with the promise of another hot day.

'Where are we?' enquired Verity after the first greetings, looking about her in some surprise after the coachman had handed her down.

'It is our old house, Miss Lambourn,' answered the Marquis, stepping forward to take her hand. He pressed it, adding softly, 'Thank you for coming. You look charmingly—as usual!'

She blushed a little, for she had, in a sentimental vein, chosen the pink gingham chemise gown and the flower-trimmed chipstraw hat which she had been wearing that far-off day when they had collided in the library doorway.

Realising all of a sudden that they were alone, she looked anxiously about. 'Where are the others?'

'The children have gone forward with Kittle. Wystan could not wait to explore the Hall. It is quite a ruin, you know, and normally he is not permitted to come here.'

He dismissed the coachman and offered his arm to Miss Lambourn, who hesitated a moment, watching the coach begin to rumble away.

'I am not sure this is right,' she said worriedly. 'I have told my patroness that at least the nurses would be here.'

'Kittle is here,' he said reassuringly, again holding

his arm for her to place her fingers within it. 'Come, Miss Lambourn. Do you distrust me?'

'N-no,' Verity said doubtfully, 'only I—I have cleared my conscience, and I do not want to burden it with a new deceit.'

'Then the sooner we join the children, the better,' Salmesbury suggested bracingly.

This seemed sensible and Verity at last consented to place her hand into the crook of his elbow. They began to stroll very gently along the rutted driveway.

'It is very much pitted, Miss Lambourn, so take care,' warned his lordship, as if it were she who stood in more danger of tripping than he with his halting step. But his cane stood him in good stead, and, although their progress was slow, it was secure enough.

'The Hall, you know, belonged to our forebears of the Middle Ages, and has been going to rack since the time of Elizabeth.'

As the Marquis talked on of the ancestors who had inhabited the ruined structure they could see ahead, pointing out landmarks as they went by, a sense of unreality began to pervade Verity's mind. That impassioned little exchange at the theatre the other night seemed as remote as something she might have wrought with her own pen. The man beside her, so far from exhibiting the loverlike ardour that had apparently consumed him then, appeared as calmly controlled as if the meeting were indeed a simple party of pleasure.

That she was herself obliged to conceal an uneven heartbeat and a certain shortness of breath did not occur to her. She thought only that her too active imagination had betrayed her into reading too much into that night's hurried exchange.

As they came close to the ruins, Braxted, poised on a fragment of wall, saw them and waved. In a moment he came running up, closely followed by Kittle with the shrieking Peggy in her arms.

'Wystan, how do you do? And Peggy! I am so happy to see you both!' exclaimed Verity, as the dreamlike feeling at once drained away.

'This is a capital place, Verity!' Braxted shouted. 'You must come and 'splore it with us.'

'Pore it! Pore it!' squeaked Peggy, although she had no idea what her brother meant.

'Well, if you like,' Verity began, but was interrupted.

'Thank you, Braxted, but I think Miss Lambourn had better keep pace with me rather than you. We don't want her dashing about in your neck-or-nothing style. She will end by breaking a limb or something, and then how should we feel?'

'Oh!' said Braxted, eyeing Verity thoughtfully. 'She don't look that feeble to me, but if you say so.'

Verity laughed. 'I dare say your papa is right. Besides, it is growing a little too hot to run around.'

'Pooh!' exclaimed Braxted disgustedly. 'Not for me. Tally ho!'

Then he was off, charging away, and hopping nimbly from rock to rock over the fallen masonry.

'Tay-o, tay-o,' echoed Peggy, as she attempted to emulate him. 'Peddy comin'!' she called as Kittle quickly lifted her and hurried after Wystan.

Verity stood looking after them, a smile on her lips, and was almost startled when the soft voice spoke behind her.

'I hope you do not mind. After having gone to all this trouble to get you to myself, I could not allow my son to take you away from me.'

Verity turned, her heart fluttering, and saw in his face that Friday night had been no dream.

He pointed with his cane to where a clump of trees

encroached on the ruin. 'There is some shade over there, and we may sit on the remains of the wall.'

They made their way through the thickly growing weeds in silence and sat, a little apart, on the low stone that jutted from the ancient foundations. Both pairs of eyes contemplated the distant figures of the children and the nurse, as they clambered about the old stones which marked out the rooms that once were there.

'You asked me a little while back what I owed you,' the Marquis said, suddenly breaking the silence. He gestured with the cane he still held, idling between his hands, towards the children. '*That*, Miss Lambourn, is what I owe you. That I am sitting here, able to watch my children at play, learning to know them again. All that is directly attributable to you.'

Verity looked at him. 'If that is so, I am glad,' she said quietly. 'Though I cannot imagine what words of mine can have brought it about.'

He turned to her then, a little rueful smile curving his lips. 'You rebuked me finely, did you not? And, not content with that, you made, in your innocent and quite understandable assumptions, such comments as made me see how selfish I had been. Very well to punish myself, but I had no right to punish my children.'

His voice had grown harsh and Verity's heart shrank within her. She put a hand on his arm. 'Pray, sir, don't, *don't* distress yourself so!'

'Distress myself! Do you think I would not suffer twice—no, a hundred times—the distress, could I but wipe out that one moment of ill-conditioned temper?'

'Oh, Mr Haverigg—my *lord*, please——'

His eyes, as they turned on her, were almost wild in their passion. '*Henry*,' he grated angrily. 'Call me Henry!'

Verity stared at him, nonplussed. She did not know

what to say, much less do, but her whole heart went out to the tortured storm within him. Without conscious thought, her fingers reached up to touch his cheek.

'Poor Henry,' she whispered involuntarily, 'don't be sad!'

In one violent movement, he caught her fingers and pressed them to his lips, shutting his eyes. Then he almost flung her hand away and pushed himself to his feet, limping some few paces off in a series of jerking steps.

Verity stayed where she was, watching him doff his beaver hat and wipe the back of his hand across his brow. She was no longer afflicted with those nervous flutterings of the heart, for her heart ached. Blindingly, as if she had not suspected it before, the knowledge came to her that she loved him. She did not know if she had the power to assuage the tempest in his soul, but at that moment she knew that she would give her life to do it.

Presently he turned and came back to reseat himself beside her, in control once more. He placed his hat on the wall beside him and rested his cane by it. Verity said nothing as he did so, waiting, willing to follow his lead, to spare him any way she could.

'I have to beg your pardon,' he said calmly. 'I brought you here to talk of that very matter, but I had no business to hurl my uncontrolled emotions at you!'

'Quite like a Gothic monster,' Verity said lightly.

He smiled. 'It must have seemed so indeed. I am so sorry.'

'Oh, do not mind it. Only consider how useful it will be to my next story!'

He laughed out at that. 'My God! A model for the villain, no less.'

'Naturally. Did you expect to play the hero?'

He looked at her. 'In this story, yes.'

Verity coloured a little, but she did not look away. 'But I thought I had explained how much of a bore I found all the virtuous heroes.'

Henry grinned suddenly, and his black eyes gleamed mischief. 'As well, then, that you have seen the worst of me!'

'Have I?' she asked shyly.

The grin faded. 'My angel, I sincerely hope so!'

A rosy glow invaded Verity's heart at this endearing form of address, but she was well aware that its use was premature. Before she could think of a suitable way to express this, however, the Marquis had begun to speak again.

'Verity, I want you to know the worst of me. That is the real reason I needed to talk to you. I want you to have no illusions about what happened here. I want no rumours, no half-truths to come between us.'

'Oh, no,' Verity protested, suddenly afraid. 'No, Henry, no! You need not tell me. It is quite unnecessary. What I have already heard is quite enough. No, I beg you, say no more!'

'I *must*,' he insisted. 'Please understand. I have no desire to distress you with a tale of horror. And it is horrible. But I cannot, will not, go further with what there is between us, unless you have heard the truth from me.'

'Well, if—if you must, then——' Verity faltered. She stopped and smiled at him. 'I'm sorry. I was being stupidly fearful. Tell me anything you wish.'

He drew a breath. 'Thank you.'

There was a pause, during which Verity could see him struggle with himself. She was tempted to say again that he need tell her nothing, but she saw, with a wisdom born of her discovered love for him, that he needed to unburden himself; that he was in fact confer-

ring upon her the greatest privilege he could by impart-
ing to her what had probably never wholly been
confided to anyone.

'It began with a quarrel,' he got out, in a light tone
at variance with the turmoil of emotion this story had
cost him. 'Margaret, you see, was a social butterfly.
She loved nothing better than to go into company,
while I—well, we need not go into that. Suffice it that
our tastes on this matter were widely divergent.'

'There is nothing in that,' Verity commented with a
laugh. 'I could name you as many as a dozen subjects
upon which my sisters and I are at variance.'

'I dare say. But between husband and wife it can
be——'

Again he shied away from revealing too much, and
Verity guessed that the quarrel he had mentioned had
not been the first to be provoked between them.

'Yes, I take your point,' she said.

'Don't misunderstand me,' Henry said quickly.
'Though I did not care for the same sort of pursuits as
Margaret, and would as lief have avoided them for the
most part, I put no bar in the way of her enjoyment. I
trust I was neither so selfish, nor so unkind. But on this
particular occasion I confess I was recalcitrant. It
seemed so pointless an expedition. Some party at a
neighbour's place—to relieve the tedium of those few
unoccupied weeks at the end of summer and before the
London little season, I suppose. I knew she had missed
much of the previous season, for little Margaret was
born then. But she had been to Bath for most of the
summer to recuperate, and I would have thought—
however, that is neither here nor there! She wanted
desperately to go and I did not. Oh, I had a reason,
though to be sure Meg thought it petty. Perhaps it
was.'

He stopped, biting his lip, and Verity, watching him,

thought that he had gone over this argument with himself many times. At the back of her mind she noted, almost in passing, his use of a pet name for his dead wife, and an involuntary pang shot through her.

'What was the reason?' she prompted quietly.

A short, mirthless laugh escaped him. 'My one fatal conceit! A race. If I have a passion, it is for driving. I flatter myself I am a dab hand at the ribbons. Nothing, it seems, has the power to curb it, not even——'

'Why should you wish to curb it?' Verity broke in, unable to bear the bitter self-accusation in his tone. 'Every man must have a hobby.'

'I should wish to,' Henry grated through clenched teeth, 'because the——the *accident* was directly attributable to that *hobby*!'

There was a momentary pause. Verity could feel his tension. Her own pulse was uneven. Her voice shook a little.

'Go on, Henry.'

Henry did not look at her. His eyes fixed themselves on a point in space, where the pictures in his mind paraded before him.

'I had arranged to run a race the following day. A friendly affair with a fellow addict, over by Faversham. I wanted to retire early, but Margaret was bored and very insistent.' He drew a breath, as if the story was becoming more painful to relate. 'We quarrelled.' He shook his head. 'A stupid affair. In the end Meg insisted she should go alone. I could not permit that, of course, and so, with a very ill grace, I gave in.'

His voice went flat. 'The party was quite as insipid as I had expected, and did nothing to improve my temper. Worse, Meg sparkled like the diamonds about her neck, and took—or so I thought—a deal of pleasure in demonstrating her enjoyment to me. I was determined to leave early and so get my rest in spite of her. She was furious and we had more words while the coach was being fetched.'

Again he paused, his breathing ragged. Verity, her own heart shrinking at what was to come, dared not utter a word.

'It was then that I—I took a false step. I could not bear the thought of a journey plagued by recriminations. I told the coachman to get up behind and took the reins myself. It was a—a *criminal* act. The act of a lunatic! For I was the worse for drink and my judgement was impaired.'

The dull ache in Verity's heart sharpened into acute pain. She longed to reach out, to hold him, to *silence* him. But she could not. Horrific as the tale was, she had to hear it.

'There was little moon that night and I drove recklessly, taking out my ill-temper on the horses and the road. Trying, I think, to give Meg the most uncomfortable ride of her life. *Which I did, God help me.*'

His voice throbbed with anguish, but he went on, jerking out the words in a disjointed way.

'There was a bridge—I was going too fast—scarcely saw it. I swerved the horses—and misjudged it. The coach swung wide. Smashed through the barrier.' He was gasping now. 'I was—thrown off. Flung to the— other side of the bridge. I hit the stone and fell— badly. Couldn't get up. I knew the coach was in the water. Meg—they told me later—hit her head. She was unconscious.' He flung his hands over his face. 'She drowned before the coachman could get to her.'

He was shuddering, his breath coming short and fast, while Verity, chilled to the marrow, sat as if turned to stone. Her befogged mind was incapable of registering anything other than the ghastly picture conjured up by the shocking events he had related. Almost as if she was a part of him, she could feel his anguish, and the mental lash with which he scourged himself.

Presently, the warmth of the hot sun penetrated the icy blanket that enwrapped her. A little shiver shook her, and she opened her clenched hands to find them clammy with perspiration. She turned her head and looked at the profile of the man beside her.

Henry was so still now, so remote, as if that iron control of his had him once more in its grip. But Verity, sensitively attuned to his emotions, felt the grief he had reawakened in the telling of the tragedy that had overtaken him. Beneath it, her own fears lurked, strengthened by this new knowledge. But she had no time now to deal with these. Henry was hurting. Henry must be comforted.

Verity reached out and took his hand, cupping it between her own as his head turned and the black eyes at last dared to look into hers again. She could not keep the quaver from her voice, nor the moisture from her eyes, but she spoke with a simplicity that touched him deeply.

'Dear Henry, it is for God to judge. For Him to decide whether there shall be retribution. If He can forgive you, can you not find it in your heart to forgive yourself?'

Slowly Henry's hand turned within her grasp and his fingers laced with her own. The black eyes were tender.

'Oh, Verity,' he uttered softly, 'what manner of girl are you? Have you no words of reproach? Do you not shrink from me in horror?'

Her lips trembled on a smile though her eyes were luminous with those unshed tears. 'I think I could never do that.'

Henry's eyes swept down to caress the smile, and back up to gaze into her own. Then he leaned towards her and swiftly pressed a light kiss on her lips.

Verity's bones turned to water and she felt oddly light-headed. On a gasp, she said, 'I d-don't think you should have d-done that.'

His face hovered still so close but she only just heard his murmured reply. 'How can I help it if you will look at me so?'

'W-what do you mean? How do I look at you?'

'Like a sleeper waking from a beautiful dream. . .to *this*.'

His mouth came down hard on hers and his arms encircled her body, crushing her to him. Something exploded in Verity's head and she was aware only of sensation: of his hungry lips drawing on hers; of the unexpected warmth of his pale cheek; of the firm muscular strength of the body locked against her chest, and moving under her hands as they groped involuntarily about his back.

She felt as if she were drowning, while at the same time a force was growing deep inside her. A force so strong that it brought a tide of heat hurtling through her veins, so that her own lips clung and moved in unison with the mouth locked with them, and she strained towards his body as if she would meld with it.

But when at last he released her, awareness came rushing back and she sprang up from the wall, and as suddenly sat down again as she discovered her knees were too weak to support her. She turned to look at the perpetrator of this devastating assault, and found him obviously equally discomposed, his chest heaving, his pale features tinged with unusual colour, and his fingers trembling as he half held his hands out to her.

'I most certainly do *not*,' she said, in a voice redolent with shock and with one hand at her palpitating bosom, 'think you should have done *that*!'

Henry's inevitable tension found relief in a burst of laughter, and Verity's blushes increased.

'I beg your pardon,' he said, valiantly trying to compose himself. 'It is uncivil of me to laugh at such a moment, I know, but—oh, Verity, you are adorable! So refreshingly innocent!' He took her hand and brought it to his lips. 'Forgive me! I had no intention, truly, of going so far before declaring myself.'

There could be no mistaking his meaning and Verity was struck dumb. The hazel eyes looked with a mixture of anticipation and apprehension into the black.

Henry smiled, retaining his clasp on her hand. 'Don't look at me so worriedly. It is rather I who should be afraid. I, who am no hero, and yet—I trust!—no villain either.'

'Don't speak of that!' Verity said quickly, suddenly finding her tongue. 'I spoke in jest.'

'Don't you think I know that? I am just a man, Verity, who has made a serious error, with tragic consequences. You asked me if I could not find it in my heart to forgive myself. More to the point, and infinitely more important, can you find it in your heart to——?'

'*Papa*! *Papa*!'

Braxted's voice, with a note of urgency that instantly took the couple's attention, broke in on them.

Verity, acutely conscious of the compromising activities in which she had been engaged, leaped up, her cheeks aflame, and turned to the boy as he came running towards them.

'What is it? What has happened?'

The Marquis seized his hat and, leaning to grope for his cane where it had fallen in the grass, he also pushed himself painfully to his feet as Braxted's jumbled explanations reached them.

'She's hurt! Fallen down. Fainted, I think. I had to leave Peggy with her.'

'Oh, thank God!' gasped Verity. 'For a dreadful instant I though you were talking of Peggy.'

'No, it's Kittle. Kittle's gone and hurt herself.'

'Where?' demanded his father, preparing to move.

'No, Henry, I'll go,' Verity said quickly. 'Show me, Wystan!'

She was gone on the words, seizing the boy's hand and running in the direction he tugged her.

'For God's sake, take care!' called Salmesbury after them, as he saw her lift her skirts and jump her way across the ground made uneven by the profusion of fallen ancient stones under the weeds. He limped gamely forward himself at an unaccustomed pace.

But Verity, already in a state of high tension, was swept by this fresh excitement into near panic, racing like the wind towards the spot where Peggy's wails pinpointed the scene of the accident.

Kittle was lying between two narrow juts of broken wall, but as they reached her they saw that she had recovered sufficiently to be able to raise herself on one elbow.

'Take care of your sister, Wystan!' ordered Verity tersely, going at once to kneel by the woman's side. 'How are you hurt?'

'It's my ankle, miss,' uttered the nurse in a faint voice. 'Twisted it, I did, as I come over the wall.'

She was struggling to sit up, and Verity moved so that she might support her from behind.

'Here, lean on me a little.'

Braxted, having collected his sister and quieted her yowls, had returned to stand by the nurse.

'I thought you were dead, Kittle!' he said, on a slightly disappointed note.

'No, Master Wystan,' she replied, 'but I did seem to lose my senses a moment.'

'Tittoo! Tittoo!' muttered Peggy plaintively.

'Only fancy if you had been dead!' said her brother, unheeding. 'We'd have had the devil of a job to get you home.'

'Be quiet, Wystan!' said Verity severely. 'Come here, please, and take my place so that I may have a look at poor Kittle's ankle.'

Braxted came, protesting, 'How can I hold Kittle and Peggy at the same time, I should like to know?'

'Sit with your back to Kittle, and she may rest against you.'

Matters were so arranged, in spite of the boy's arguments, delivered against his sister's interjections, and Verity moved to examine the injured part.

'At least there is no swelling,' she commented, as she gently moved the foot.

Kittle cried out. 'Ooh, miss, it do hurt!'

'I'm sorry. Well, it does not seem to be a bad sprain, thank God. Let us see if you can stand.'

With a good deal of puffing and blowing and groans on the part of the patient, which caused Peggy to break out in tears again, crying, 'Tittoo, Tittoo,' so that her brother had his work cut out attending to her, Verity managed to get the woman on to her feet. By this time the Marquis was seen to be coming up with them.

'Can she walk?' he asked without preamble.

'We have not yet tried,' Verity responded, adding to the nurse, 'See if you can put your foot to the ground.'

Kittle did so, but raised it again, wincing.

'Very well, you must lean on me and hop,' Verity instructed practically. 'We will go this way to avoid the stones.'

'Let me lead,' Salmesbury advised. 'You will not go faster than I in that condition, and I know the way out of this labyrinth of a ruin.'

By a circuitous route, they came out of the ruin itself and traversed its environs to arrive at the trees where

the Marquis had left the phaeton with its horses
tethered so they might crop the bushes.

Kittle was very apologetic and expressed herself as
feeling extremely foolish and low at having spoiled the
party of pleasure.

'Stuff!' scoffed Verity. 'We will take you back home
and have this ankle seen to.'

'Oh, no, miss! Oh, please, miss,' begged Kittle. 'I
couldn't never forgive myself if you was to go to such
trouble. No, indeed.'

'It is no trouble, I assure you. His lordship will not
mind driving us all, I am sure.' She threw a smile at
Henry as she spoke. 'Driving is his passion, after all.'

He smiled back, but, before he could respond, Kittle
was off again.

'Oh, no, miss. His lordship is very kind. But I don't
want to spoil the day, miss. If only his lordship might
consent to take me up, the children could stay with
you, miss, couldn't they? At least until Bradshaw
comes back with his lordship.'

'Now that,' put in Henry in a pleased tone, 'is an
excellent notion.' He gave Verity a meaning look. 'I
think there is no need to end our day out so soon.'

Realising that he meant to continue their interrupted
tête-à-tête, Verity felt the colour steal into her cheeks.
But she made no comment, merely falling in with the
plan, helping Kittle into the carriage and making sure
she was comfortable.

'I'll be back in no time,' Henry promised. His eyes
signalled to Verity a fleeting intimate message that this
reassurance was meant for her. Then he drove away.

Verity, her heart fluttering, turned to find Braxted
trying to stifle a fit of the giggles as he held little Peggy
back from trying to run after the vehicle.

'What is the matter?'

He grinned. 'I was only thinking, now there are two old crocks!'

Verity could not help but laugh, but said, as she stooped to pick up Peggy, 'Yes, very well, I know it is amusing, but it is not at all a proper sentiment, so don't repeat it, I beg of you!'

'I won't. Can I go off again now? I haven't finished my 'sploring.'

'Very well, but keep within sight.'

Peggy, stunned into silence by these rapid events, remained so for a few moments in the novelty of finding herself in a strange embrace. But as she noticed Wystan darting about the ruins, she wriggled, signifying her desire to be released in no uncertain terms.

'Peddy go down! No 'old Peddy. Peddy want to pay. Down! Down!'

Verity, unable to keep hold of the wriggling bundle, was obliged to put her on the ground. Peggy immediately stumbled off after her brother, but Verity was easily able to keep within a few feet of her.

Her mind once more at leisure, she found her thoughts flowing back to the memory of Henry's kisses. A sharp tug inside her brought back the feel of his passion and she found herself longing to feel it again. It seemed as if her wish was to be granted—if he had really been about to offer. She had been so sure at the time, but now——

An alien sound, coming in above Braxted's muted shouts and Peggy's shrill responses, broke into her absorption. Hoofbeats, muffled by the grassy ground.

She looked about, trying to identify where they were coming from. Suddenly a pair of horsemen erupted from the trees beyond the ruins, coming out of the forest that ran through the whole estate.

Verity stood watching them come for the space of a few seconds. Then, spurred by an intangible sense of danger, she closed the gap between herself and the little girl, lifting the infant as Braxted came running towards her, impelled no doubt by the natural curiosity of childhood.

The horsemen were trotting directly towards them and Verity called out to the boy. 'Wystan, hurry! Come here to me!'

The two horses slowed to pick their way over the stones and Verity grasped the boy's hand and held it tightly.

'Who are they? What do they want?' asked Braxted, a touch of fear overlaying the excitement in his voice.

'I don't know,' Verity replied, eyeing them nervously.

Without quite knowing why, she began to back away. Her heart was thudding and she could feel Peggy stirring uneasily as her fright communicated itself to the little girl.

Then everything happened so fast that she was never able afterwards to recall exactly the sequence of events.

The horses suddenly speeded up. With one accord, she and Wystan turned to run and Peggy set up a whimper. Verity let go the boy's hand and he dashed headlong for safety among the ruins. He was not quick enough.

With a cry of alarm, Verity saw one rider lean down and scoop up the child with one hand, hoisting him, kicking and screaming, across his saddle, while the other swung his leg over his mount and prepared to leap down.

Next instant, she was knocked to the ground and Peggy torn from her arms. Dazed, she scrambled up. Too late! The brute had remounted and was already away, the infant clutched in one strong arm.

Verity ran screaming after the horses in a fruitless,

CHAPTER NINE

SOBBING for breath, Verity came to a halt, clinging on to the nearest tree as her brain signalled the utter futility of this insane chase.

She must think! The children were gone. Kidnapped. Henry could not return for some time, but she would do better to wait. Oh, Wystan! Little Peggy! What in the world would Henry say? All he had endured, and now this! Tears dripped unnoticed down her cheeks as she dropped to her knees, desperately trying to think clearly in spite of her bursting lungs.

In a few moments she had recovered sufficiently to get up again, and with the recovery of her physical strength her faculties began to function more coherently. One thought emerged clear and strong. Help. She must get help. There must be a dwelling hereabouts, estate people or forest workers. Something!

Her frantic gaze searched the surrounding area, and, finding nothing, focused further afield, beyond the immediate confines of the ruins, over the trees and down into the valley.

A plume of smoke curling into the distant air impinged itself on her consciousness. The gypsy encampment! Her heart contracted. Gracious heaven, could the men have come from there? Into her mind's eye came the image of the gypsy she had first seen the day she met the children. Could he have meant to take them then? Had she thwarted his design?

Her too ready imagination presented her with a horrific, impossible picture: the gypsies, knives aloft, greedily gazing upon the two small bodies, lashed to a

makeshift spit which turned over the leaping flames of
an open fire. And riding around them all, the triumphant horsemen she had just seen.

Instantly she snapped out of the picture. Fool! she
scolded herself. To allow her absurd realms of Gothic
fancy rein at such a time! *Those* men were not gypsies.
The mental image imprinted on her mind proved that.
Old slouch hats and frock-coats, gaiters over their
shoes. They were rustics, working men, not gypsies!
And the gypsies, she remembered, common sense
reasserting itself, were camped on the Marquis's land.
It would be sheer suicide for them to attempt a crime
of this nature, even if they had the inclination—which
she refused to believe. Time and past that such stupid
prejudice was set aside.

She looked towards the valley, straining her eyes,
almost unconsciously beginning to move in the direction of the gypsy camp. From here she could see over
the trees to gauge the right path to take. The forest
was thin above the valley and the distance did not
appear very great. But Verity hardly thought of all this
as she began to walk purposefully towards the dipping
edge of the land. The children were in her mind, and
suddenly it seemed that the gypsies were the nearest
available source of help.

The sun had risen high by now and even in the light
cotton gown, Verity was uncomfortably hot. Strands of
hair under the now lopsided chipstraw hat clung
damply to her flushed cheeks, and in her scrambling
haste she stumbled once or twice on the uneven
ground. By the time she came out of the forest the
pink gingham gown was dirtied over, ripped in several
places, and she had scratches on her face and her
ungloved hands from the swishing greenery she had
thrust carelessly aside to clear her path.

From here she could clearly see the little clutch of

gaily painted caravans a little below where she stood. But she was still some way off and a sigh escaped her. She wondered, with an involuntary pang, if Henry had returned yet, and what he would do when he found them all gone. She thought, as she plodded on, that he might at first suppose them to be playing a trick, and waste a deal of time hunting fruitlessly about.

Could she but have known it, the Marquis was at that very moment staring from the seat of his phaeton in utter perplexity at the distant figure he could just glimpse, moving at a jogtrot in the direction of the gypsy camp, her hat bouncing on her shoulders, held on only by the ribbons about her neck.

There was a spot on the route from Braxted Place to the ruined manor of Haverigg Hall where the forest dipped so low that a clear view of the valley was obtained. Salmesbury's idle gaze had been caught by something familiar about the hurrying figure and he pulled up, uttering a shocked expletive.

'Good God! What in the world——?'

Bradshaw, the second nurse, who was up beside him, pleased to find herself a member of the expedition after all, glanced enquiringly up into his face. 'My lord?'

The Marquis pointed. 'See there! That is Miss Lambourn.'

The woman peered, frowning. 'But she don't have the children with her, my lord!'

'Exactly. She would never have left them. Damnation! They must have run away.'

'Oh, no, sir, surely not!' protested Bradshaw. 'Master Wystan thinks that highly of Miss Lambourn, my lord. He's talked of her often. I'm sure he'd never serve her such a trick. And with Miss Peggy, too!'

'You're right,' agreed Salmesbury, a heavy frown descending on his brow. 'He could never have outrun Verity while carrying the babe.'

'What does it mean, my lord?' asked the nurse anxiously.

'I don't know, but I have a fearful suspicion. We must go back at once!'

So saying, he began to turn the horses to face in the direction of Braxted Place again, revolving plans in his head, while his heart ached with dread.

They were waiting for her when she got to the camp. She had seen them gathering at the edge of their circle of caravans, one by one as the word passed round of a stranger on the way, intrigued no doubt by her haste and her unkempt appearance.

A knot of nervous tension settled in the pit of Verity's stomach as she searched among the tanned, impassive faces for some sign of warmth. Even the few ragged children who ventured out of the camp towards her exhibited a surly, silent hostility.

No one spoke as Verity came up, slowing her pace the last few yards, to come to a faltering halt before the seemingly solid phalanx of humanity that barred her progress. In fact there were less than a dozen, men in breeches and waistcoats with colourful handkerchiefs knotted about their necks, women in simple layered skirts and light embroidered tops. No bright scarves in evidence here, for this was everyday and they must keep them for best, like the villagers with their special Sunday clothes for church.

Verity looked from one to the other, and proffered a tentative question. 'I need help. The Marquis's children. They've been taken. . .kidnapped. . .please, can you help me?'

The faces were blank, shut in. They merely stared at her and said nothing.

Verity swallowed on a dry throat. Dear Lord, make

them understand! she prayed silently. Desperation entered her voice.

'I'm not your enemy. I was alone with the children for a very short time. Two horsemen came out of the forest and took them. I saw your camp and ran down to see if you could help. *Please*.'

Not a flicker. As a clan, these people were so oppressed, so isolated, that even this innocent appeal failed to break through the wall of prideful, silent enmity they had learned, through bitter experience, to present to strangers.

Verity wanted to run away. She wished she had after all waited for Henry. But she was here, and the thought of the fear and horror that the children must be experiencing even now drove her to hunt her mind for inspiration. It came.

'There's an old woman who tells fortunes. I met her at Tunbridge Wells, at the fair. Is she here?'

There was a sudden change. Here and there the gypsies exchanged glances, shifted position.

'You know her?' Verity went on eagerly. 'I can't recall her name. An old gypsy. . .yes, something like *Mary*, was it?'

The relaxation could be felt. The stern poses eased and even a few mutterings could be heard. Verity caught one and it jogged her memory with the errant name.

'Mairenni!' she said triumphantly. 'That was it. Old Mairenni, she called herself. Oh, please, take me to her! She told me there was trouble and sorrow ahead. Now it has come. She'll help me. I know she will!'

One of the men stepped forward a pace and jerked his head, signifying that she should accompany him. He waited only to see that she understood, and then turned to stride off into the circle of caravans. As Verity followed, the tableau the gypsies made began to break up and shift. In a moment the little group had dispersed about their various businesses, and Verity was more or less alone with her guide.

Old Mairenni must have been waiting for them, apprised by some earlier messenger of the advent of this stranger. She came out of her caravan as they approached and stood on the top step, peering down.

'And is it we'm suspicioned, dearie? Will ye find yon childer stowed away in one o' we wagons, eh?'

'You know?' Verity asked, amazed.

The crone cackled. 'Aye. But there ain't nothing in that, dearie. Young 'un here brought yer tidings.'

She clicked her fingers and an urchin crept out from under the wagon, grinning cheekily up at Verity. She smiled at him automatically, but went to the steps, closer to the old woman.

'Will you help me?' she begged urgently.

'How? Is it the likes o' we be knowing anything worthwhile? How be we going to help?'

'I don't know how,' Verity confessed. 'But I feel sure you could—if you wished to.'

Mairenni stared down at her for a moment, her old eyes inscrutable as she scanned the face below her. Then she broke into her cackling laugh, and swinging a gnarled hand, called out in a cracked voice.

'Peneli! Ho, there, boy!'

Verity looked round to find that the man who had led her here had retired to stand some distance away, not quite out of earshot. Now he came forward, and an abrupt realisation jolted Verity's mind. It was that very same gypsy!

'Upon my word!' she ejaculated. 'It was you!'

His mouth curled sardonically, marring his handsome features. His voice was rough and deep, his accent as thickly overlaid with the west-country twang as was that of the old woman. 'Is it I took the Markiss's childer, then?'

'No, no, I didn't mean that,' Verity said hastily. 'But I have met you before. At least, it was you, was it not, that day I found the children on the road?'

'Aye,' he agreed, his dark eyes roving insolently over her face and figure. 'Thought I meant 'em harm then, you did.'

Verity could not deny it. 'I admit that I was afraid. But I later repented of such a hasty conclusion. It was wrong of me, very wrong, and I beg your pardon.'

He shrugged. 'Can't be blaming ye. It's like yer kind. What do ye know of us Romanies?'

'Nowt she knows,' interrupted Old Mairenni. 'Enough now, Peneli. Come to we for help, she has. Is it our way to refuse? Go now. Take her. Likely news to be found at yon thievin' ken.'

Mairenni was evidently a person of some power, for the man Peneli merely nodded, and once again jerked his head to Verity and moved off. She paused to smile up at the old woman.

'Thank you. I hope you will allow me to come here again to visit you.'

The woman showed her gapped teeth in a grin. 'You'm welcome, dearie. Fortune smiles on ye, don't she?'

Then she waved the girl off with a sweep of her hand and turned away. Verity could hear her cackling as she turned to hurry off after Peneli.

The man led her to a spot behind one of the caravans where a clutch of ponies was grazing in a makeshift corral. He laid a hand on the roped gateway and turned to the visitor.

'Ye ride?'

Verity sighed. 'I'm afraid not.'

The Reverend Harry Lambourn kept but two horses,

one to draw the gig and another for his own use. His
purse did not run to mounting his bevy of girls.

The gypsy's lip curled in that disparaging way, but
he merely said, 'It'll have t'be donkey. And fix you'm
hat. Hot, it be.'

Verity obeyed, retying the ribbons, but without
bothering to prettify the bow. In a few minutes she
found herself sitting rather precariously on the blan-
keted back of an overfed creature, who plodded behind
Peneli's pony at the end of a leading rein. The position
was ignominious, to say the least, but Verity did not
mind that. Her whole preoccupation was with the
children, and she could only hope that wherever Peneli
was taking her would bring her closer to finding them.

She was glad, nevertheless, to see that, once out of
the valley, they very quickly left the main road and
travelled crosscountry via a series of byways. She was
in no fit state to be seen by chance wayfarers. She
would have liked to converse with her dour companion,
ask where they were going, but their relative positions
made speech impossible.

They had been travelling for what seemed an age
when Peneli slowed the pony's pace, allowing the
donkey to come up alongside. His dark face looked
down at Verity, expressionless.

'Can ye tell me why I should help ye to find yon
Markiss's childer?'

A wild pulse began to pump in Verity's heart, but
she met his gaze unflinchingly. 'You are camped on his
land.'

'Be it we owe him a favour, then?'

'Perhaps.' Verity drew a resolute breath and went
on firmly. 'But I think you will rather help me from out
of a warm heart. The same impulse of charity that led
you to approach his children that day we met. For you

knew who they were, and you were going to help them then, were you not?'

'Aye,' he agreed, his voice devoid of any expression that might give her a clue to his thoughts. 'Would've took 'em home.'

'Why didn't you *say*?' Verity burst out.

He shrugged. 'Who'd believe a gypsy? Blame us first, ask questions after.'

She was obliged to admit the truth of this. A stupid prejudice, and she had fallen victim to it herself. But there was little point in discussing it. She turned the subject.

'Where are you taking me?'

'Inn up yonder. Fiddler's Haunt, they calls it. Place of thieves and vagabonds.' He grinned maliciously. 'The likes of we.'

Verity ignored the taunt, but put an anxious plea. 'I beg you will not leave me there.'

'Don't fear on't. Mairenni sent me with ye. Mairenni's word is law.'

'Is she the—the chieftain?'

Unexpectedly, he gave out a loud guffaw. 'Nay. She'm me mam. We be all her childer, or her childer's mates.'

Verity was silent, thinking how odd it was that one should think differently and fearfully of a people whose core of life was in fact very similar to one's own. Old Mairenni, the matriarch, living among her own close-knit family, just as her own and her sisters' lives revolved closely around her father.

Their arrival minutes later at the Fiddler's Haunt put paid to such idle whimsy. It was a disreputable establishment, dilapidated and dirty, a place at which no respectable person would choose to bait. Scrawny livestock roamed its yard, scratching for food, and a slatternly maidservant scoured pans under the pump.

Peneli tethered the mounts and led the way into the dark interior. The large taproom stank of stale drink and tobacco, and a haze of smoke from a dozen pipes dimmed what little light filtered through the grimy windows.

Verity, sticking close to her guide, felt the eyes that appraised her from the shadows hunched on benches in dark corners. She was thankful that her own dirt and disorder allowed her to blend into the scene.

She would have been more fearful still had she known that those unseen eyes easily saw beyond a few mere rips and smears of dirt. The indefinable quality that characterised her was obvious to those whose callings demanded an ability to sum up all chance strangers encountered in the course of their dubious careers.

Peneli moved to the counter, found a chair and bade his fair companion sit and be silent. Verity obeyed, feeling lonely and exposed as he left her to saunter from one group to another, muttering in a low tone with those he met.

As Verity watched him, her fear erupted in a dreadful vision: the shadows in the corners creeping forward, surrounding the shrinking heroine, their grimy, sweat-shining faces flickering evilly in the lanterns held in one or two hands, closing in on her, lasciviously smiling, licking their lips in anticipation at the thought of their evil intent. One filthy paw reached out to the beautiful young girl's face and she opened her mouth to scream.

'Don't fear!' said Peneli's deep voice, his rough tone low and soothing.

With a start, Verity came to herself to see the gypsy regarding her intently, beside him a thick-set man who was eyeing her with undisguised interest. She caught herself up on a gasp, annoyed with herself for having once again given way to her propensity for daydreaming. She felt clammy and cold, and realised that she was allowing fear to rule her.

She drew a steadying breath, threw a glance of reassurance at Peneli, and boldly stared back at the man he had brought, taking in the heavy jowls and the broken nose. Something clicked in her brain.

'Gracious heaven!' she ejaculated. 'Why, you are Sam Shottle!'

He looked taken aback. 'How come you knows me name, missie?'

'You were pointed out to me at the diversions. The fair, you know, the other day.' She got up, her voice eager. This was the man who had been talking with the children's nurse that day, the man who had been identified by the boy Jed.

'This is fortuitous, for you are acquainted with Kittle. And you've seen the children. Surely, surely, you can help me? Has he told you? They've been taken, but they can't have gone far. And perhaps you know people who will have information. The Marquis will pay well, I know that.'

Sam Shottle scratched his chin. 'Well, I don't know, missie. Did hear talk of summat o' the kind. No notion they meant the Markiss's children, mind.'

'You know something? Oh, pray tell me!'

'Not to say *know* exactly,' Shottle said cautiously. 'Heard talk, I did. That's all.'

'But *who*? Who talked? Can we not consult them?' begged Verity, oblivious now to the unsavoury surroundings.

Shottle looked dubious. 'Don't know as how——'

'*Please.*' Driven to desperate measures, Verity seized on the most persuasive argument she could think of. 'I can guarantee you a reward, for I am—I am to *marry* the Marquis.'

She was aware of a concerted reaction through the

stuffy room. Murmurs and movement rippled from man to man. Sam Shottle's keen eyes gleamed with a new light.

'Are you, now?' he said in a ruminating tone. 'That's different, that is. Reckon I'd better take you to see Olly Hargate. 'Tis him and Jim Brigg as I hear a-gabbling o' them there nippers.'

'Do you mean you know where they might be found? Oh, thank heaven!'

'I don't say as I *know* exactly,' pointed out Shottle with his usual caution. 'I'm saying as how I can take you to Olly Hargate, that's all.'

Verity smiled in relief. 'That will do for a start.'

She was thankful to come back out into the bright sunshine, for the foul air of the Fiddler's Haunt was more overpowering than the heat outside. Peneli the gypsy accompanied them for a little way, and then handed the donkey's rein to Sam Shottle.

'You're leaving us?' Verity asked, disappointed.

Peneli turned his impassive stare upon her. 'B'ain't fitting. Remember, blame first, questions after.'

Verity sighed. She understood. There was trouble brewing. The gypsies could not afford to become involved. Especially when it concerned the man whose land they were currently occupying.

Peneli told her she could borrow the donkey. 'When you'm done with he, let he go. Him'll find his own way.'

'Nothing of the sort!' Verity said indignantly. 'I shall bring him to you. Or at least send him with a messenger.'

She thanked the gypsy warmly for his help, but as he rode off in the opposite direction her heart sank and she looked with growing apprehension at the burly back of her new guide as he plodded on foot, the leading rein grasped firmly in his hand. The words of young Jed, Wystan's friend the climbing boy, came back to her unpleasantly. 'He beginned by thievin' and poachin'. . . Reckons to make his fortune. . . *He'll end in Botany Bay*.' Into what hands had she delivered herself?

The way to the establishment inhabited by this Olly Hargate appeared to Verity even more circuitous than the journey she had taken to the Fiddler's Haunt. But at last they came to a cottage. Shottle led the donkey around to the back and Verity was able to see that it was practically derelict and, she realised with a quickening of her heartbeat, extremely isolated.

There was a species of small barn off to its rear and to this Shottle turned his steps, pointing ahead, and saying gruffly over his shoulder, 'You better hide in there, missie, while I finds out if Olly knows summat.'

Verity eyed the barn with misgiving. 'Why should I do that? If he's here, he must have seen us arrive.'

'Likely he's asleep. Or drunk,' said Shottle sapiently. 'Else he'd have come out by this.'

He was still leading the donkey towards the rickety-looking barn, and, quite suddenly, a sound like muffled crying came to Verity's ears.

'What's that?' she demanded suspiciously, and, without waiting for aid, pushed herself sideways and slid off the donkey's back.

She landed awkwardly, but was up in a second, running to the barn as another, more distinct sob reached her.

'Wystan! Wystan! Are you in there?' she called out, frenziedly rattling the locked door.

There was silence from within. Then a muffled, hoarse shrieking broke out. Eyes blazing, Verity turned on Sam Shottle.

'Open this door! *Now*.'

With a nonchalant air, Shottle dug into a deep pocket

and, smiling, brought out a key which he twirled ostentatiously.

'Open it,' Verity repeated, in a voice trembling with rage, far too upset to take in the implications of his actions.

The man unlocked the door and tugged it open with a flourish. Verity ran inside, peering in the sudden gloom. On a heap of sacking at the far end Wystan was lying, hands and feet bound, a scarf about his mouth, while near him was Peggy, peacefully asleep.

'Oh, my poor darlings!' Verity cried out in distress, and dashed forward.

The door behind her slammed shut, and the key turned in the lock.

'My lord, I beg you to listen to reason!' the secretary said urgently, going so far as to lay a restraining hand on the Marquis's arm.

'Reason?' Salmesbury repeated, a dull agony in his black eyes. 'My children are gone, and Miss Lambourn after them, and you talk to me of *reason*!'

'My lord, Miss Lambourn's visit to the gypsy camp was to seek help. I am sure of it.'

'Then why won't they *answer*? Damn them all to hell!'

Henry shook off Inskip's hand and threw his arm across his forehead. The headache was blinding and he could not think. On his return to Braxted Place, he had raised the alarm, and would have gone on to the gypsy encampment immediately, had not Inskip persuaded him that a groom on horseback would travel faster—and perhaps glean more information, though that thought he kept to himself. But Hoff, the only groom Salmesbury would trust, had met with the same wall of silence that had greeted Verity. The gypsies responded equally to either pleas and threats with nothing but blank stares. Hoff had been obliged to concede defeat.

Meanwhile, from the headquarters of the massive office, the secretary had organised a comprehensive search of the estate, and the news of the kidnap had spread like wildfire through the district.

It was oddly disquieting to watch the distress accumulating in his employer's face in these opulent surroundings. The green and gold décor, the gilt ornamentation to the mantel and the ceiling, and the elegant proportions of the furnishings seemed incongruous set against the dark shadow of anguish that was the Marquis of Salmesbury.

Inskip exchanged concerned glances with the chaplain, Eastleigh, as their master staggered blindly to his chair, and, leaning his elbow on the rich wood desk, dropped his aching head into his hands.

'My lord, can I get you anything?' Eastleigh asked anxiously, coming forward.

Salmesbury raised his head and shook it briefly, his pale features drawn, his eyes haggard as he sat kneading his brow. 'I have the headache.'

'I am not surprised, my lord,' Eastleigh said sympathetically. 'Shall I send for a composer, perhaps? Laudanum?'

'*No*,' Henry snapped. Then, recollecting himself, he summoned a brief smile and said more gently, 'No, thank you. I have no intention of returning to that particular slavery.'

He had taken so much of the pain-killing substance during the worst of his nightmare experiences that he had almost become an addict. It had been Hoff, that bluff, scolding nursemaid of a groom, who had saved him, dashing the glass from his hand, forcing him to do without it and learn to overcome by sheer force of will both his physical and mental agonies.

'Will you not lay down a little on your bed?' pursued the chaplain. 'Mr Inskip and I will——'

'Eastleigh, I know you mean well,' interrupted his lordship, 'but I pray you to bear with me. How could I possibly rest in these circumstances?' He turned, with determined calm, to his secretary. 'Inskip, what do we do next?'

'I am still waiting for all the men to report in, sir. Someone may have gleaned information by now that may give us a lead.'

Salmesbury nodded. 'Very well. But if there is nothing——'

A knock at the door broke into his thoughts and he automatically called out permission to enter. A head poked round the door. It was Bradshaw, the gaunt-looking nurse Inskip had hired with the intention of supplanting Kittle once Lady Margaret had become accustomed to her presence.

'I beg your pardon, my lord, for disturbing you at such a time,' she said diffidently.

'Well, come in, come in!' said the Marquis impatiently. 'What is it?'

The nurse edged into the room and carefully shut the door. 'I'm not sure as it's anything important, my lord, only——' She stopped, biting her lip.

'Well? Out with it!'

'It's Miss Kittle, sir. I can't find her!'

'Oh, my God, not another one gone!' Inskip muttered under his breath. Then, more loudly, 'What do you mean, Bradshaw?'

'Well, sir,' she said, turning with obvious relief to relay her story to this less intimidating auditor, for the Marquis's haggard aspect was daunting, 'she was laid up with this ankle, sir, as you know. One of the maids was with her in her room, applying cold compresses like you instructed, sir. Then the maid left her to sleep as Miss Kittle begged her to do. But when I went up to tell her as how the children were gone, sir, she weren't there. And no sign of her in the house.'

All three men stared blankly at her, as if they could not fathom why she should come bothering them with such a matter at such a time. Bradshaw looked from one to the other, and then addressed herself once more to the secretary.

'I just thought it odd, sir, that's all.'

Inskip frowned. 'Foolish, anyway. I dare say she has got wind of the present situation some other way. She would be naturally anxious. Perhaps she has got up to help search.'

'But she couldn't hardly walk, sir!' protested the nurse. 'Leastways, that was what it looked like.'

The black eyes, suddenly keen, looked across at her. 'What do you mean?'

Bradshaw ventured a little closer to the desk, her intelligent eyes searching his face. 'My lord, it ain't my place, perhaps, as I'm only the junior, but I can't say as I've been easy in my mind.'

'Go on,' Salmesbury said, one hand still pressed to his heavily frowning brow.

'It's just that I overheard Master Wystan one day, talking with that little friend of his. They were saying as how——'

'Just a moment, madam,' interrupted the cleric, in a voice that suddenly made him appear very much the stern tutor. '*What* friend? Master Wystan has no friends his own age.'

He did not see the spasm of sudden pain that crossed his employer's face, or the understanding look in the secretary's eyes as they rested briefly on Salmesbury and noted this reaction to the fresh arrow in his touchy conscience. But then both men lost this fleeting instant of recognition in interest at what the nurse was saying.

'It's a village boy called Jed. I think he's the sweep's lad, for I've seen him with the man. But he is certainly very well known to Master Wystan by their conversation. For they were discussing Miss Kittle's personal affairs, my lord, and laughing over what they thought was—well, a-*courting*, sir—with this terrible *bad* fellow. The boy Jed referred to him as one Shottle.'

Three sets of puzzled eyes exchanged glances.

Inskip shrugged. 'The name means nothing to me, my lord, but I could make enquiries.'

'Good God, what is the use of that?' exclaimed Salmesbury impatiently. 'No, no. Send someone to find this sweep's boy and bring him to me at once. Let us go to the horse's mouth, for God's sake!'

'Certainly, my lord,' the secretary said smoothly and left the room at once, pleased to find that with the possibility of a lead his employer's faculties were rising out of the despair that gripped them.

When he returned to the office, he found the Marquis on his feet and coldly determined. He handed a sealed note to Inskip.

'Have Hoff deliver that at once to the captain of the district militia. Whatever may come out of this boy's testimony, there is one thing we do know. Miss Lambourn went to the gypsies and subsequently disappeared. If they will not volunteer the information we seek, then let them be persuaded by other means. We will see how they answer to the barrel of a gun.'

CHAPTER TEN

WYSTAN talked non-stop as Verity wrestled with the bonds about his wrists and ankles. It was as if the pent-up fear was released by this outpouring of the tale.

'I couldn't breathe 'cause he had me hunged over the saddle, head down, and that was the worst of it. But when he tried to right me, I screamed and kicked him. And I shouted him Papa would have him throwed in prison an' transported if he didn't let me go! That's why he put the scarf round my mouth, and then I kept on kicking and he had to tie me up.'

'Gracious, how brave you were!' Verity exclaimed, pulling loose the final knot and setting his legs free.

But Wystan did not jump up as she had expected, only leaning down to rub his sore ankles.

'Yes, but I was afraid,' he admitted. ''Specially when they put us in here, 'cause Peggy had stopped crying by then, and——' his voice faltered a little '—and they hadn't tied anything round her mouth and—and she didn't wake, and——' A sob tore from his throat and he suddenly hurled himself into Verity's arms, crying out into her shoulder, 'Oh Verity, I—I th-thought Peggy was d-*dead*!'

He broke into a storm of weeping, while Verity held him close, her own eyes wet as she remembered with a bursting heart that he was only a little boy, with no mother, and no one to comfort his little distresses. Only this major disaster had had the power to break through his enforced reserve, and show that death held real terror for him, for he knew its merciless rule at first hand.

189

'There now, my darling,' she crooned, rocking him gently. 'There now, my love. Verity's here, sweetheart. Verity's here now. There, darling.'

But it was only a sudden loud wail from his little sister that brought Wystan's head up from her shoulder, and turned his tears to laughter. The baby had got on her feet and was standing beside them, mouth wide, little face screwed up in the way infants had, ready to let out another protest if she did not get instant attention.

'*She* ain't dead!' he gurgled, letting Verity go and brushing the wet from his cheeks. 'Are you, Peggy?'

But Peggy wanted her turn on the comforting bosom. 'Peddy sit. Vetty 'old Peddy now!' She held up her little arms to be lifted.

'Come along, Peggy,' Verity said, smiling, and taking the child on to her lap. 'There, is that better?'

Peggy did not bother to reply, only signifying her deep content by shoving a thumb in her mouth, and snuggling against the soft breasts. Verity looked up to see Wystan surreptitiously wiping his eyes with his handkerchief, and tactfully refrained from comment. Instead she adopted a brisk, though playful tone, designed to keep fear at bay.

'Now, Wystan, we cannot stay here. We must think. If we were writing this as a story, how would we procure our escape?'

Braxted's eyes lit with interest, and he jumped up to examine their prison. 'We have to 'splore first.' He ran to the door. 'Locked. That's no good.'

He looked up and his eye brightened. His voice held a note of excitement. 'Verity, there's a kind of window up there!'

Verity got up, still holding Peggy, and came to join him. The sacks they had been sitting on were under a kind of loft which covered one end of the small barn.

From the door they could see above it a square hole, open to the outside.

'Gracious, I believe it is a hayloft, and that is how they load the stacks. You see, they throw them from that opening straight on to the cart below. It saves a great deal of carrying.' Her eye ran across the edge of the loft. 'There should be a ladder.'

'There is,' exclaimed Wystan, 'only it looks broked.'

From one end of the hayloft two parallel lengths of wood ran down to the floor, but there were only a couple of crossbars at the bottom to show that it had ever been a ladder. The rest were missing.

'So that is why they did not concern themselves over the window,' sighed Verity. 'We cannot get up there.'

'Yes, we can! At least, I can.'

'Wystan, you can't climb a ladder without steps.'

'Yes, I can,' insisted the boy, dashing off to test the two wooden struts. 'Jed taught me to climb the chimbleys. This is just the same. You brace yourself each side and pull up.'

Without more ado, he jumped up those first two cross-bars and set his feet either side, bracing against the struts.

'Oh, take care!' cried Verity anxiously, darting forward.

'S'all right. I'm good at this.'

In only a few moments he had proved his boast, moving with remarkable swiftness up between the two parallel struts, pushing himself higher, gripping with his hands and sliding his feet up again. It hardly seemed any time before Verity's jumping heart was steadying and he was perched on the loft, grinning down at her.

'See?'

'Excellent!' applauded Verity, and did not spoil his triumph by asking the questions in her mind. How in the world was she to get up there herself? Though perhaps she might somehow lift Peggy. At least the children could get away. But how could they find their way alone?

Wystan, flushed with success, was already moving across the hayloft. 'I'll have a look through the window.'

Verity moved back so she could see him as he crossed over to look out of the hole.

'It's a long way down,' he began dubiously, and then Verity saw him stiffen. He ducked down and began crawling back towards the edge.

'What is it?' Verity asked, her pulse quickening.

'There's a man out there!' hissed Wystan fearfully.

'Oh, gracious heaven! Did he see you?'

'I don't know.'

'Why Wissen up dere?' asked Peggy suddenly in a piercing voice.

'Ssh!' Verity begged, quickly putting a hand across her mouth. Then to the boy, she asked, 'Is it one of the men who brought you here?'

'No.' His voice took on a note of puzzlement. 'He looks like a gypsy.'

Hope sprang up in Verity's breast. Peneli! He had not deserted her.

'Quick, Wystan!' she said urgently. 'Go to the window and call to him. If I am not mistaken, he has come to help us.'

'Why should he?' Wystan demanded suspiciously. 'I don't trust gypsies.'

'Do as I say!' Verity ordered, anxiety sharpening her voice. 'You trust me, don't you? He is not here to harm us, I promise you! He has already helped me today. Without him, I would never have found you. I thought he had gone home, but he must have followed us here.'

Dubious still, Braxted crept back to the window and cautiously looked out. The gypsy was right below him.

'Ho, young master! Is the lady in there?' he asked without preamble, his tone low.

'Yes, she is,' Wystan answered back. 'She says you've come to help us.'

'Aye,' agreed the man, phlegmatic as usual. 'Be there any rope in there?'

'Wait, I'll look.' He was soon back. 'No, there ain't. Nor downstairs, Verity says.'

The gypsy looked up. 'Mebbe some cloth we can tear?'

'There's lots of sacks,' Wystan offered.

'Aye, that'll do. Get it, young master. Many as ye can.'

Verity had by this time deposited Peggy on the floor, and she gathered up sacks and threw them to the boy, glancing frequently at the door and listening for the sound of footsteps. Peggy contributed her mite, dragging a sack laboriously from under the loft. Verity thanked her and threw it up.

'Tell Peneli,' she instructed Wystan as she continued with her own efforts, 'that I cannot get up there because of the broken ladder, and we cannot get Peggy up either.'

Peneli listened as the boy relayed this problem, meanwhile ripping the sacks apart, nicking them with the point of a knife produced from some recess in his boot, and tearing down their seams with all the strength of his brawny arms. He made no comment on Wystan's words, but threw up the end of his improvised rope of knotted sacking.

'Now, young master, see if ye can find a beam low enough for ye to get this over.'

Eager to do everything he could, and fairly blazing with mingled apprehension and excitement, Braxted searched the roof above him. But to his disappointment he could not reach high enough, and a couple of attempts to throw the heavy rope produced so much thumping that Peneli told him to desist.

'Ye'll bring yon bad 'uns out on we, boy! Look ye, take rope and tie it side o' yon ladder ye spoke of.'

Crestfallen at his failure, but sufficiently frightened of his captors to refrain from argument, Braxted took the end of the rope around one of the wooden struts and tied it with one of the useful knots Jed had taught him.

'Tight, is it?' Peneli asked, testing the pull with all the nonchalance of his race, as if they had all the time in the world.

'Tight as I could,' the boy confirmed, and watched in fascination as the gypsy climbed up to him, his feet literally walking up the outer wall as he pulled himself to the window. In a moment he was standing in the loft, half bent under the sloping roof.

'Oh, Peneli, thank heaven you are come!' called Verity from below, in accents of heartfelt gratitude. 'Did you follow us?'

'Aye, but you hush now!' he admonished her sternly. 'Yon thievin' coves'll hear!'

'I'm sorry,' Verity whispered contritely. 'What do you want us to do?'

He slung his lengths of sacking over a beam and threw them down to her. 'Tie up yon babe, quick.'

Verity did so, slipping the rope under Peggy's arms and tying it tight.

'*No*. Peggy no like!' shouted the infant, pulling at the bonds which were all too reminiscent of the times Kittle had tied her between two trees. 'Off! Off!'

'Ssh!' Verity begged hastily, crouching down to put a restraining hand over the child's mouth. 'Wystan's waiting, Peggy. Don't you want to go up to Wystan?'

Peggy turned her little face up, staring the long, long distance from her tiny height to where she could see her brother's face hanging upside-down over the edge of the loft.

'Wissen?' she asked uncertainly. 'Peddy up?'

'Come on, Peggy!' he called softly, knowing his exhortations would move her. 'Come up here, Peggy. It's good up here. Let the man bring you up now.'

Peggy beamed. 'Peddy up. Dood up 'ere. Man bing Peddy up *now*.'

'All right,' Verity said, nodding to Peneli.

'Lift 'er high,' instructed the gypsy.

Verity held the infant up as high as she could, feeling the weight taken out of her hands as Peneli drew in the slack. Then with a sudden, swift tug he swung the child up above the level of the loft, and, loosing the rope, grabbed her out of the air with both hands.

'Gracious heaven!' Verity gasped, her own hands automatically stretching up as if she would catch the infant from a fall.

'A capital catch!' Braxted cried, and received a light cuff for his pains.

'Hist, will ye? And take 'er while I get the missie.'

'Sorry,' muttered Wystan, abashed, hastily relieving the man of his sister and undoing the knots about her little body.

Now it was Verity's turn. As Peneli was preparing, she ran to the door and listened, trying to peep through the keyhole, convinced that some sound of their activities must reach the cottage nearby. But there was complete silence.

'I suppose they haven't gone away somewhere?' she suggested as she came back to below the loft.

'Nay,' the gypsy decided. 'Seen 'em, I would. Now, missie. Take yon rope and tie a loop around ye, and hold tight as ye can.'

Obeying, Verity began a silent prayer, unable to see Peneli as he braced himself against the wall at the back of the loft. Without warning, she felt the sacking tighten about her back, and her arms stretched as the improvised rope began to rise. Her feet left the floor, and she held on for dear life, suspended precariously in the air, as each jerk on the rope dug into her back and under her arms and pulled her a few more inches towards the loft and safety.

She closed her eyes briefly, opening them again as she remembered that she would be close to the edge of the wooden platform. If she didn't look she might easily hit her head. There was no room in her thoughts now for the captors who might burst in any second to prevent this extravagant and complex escape. All her mind was concentrated on the effort of remaining calm, refusing to look down, and waiting for the end of this dreadful ordeal.

In reality, the passage to the loft occupied the space of a few brief moments, but they felt to Verity like hours, and as she came up above the surface of the platform she scrambled with unseemly haste to swing her legs to safety. Rolling on to the planks, she lay there a moment, breathing raggedly, her heart sickeningly loud.

'Well done, Verity!' she heard Braxted say. 'Isn't this the most 'citing thing ever to happen to you?'

Verity had barely strength to shake her head, but she looked up to find the gypsy's expressionless eyes upon her. That gave her courage, and she forced herself to sit up.

'What now?' she asked in a far from steady voice.

It seemed to her there was a gleam of mischief in his eyes. It reminded her poignantly—and unbearably!—of the amusement that showed so often in Henry's black eyes, and she was obliged to swallow on a rising lump in her throat. Poor Henry! Whatever must be his feelings now? The thought spurred her to urgency, and she did not even protest in silence to herself when the gypsy spoke.

'Ye to go first. Down t'other side.'

Gritting her teeth, and keeping Henry's pale, haunted features firmly in her mind, Verity hoisted her petticoats indecorously high and climbed out to sit on the ledge of the opening. She felt the slack pull up behind her and, easing her rear forward, let herself go.

The sharp tug under the arms was painful, but she made no sound, only pushing herself away from the wall as she was lowered down to the ground. In fact the descent was far easier than the appalling lift. Or perhaps, she thought, as her feet touched safely on to terra firma, familiarity lessened the giddying sensation of helplessness.

Once she was freed of the rope, it proved a simple task for Peneli to lower the infant down to her. Wystan shinned down the rope like a monkey, and Peneli himself made as easy a job of it as he had of climbing up.

They left the rope hanging down the back of the barn and, creeping to the edge, peered round to see if there was as yet any sign of pursuit.

'Well, I don't suppose they would open the door unnecessarily,' Verity guessed in a soft voice, once they had ascertained that their captors were still ensconced in the cottage. 'For they neglected to tie me up and they don't know but what I might prove troublesome.'

Nevertheless, she held her hand over Peggy's mouth as, following Peneli's lead, they entered the undergrowth behind the barn and crept through it, well hidden by trees as they skirted the cottage. They could see a light within the dim interior and in front of it were two horses tethered close by.

'Let's hope they don't take it into their heads to check on us too soon,' Wystan said.

'Better waste no time,' Peneli advised, and set off.

Neither Verity nor the boy could resist several furtive glances behind them, but the gypsy did not look back once, and seemed to know by the sound that his little band of runaways was still with him. He led them deeply into the shelter of the trees for some little time, but at length they came across his pony, quietly standing, and realised he knew exactly where he was.

'Gracious, there is your donkey!' Verity exclaimed, catching sight of the animal. 'How in the world did you come by him?'

'Man Shottle let he go after locking ye up. I called he by special whistle.'

'Then you saw it all?'

'Aye. Saw his eye when ye told him ye meant to wed Markiss. Knew he meant harm.'

Braxted turned round eyes upon her. 'Are you going to *marry* Papa, Verity? Why, that is a capital notion!'

'Hush, Wystan,' Verity begged, blushing. 'Nothing is settled as yet.'

'Yes, but I think you ought,' said the boy, unheeding. 'Then you could come and live with us at the Place.'

'Yes, yes, but it is not at all certain. I only said it was to induce that horrid man to take me to find his associates.'

'Aye, and filled him's mind with more schemes to bleed yon Markiss,' put in Peneli roughly.

'It was stupid, I realise that now,' Verity said apologetically. 'But I cannot regret it, for we have the children safe.'

Soon she was seated on the donkey again, a delighted Peggy tucked before her, supported by her arm, while

Wystan sat in a similar position with the gypsy on the pony.

The boy had evidently been turning her words over in his mind, for he suddenly demanded, 'Verity, if you and Papa were to be married, would you be our new mama?'

'Only if you wished it,' Verity replied, adding anxiously, 'but I repeat, Wystan, it is not a settled thing at all. You should not know anything about it, and I absolutely forbid you to speak of it again—to *anyone*.'

'But shan't I tell Papa how Peggy and I would like it? That would make him——'

'*No!*' Verity cried, alarmed. 'Upon my word, if you repeat *one word* of this conversation to your papa, I declare I shall never speak to you again!'

'Oh, very well,' consented the child reluctantly, 'but I——'

'*Wystan*. If you will not do as I ask, I shall think you unable to keep a secret, and I shall never be able to share one with you—*ever*.'

'I *can* keep a secret!' he objected indignantly. 'I never telled no one about Jed, did I?'

'No,' agreed Verity, trying for a calmer note, 'and of course I know you will respect my secret, too.'

''Course I will,' Wystan said importantly. 'Only if you *do* decide to marry Papa, will you tell me?'

Verity laughed. 'I should have to, shouldn't I? Now pray don't mention the matter again.'

Fortunately, or perhaps intentionally, he was diverted then by Peneli, who asked him how he had been captured and if he knew the people who did it.

'I should say I do! At least, not eggzackly, but I'd wager I know who made the plot. It was Kittle!'

'Tittoo!' cried Peggy, catching the name. But the others were too involved in discovery to heed her.

'Upon my word, Wystan, I believe you are right! There was not even a swelling on her ankle. She had no more sprained it than I had.'

'But she pretended so as to give those men a chance to get us.'

'And Sam Shottle is Kittle's sweetheart, according to young Jed. That proves it, for it was certainly he who captured me,' Verity agreed. 'I never did like the sound of that Kittle. What a dreadful thing for such a trusted servant to do!'

Dissecting the supposed ramifications of the plot, they hardly noticed the journey. But by the time they came to the gypsy encampment they had begun to feel tired and hungry and Peggy was whimpering incessantly, in spite of both Verity's and Wystan's efforts to distract her. It must be many hours since any of them had eaten, Verity realised, her own stomach acknowledging the fact.

As they descended into the valley, however, bodily wants were once more swept aside when Peneli suddenly brought his mount to a standstill and uttered an imprecation in the Romany tongue.

'What is it?' Verity asked.

Even as Wystan answered for him, she saw for herself the band of redcoated soldiers surrounding the huddled group of gypsies, while to one side, slightly in front of a number of people who were recognisably of his entourage, stood a familiar figure, leaning on a cane.

'Papa's called out the militia!' Raising his voice, Braxted yelled, '*Papa*! *Sir*! We're here! We're back!'

Faces turned towards them as Peneli clicked his tongue and the little cavalcade began to move again, faster now. Faces of surprise and delight. Except for those of the gypsies, which remained sullen and shut in. Except also for that of the Marquis himself, who stared in shocked disbelief, his pain-racked mind capable only of registering that his children and Miss Lambourn were accompanied by the gypsy, without taking in the fact that they were safely restored to him.

His overwrought nerves were discharged in a blast of invective delivered in a voice of molten rage.

'You *villians*!' he began, launching himself forward to burst through the ranks of soldiery, to confront the band of gypsies. 'You knew all the time! You lying, vicious nest of evil! You knew, you *knew*. How *dared* you deceive me?'

He swung himself about and flung out an arm to point at the man who sat behind his son, and did not even see the way the boy's big blue eyes gazed at him in horror and fear.

'Captain, arrest that man! Arrest them *all*. Shoot them! Do what you will with them. But *get them off my land*!'

He stopped, breathing hard, his black eyes wild.

Into the breathless hush that followed his words came Verity's voice, deeply shocked. 'Henry, are you mad? You cannot mean that!'

She slid from the donkey's back, still clutching the infant Peggy, and ran forward.

'I'll take the babe, ma'am,' said a voice, and, turning, she found Bradshaw in her way.

Relinquishing the child at once, Verity moved to where the Marquis still stood, his wild glance roaming over gypsies and soldiers alike, seeing no one. Verity's face swam into focus before him, but her anxious words did not reach through the fog in his brain.

'Henry!' Verity was saying urgently. 'Peneli saved us! Don't you understand? He helped us to escape.'

Recognition flickered briefly in the dark eyes, and he half put out a hand. Then he staggered a little, dropped his cane, and in an anguished voice cried out, '*Hoff*!'

Verity leapt forward as he reeled, but the faithful groom was before her, catching him as he fell.

'*Henry*!' Verity shrieked, as his eyes rolled and closed. 'Oh, my God!'

'It's all right, miss,' Hoff said soothingly. 'I'll see to him. Been too much for him, that's all.'

So saying, he lifted the unconscious man in his brawny arms as if he had been a child, and walked towards the phaeton. Verity, tears in her eyes, would have followed, but was intercepted by the secretary.

'Leave him, Miss Lambourn,' he said, low-voiced. 'Hoff knows exactly what to do for him.'

'You are his secretary?' Verity asked, her voice shaking.

He bowed. 'Inskip is my name.'

'Will Henry—will he be all right?'

'There is no cause for alarm,' he assured her. 'His lordship has had a stressful day. To lose the children was, I think, too severe a reminder of the past.'

'Yes. . .yes, of course.' Struggling to control her agitation, she looked to where the soldiers still guarded the gypsies. The need to right a wrong gave her courage. 'Mr Inskip, you must have the soldiers set the gypsies free! But for them I would never have found the children, and but for Peneli we might still be immured in that wretched barn.'

'I understand, ma'am, but unfortunately I have not the power to countermand his lordship's orders,' said Inskip apologetically.

'Oh, stuff! His lordship was not himself. Anyone can see that. Besides, the soldiers would be far better employed in getting after the villain Shottle and his gang.'

'Shottle? So young Jed was right!'

'Telled you so!' piped up a new voice, and the climbing boy pushed in, accompanied by a rather subdued Lord Braxted. 'Wys been tellin' me as how you come'd after 'em, bold as brass. A right one you are, missie, and no mistake!'

Verity smiled as Inskip chimed in, 'We all echo that sentiment, Miss Lambourn! What we should have done without you, I dare not think. Now I had better see the captain.'

When appealed to, pleadingly by Verity and eagerly by Wystan, the captain of the troop scratched his chin and demanded the full story. He was told it by Braxted, with footnotes added by Verity to clarify several points that became muddled in the telling.

'Seems we'd better get after this enterprising fellow Shottle,' he said good-humouredly when they were done. He cocked an eye at Verity. 'Think your gypsy friend would consent to show us the way?'

'You mean you are not going to arrest them, nor throw them off his lordship's land?' she demanded, her heart lifting.

'In view of your evidence, ma'am, I can't do that. At least, I can't arrest the man. As to seeing the gypsies off, well, I'd need a *written* authority from the Marquis,' explained the captain, with a broad wink. 'I'll ask him again when he's recovered from his—er—illness.'

'Thank you!' Verity said, from the heart, for she knew that Henry would not repeat his request once he knew the full story. Besides, she would ask him not to. That is, she thought fleetingly, if, after today's telling exhibition, Henry and she were ever to talk again. She pushed the idea aside and turned back to the captain.

'Wait! I will ask Peneli if he will take you to the cottage.'

She swung about to look for the gypsy and found

that, with the soldiers' guns no longer trained upon them, the clan had backed up to stand in a ragged line across an opening between two wagons, as if in readiness to defend their very small island against the threatening storm.

Searching for her saviour's tall person, Verity's gaze went from face to face and found nothing.

'Where is Peneli?' she asked of the blank countenances giving her back look for look. 'You need not fear me. Tell me, pray!'

A racked voice called out from behind the barrier. 'Ho, there, dearie! Come ye in.'

It was Mairenni, her clawed palm beckoning. Smiling in relief, Verity pushed through the unresisting gypsies, realising that it was the matriarch rather than their possessions they sought to protect. She thought suddenly, with a wave of tenderness for their loyalty, that Mairenni had not been among the group herded by the militia.

Peneli was beside his mother, his dark face brooding and sullen. 'Yon Markiss don't deserve ye.'

'Don't judge him too harshly,' Verity begged quickly. 'He has suffered greatly, and is still not truly recovered. He did not mean it and will be sorry presently, I promise you.'

Old Mairenni's knowing eyes twinkled up at her. 'Excuses for he ye'll be making, if he do chase us off the valley.'

'He won't,' Verity said confidently. 'I *know* him.'

'Aye,' Peneli nodded. 'Likely ye do, seeing as how you'm to wed he.'

Verity coloured. 'That is another matter.'

The cracked old voice of his mother intervened sharply. 'Don't ye pay no mind to them visions o'yourn, dearie! Leading ye false, they be. Mark old Mairenni's words.'

Biting her trembling lip, Verity put out a hand to take the old one held out to her in kindness and friendship, but she avoided the subject. 'I owe you both so much, but I must ask yet one more favour.'

Peneli nodded as if he read her mind. 'Take yon redcoats to cottage, is it?'

'Would you?'

'Aye. Finish job proper like. Mind, if it weren't for ye——'

She smiled tremulously. 'I can't thank you enough.'

'Enough it is,' interrupted old Mairenni. 'Get ye gone, Peneli, boy! And as for ye, dearie, go on home. Eat, sleep.' She wagged a finger in Verity's face. 'And enough o' setting you'm head alight, eh?'

'I will try,' Verity promised, and left her, but unfortunately, she could have said, her head was already very much alight.

When she rejoined Inskip, she discovered that both Wystan and Peggy had been taken home to be fed and rested, and only the secretary was waiting for her. She realised suddenly that she had not even seen Hoff the groom drive his master away.

'His lordship would never forgive me, ma'am,' Inskip told her, 'if I did not see you safe home, so I have called for the carriage to take us.'

'That is kind,' Verity said, adding, 'but I will not trouble you to escort me. I can quite well go alone.'

Inskip smiled. 'I have no doubt of that, Miss Lambourn. But you will appreciate that I am very happy in his lordship's employ, and would not care to find myself summarily dismissed!'

Verity did not laugh. She stared up at him, trouble in her face, but said nothing more until they sat in the privacy of Salmesbury's coach. She was near sick with hunger and fatigue, and, with the sun just beginning to sink, a chill was seeping into her bones and she was glad of the rug which the secretary tucked about her. But now that all need for action was past, the apprehensions that she had kept at bay came creeping in, wreathing her tired mind in a whirling onslaught of questions.

She sought in the dimming light for the secretary's profile and spoke with a quaver in her voice. 'Mr Inskip, will you tell me something?'

He turned his head, but she could not see his eyes, for which she was thankful.

'If I can, Miss Lambourn.'

'The—the Marchioness. Was she. . .very beautiful?'

There was a pause. Verity held her breath.

'I would not have said,' Inskip began carefully, 'the Lady Margaret was a beauty exactly. She was extremely pretty. The children are very like her, you know.'

'Then she must indeed have been pretty,' commented Verity in a neutral tone. 'He must have counted himself a very lucky man.'

Inskip said nothing. There was much he could say, but he had no idea how far matters had gone, although he could hardly fail to be aware of his employer's interest in Miss Lambourn. He did not want to prejudice the situation by any untoward comment. But all of a sudden, Miss Lambourn turned to him, speaking fast, almost as if she *must* speak.

'It is evident, even had he not told me, how distressed he has been! But his agony of mind, this *passion*—is it all since the accident? Was he—was he *happy*. . .before?'

It was a moment before Inskip said anything, but again his voice was careful. 'I think he was *contented*.'

To his surprise, Verity gave a rather hysterical little laugh. 'Upon my word, Mr Inskip, you are the perfect secretary! You answer my questions and yet you tell me *nothing*!'

'What would you have me say, Miss Lambourn? I am groping in the dark.'

'I would have you say that I may exorcise a ghost!' Her voice cracked. 'Oh, Mr Inskip, what am I to do? It has all happened so very fast, and I thought—up until tonight I thought it would all be well. I thought I had the power to *recover* him. But the hurt runs so very deep! It is much, much worse than I had imagined. And I am afraid. . . I am so afraid!'

Not knowing what else to do, Inskip put out a hand to grope for her arm and press it sympathetically. He felt for her distress, but was unable to offer a single word to assuage her fears. He had seen all too clearly for himself, and many times, the anguish that tormented his employer. How could he reassure this innocent young girl, brave and resourceful though she was, that her love—for he could not doubt that she loved the Marquis with her whole heart—would be enough?

Verity arrived back at the lodgings in Tunbridge Wells in a mood far other than that in which she had set out that morning. But it was still necessary to explain her sorry state to her patroness. Her hair was in a tangle, her hat on askew, and her pink gown in ruins.

'Good God in heaven!' ejaculated the old lady on catching sight of her. 'What in the world have you been doing, child?'

Maria Polegate, who had been dining with her friend, sat staring, her eyes nearly popping out of her head, bereft for once of words.

'It is a long story, ma'am,' Verity uttered, sinking into a chair. 'The children were kidnapped.'

'Mercy me!'

'Lord save us!'

'Tell us all about it at once!'

Neither old lady was prepared to waive her burning curiosity, in spite of Verity's plea of exhaustion.

'You may well be tired! And hungry, too, I dare say,' said Lady Crossens. 'You had better come to the table. I will tell the woman to bring the remains of dinner.'

'Oh, no, please,' Verity begged. 'I could not swallow a thing!'

'Pish and tush! You will take at least some cold meat and some bread and butter. A dish of tea, too. It will do you all the good in the world!'

'Yes, indeed,' corroborated Mrs Polegate, 'there is nothing like tea to refresh you after a fatiguing day. And after such adventures as you have had! You will feel very much more the thing after you have drunk it, I promise you.'

Fussed over and bullied into partaking of a little of the food that was presently brought, and thankfully gulping down a cup of hot tea, Verity found them to be right. She did feel a deal better, and was able to rouse herself sufficiently to deliver a fluent account of the day's adventures.

When she had finished, and the two elderly ladies had done exclaiming and blessing themselves, they drove her to bed and tucked her up, confident in the belief that she would drop asleep in minutes. Verity was so tired that she thought so herself.

But the instant she was alone, the doubts that had been relegated to the back of her mind came flooding in to plague her. And Henry's eyes, wild and anguished, just before he sank unconscious into his groom's arms.

Verity turned her face into her pillow and wept.

Could she have been transported by some magical

means to Braxted Place, it might have resolved all her doubts. For her beloved Henry Haverigg, threshing in his huge four-poster bed in an agony of mind which sent shivers of fear through the heart of the faithfully attendant Hoff, uttered such words as must have brought welcome balm to her heart.

CHAPTER ELEVEN

'WHAT did I *say*?' begged the Marquis, his grip demanding about his faithful henchman's wrist.

Hoff eyed him uncertainly, unwilling to trigger off another such storm as he had witnessed last night.

The black eyes burned at him. '*Tell* me.'

The man sighed. He never had been able to resist that dynamic, compelling look. 'You were calling for that there Miss Lambourn something pitiful, me lord.'

It was the simplest way he could think of to describe the harrowing groans of his master as he called out for the girl as if she had been a goddess, empowered to *deliver* him—as he had begged—from the torture of his own mind.

But Henry stared at the groom, his expression perplexed. Then he shook his head angrily and gripped the wrist he held more tightly.

'Not that, fool! Do you think I can't remember that? My God, she walks in my mind day and night, and if I talk to her in my semi-delirium it is not to be wondered at!'

'Talk!' echoed his henchman scoffingly. 'Aye, if you want to call it that. But I never heard no conversation like it, nor I never will!'

The Marquis reared up in bed, releasing his grip on the man's wrist only so that he might grasp him by the shoulders, the better to bellow into his face.

'Because I know that if *she* were here beside me I could be *calm*! *Don't you understand*?'

He released the man and fell back upon his pillows, closing his eyes. His voice came tiredly, wretchedly.

'No matter how monstrous my actions, how bizarre, she, like you, dear friend and comforter——' with a flicker of a smile to the groom as those eyes flew briefly open and shut again '—she will not blame me. She knows me. It is as if she has always known me. And I her.'

His eyes opened and the energy mounted in his voice. 'Whatever I may have said, Verity knew I did not mean. But not so the gypsies, Hoff!' He was leaning up on his elbow now. 'What did I say to the gypsies? That is what I am asking you.'

'Ah!' said Hoff heavily, and nodded his head. 'You tried to have that there capting of militia arrest 'em. Said as how you didn't care if he shot 'em, only so as he got 'em off of your land.'

Salmesbury sighed, covering his eyes with one hand. 'And to them I owe the safety of my children and of Verity herself. Oh, *God*!' He sat up, preparing to throw off his covers. 'I must see them. God send the captain did not obey me!'

'That he didn't, me lord,' soothed his henchman, but put out a hand to prevent him from leaving the bed. 'But you'll not get up today, me lord!'

Salmesbury sank back, for he was indeed fatigued. He must see the gypsies, however. A picture of the previous evening was in his mind, and abruptly he saw again his son's face where he sat on the pony before the gypsy. Oh, God! *Wystan*. What had he thought?

'Hoff!' he said urgently, his hand going out. 'The children! How are the children?'

'Don't you worry your head over them, me lord. Fit as fiddles, both of 'em!'

'I must see the boy,' muttered Henry, once more attempting to rise.

'No, me lord, no! Stay put and rest, I beg you. You

know Dr Claughton said as how you didn't ought to get up.'

'To hell with Dr Claughton! I shall certainly get up.' He paused, an odd look in his black orbs. 'No, wait. I shall rest then, Hoff, and rise a little later. But first be so good as to fetch the children to me.'

This was so unprecedented that even Hoff could not forbear a shocked gasp. '*Here*, me lord?'

'Yes, here,' responded the Marquis, and grinned suddenly. 'Let them see another side of their father for once, and realise that he is but a mortal man.'

Hoff privately thought that what they would see, coupled with what they had witnessed last night, was more likely to convince them that their father was demented. For besides his crumpled nightshirt, and the blue smudges under his eyes, Henry's motions of the disturbed night had rid him of his nightcap, leaving his long brown hair falling about his shoulders in disarray.

Nor was the groom entirely mistaken. A few minutes later, he returned to his master's chamber with the infant Peggy in his arms, and Wystan lagging a little in his wake. The boy stopped short at sight of his father's dishevelled state and his jaw dropped open.

His eyes goggled a moment. But the slight figure in the bed leaned forward from the bank of pillows, and smiling, held out his arms. In instinctive reaction, Wystan gasped, '*Papa*!' and then ran to the bed to find himself enfolded, for the first time he could remember, in this man's strangely comforting embrace.

His sister Peggy, needless to say, no sooner saw her brother locked in those unfamiliar arms than she set up a jealous shriek.

'Me too, me too! Peddy want 'ug. 'Ug Peddy *now*!'

Both father and son burst out laughing, breaking apart. Soon both children were ensconced on the bed, a fatherly arm about each, while Wystan poured out

the tale of their adventures the day before. Verity's
name figured largely, and at last Henry became aware
that every time his son mentioned it, he looked sideways at his father.

Had the boy guessed, then? Henry wondered. Well,
why not? He was no fool. But Henry had no intention
of discussing his plans as regards Verity Lambourn
until he had settled everything with the lady herself.
For although he could not doubt but that she recipro-
cated his affection, he was by no means certain of his
acceptability as a husband.

There were the strange views she had expressed on
marriage, and her wish to work at this writing—
although she could as well pursue *that* married to him
as not. More easily. Moreover, could she be expected
to overlook the past? The dark shadow of Meg's
accident would always be there, even when not in
mind, in the legacy of his physical punishment. It was
very well to know and respect the integrity Verity
possessed, but might it not lead her to discard him?
For he was unworthy, God only knew! And she was
too honest a soul not to recognise the shoals ahead.

Inwardly sighing, he refocused his attention on the
boy's face, realising that he had stopped speaking.

'I'm sorry, Wystan. What were you saying?'

Braxted frowned. 'You went away. In your head, I
mean.'

The Marquis tightened his hold about the child's
shoulders. 'I did. I beg your pardon.' He paused,
looking into the blue eyes, in which he recognised
uncertainty. 'Wystan, if you find me sometimes
strange. . .distanced. . .or perhaps a little as if I have
lost my senses, I pray you don't ever think it means I
love you less. You and Peggy. You see, when your
mama. . .died——' bringing out the word with diffi-

culty '—I was very much at fault. I am still learning to
live with that. Do you understand at all?'

The boy nodded solemnly. 'I think so. You get a bit
broody-like.'

'That is it exactly.'

Wystan looked at him a moment longer, and then,
so abruptly that it startled Henry, his face broke apart
in a wide smile. 'Well, you won't much longer. *She'll*
see to that.' Then before his father could respond, he
turned to his sister. 'Won't she, Peggy? She'll see to
that.'

'Wissen see to dat,' shouted the infant.

'Not Wissen, silly! Ssh, it's a secret. Peggy not to
tell.'

'Issa seekit. Peddy no tell.'

In a moment, the two of them were jumping on the
bed, both shouting Peggy's version, 'Seekit! Seekit!' at
the tops of their voices. Called to order by Hoff, who
was afraid they might land on his master's injured leg,
they tore round the room in boisterous spirits while the
Marquis lay against his pillows, laughing, all the gloom
vanishing from his features.

A couple of hours later, having partaken of a belated
breakfast together, the Marquis and his son, with Hoff
aboard at his own insistence, were perched in the
phaeton, driving down into the valley towards the gaily
painted caravans.

They must have seen him coming, for as he brought
the carriage to a standstill, he saw them gathering in
knots, coming from inside the circle, to stand, arms
folded, presenting him with the same hostile silence
that had greeted Verity.

The Marquis refused to be intimidated. He climbed
unhurriedly from the phaeton, took up his cane and
limped towards them. Stopping a few yards before
them, he looked from face to face as if he sought to

memorise them. They stared back impassively, but he could feel the vibration of loathing directed towards him. At last he began to speak, not in the manner of one addressing an audience, but looking first at one and then at another, appealing directly to each.

'I am come to retract the words I spoke to you last night. I do not seek your friendship, for I know that is impossible. But perhaps I may at least mitigate your hatred, and pray you to try to understand.'

There were the faintest flickers of the eyes, one to another, in silent communication. Salmesbury had evidently chosen an acceptable tack.

He held out his hand to Braxted, and the boy put his own into it. 'But for one of your number, this child, together with my daughter, would not be here with me today. For that you have my everlasting gratitude, and you may ask of me what you will.'

One of the gypsy women spat suddenly. 'We don't want no reward o'yourn, Markiss.'

'I don't blame you,' Salmesbury sighed. 'Very well. I will make no excuses, and I will offer you nothing. Believe me only when I say that what I spoke last night came from my distress of mind, and from nothing else. And accept also my assurance that as long as I am alive you and yours will ever be welcome on my land.'

With that, he turned away and began limping towards the carriage. A shout from behind stopped him.

'Ho, there, Markiss!'

He turned, and saw that one of the men had come forward. He was a tall, burly fellow with thick black hair waving down to his shoulders.

'That's Peneli,' whispered Wystan. 'The one who helped us escape.'

'You want me?' Henry asked of the man.

'Not I,' Peneli said proudly. He jerked his head. 'It's me mam.'

A hand reached up and clipped him smartly across the ear. Old Mairenni pushed past him, muttering, 'Keep civil tongue in you'm head, boy!'

She came on and Wystan backed away, for she was odd enough and sufficiently witch-like to frighten a little boy. She paid him no attention as he went to the phaeton to seek refuge with Hoff, but came up to the Marquis, standing before him and squinting up into his face, her lined features questioning.

Henry frowned. 'We have met before, I think.'

'Aye, at fair,' she answered.

'Why, you are the woman who told fortunes!'

'That I am, master,' she nodded. 'Don't ye pay no mind to these 'un.' She gave that characteristic gypsy jerk of the head to indicate the gypsies behind her.

The Marquis flicked a glance at them and found they had begun to disperse. 'They have every right to be angry with me.'

'B'ain't angry, master. Glad they be as to find ye don't mean to throw we off you'm land.'

'They have a strange way of showing it,' Henry said with a brief smile.

'Ah, master! Ye don't understand Romany ways. Besides, knowed it we did, what ye say. She told we.'

'She?' he repeated, knowing very well what the woman meant.

'Don't ye judge he too harshly, she say,' the matriarch went on, without answering his question directly, but with her watchful eyes studying him covertly. 'He have suffered, she say. Sorry he'll be when he'm back to his senses.'

'She said that?'

'Aye. And she be right.'

Henry nodded. 'She usually is.'

Old Mairenni frowned, and her clawlike hand reached out to pluck at his sleeve. 'Aye, but she be all wrong now, mark my words!'

'What do you mean?' he said quickly, his black eyes staring into the crone's beady ones.

'I mean as how you'm at crossroads, Markiss! Wrong turn now, and—whisht!' She drew a thumb swiftly across her throat to indicate an end.

As Salmesbury stared at her, his heart began thumping oddly, as if some echo of his own fears were put here into words. His voice was unsteady. 'Fortune could not be that unkind.'

'Aye, but she can,' argued Mairenni, and her cracked voice took on heat. 'Only it *ain't* fortune, master. She be feared. Seeing them pictures in her head, she be. Told her to pay them no mind, I did, but she be stubborn. Ye be warned!'

She turned to go, but Henry reached out a hand to restrain her. 'No, wait!'

Halting, she looked back. 'Aye?'

There was a pause, but then he laughed a little and shrugged. 'You're bewitching me, old woman! And I have no notion what all these nonsensical omens and warnings of yours mean.'

She cackled at him. 'Ye'll pay them no mind anyhow! But don't be a-feared, master. Promised her all, I did—*after* the tears.'

Then she left him standing, snaking away, her bent old bones carrying her in a kind of zigzag path to the caravans, as she sang a snatch of some unknown song in a high-pitched voice that cracked with every other word.

The Marquis watched her go, still smiling, but oddly disquieted by the possible significance of her discourse, for he felt as if something important had slipped away from him in the jumble of her words.

* * *

Two days after Monday's ill-fated expedition to Haverigg Hall, the humdrum life of Tunbridge Wells had forced on Verity an appearance of outward calm. It was obvious that the wagging tongue of that inveterate gossip, Maria Polegate, had made her the cynosure of all eyes. Besides, the story of the kidnap had already made its way to the genteel circles of that avidly curious little town before ever Verity had arrived home at the end of that fateful day.

Verity could see the whispering behind fans, the nods in her direction. But somehow it had ceased to be so important set against the juggling, the see-saw imbalance of her mind and heart. Coupled with the worry over how Henry was after that dreadful collapse, the indecision into which she had been thrown was almost unbearable. She knew that Lady Crossens was narrowly watching her, but she had shut herself in from any attempt to divine her trouble.

'Papa always says,' she told her image in the mirror, 'if you have doubts, *don't*. But oh, Henry, can I *bear* to refuse you?'

She watched in fascination as her hazel eyes in the mirror brightened, and the moisture crept down her cheek as the picture came to her mind of his wild eyes closing as he fainted into his groom's arms. She wondered how, if at all, she would hear news of his present health.

'Perhaps I will not have to refuse him. Perhaps he will not ask me. Perhaps he is. . .*incapable* of asking me—of *remembering* me! Perhaps it is only the image of her, Lady Margaret, that fills his mind, and I—I have no longer a place there.'

Her face in the glass blurred and she searched her sleeve for a handkerchief.

'Verity! Verity, we shall be late!'

The voice of her patroness calling from the corridor caused her quickly to wipe away the giveaway tears.

'Coming!' she replied, hastily patching over her damp cheeks with a dash of Hungary Water, and checking the mirror for reddened eyes.

They were engaged with Richard Cumberland, who was to read to them his latest play.

'Not that I wish to hear it,' as Lady Crossens had confided to her friend, 'for it is sure to be tedious in the extreme. But it may serve to take the poor child out of herself.'

'Oh, yes, indeed, Emilia,' nodded Mrs Polegate. She sighed deeply. 'Such an unhappy state as she has got into. Just when we thought all was in train for the brightest of futures!' For it had not been long before the lady had wormed her old crony's secret hopes from her. 'What can have happened, do you suppose?'

'I am not going to speculate, Maria,' her ladyship said sharply, 'and nor are you! When she is ready, she will doubtless confide in me.'

If Mrs Polegate thought otherwise, she did not say so, but continued to wonder and suggest, in spite of her friend's prohibition. When she saw Verity come into the Assembly Rooms with her patroness, however, making for the corner where the playwright and his prospective audience was awaiting them, she thought perhaps Emilia had exaggerated, so well in hand did Verity have herself.

But if she fooled Mrs Polegate, there was one other whom she decided had seen through her, for surely it was not chance that led Sir John Frinton into an impish attempt to draw her into laughter?

'Now, Miss Heroine,' he said gaily, coming up to the group and rudely pushing past the bulk of Richard Cumberland, who had been about to offer Miss

Lambourn a seat. 'Don't you think you had better entertain us with an account of your great adventure?'

Verity, who wanted nothing less than to talk about the kidnap, at once put in an objection. 'Oh, no. Here is Mr Cumberland who has been so kind as to invite us to hear his play. I am sure it will prove entertainment enough.'

'Oh, do you think so?' asked Sir John blandly, eyeing Cumberland with one eyebrow raised. 'For myself, I should have thought *anything* else—I mean——' correcting himself in so clumsy a fashion that no one could doubt that his slip was deliberate '—of course, I should have thought *your* real-life adventure might prove of more general interest, and—er—stimulation.'

Cumberland was swelling with indignation, as people began to snigger around him. 'I will have you know, sir, that Miss Lambourn herself expressed an interest——'

'Quite, quite!' agreed Sir John, silencing him effectively, and noting with a pleased glance round that several of those within earshot had gathered about the group, ready to enjoy his wit. He would not disappoint them, even if his real object was to divert one particular young lady.

'But really, now, Cumberland, I think you are missing an excellent opportunity. Only consider, my dear fellow! Here is Miss Lambourn, the prettiest little heroine you could hope to find, full of a wonderful tale of romance and adventure—complete, I may say, with the innocents she managed to rescue, which as you must know is *always* a dead cert with audiences—and all you have to do is seize the story and fashion it into a play.'

There was a ripple of amusement, and Sir John's eye gleamed. He pursued his quarry relentlessly. 'Not that I mean to suggest, dear Cumberland, that your own plots are in any way devoid of excitement. Nor, of course, that you are in the habit of stealing ideas from others.'

As this was precisely the opinion of everyone present, most of whom had at some time or another been subjected to the unutterable boredom of the gentleman's productions, it provoked a deal of suppressed hilarity.

'How dare you, sir?' demanded the author, outraged.

'But my dear fellow, have I said anything amiss?' enquired Sir John innocently, glad to see a tiny smile on Verity's lips.

But Mr Cumberland had had enough. Turning his back on his tormentor, he addressed the prospective audience. 'If you are ready, ladies? Perhaps if you would sit here, Miss Lambourn.'

She was very glad to do as he asked, for although she was amused by Sir John's reprehensible behaviour she had no wish at all to relate the story of her adventures.

'Yes, do let us begin,' she said with an assumption of eagerness. 'Pray go away, Sir John, if you do not want to hear the piece.'

He bowed. 'Your wish is my command.'

Behind him Mr Cumberland portentously cleared his throat, and began, 'The scene is set in the Roman forum. . .'

Sir John and his group of admirers beat a hasty retreat, but Verity dutifully remained sitting to listen to the play with every evidence of enjoyment. The fact was, however, that she scarcely heard a word of Mr Cumberland's piece, and could not even have said what it was about had she been questioned. She came to herself with a start when the master of ceremonies, Richard Tyson, gently touched her arm.

'There is a young gentleman to see you, ma'am,' he said in her ear. 'Lord Braxted, he says he is.'

Verity sat up with a jerk, forgetting to lower her voice. 'What? Where?'

She realised the playwright had ceased speaking and was gazing at her in a pained way.

'Forgive me, Mr Cumberland,' she said quickly, 'but I am obliged to leave you for a space.'

He looked annoyed. 'I will await your return.'

'No, no, pray don't,' she begged. 'Do let the others hear it. I am sure Lady Crossens and Mrs Polegate——'

She broke off, as glancing at each lady in turn, she discovered both to have nodded off, their heads sinking on to their chests. 'Oh, dear! Oh, I am so sorry. But I *must* go.'

She rose on the words and followed Mr Tyson to the entrance of the Assembly Rooms where she at once saw Wystan standing with the secretary, Mr Inskip.

'Verity!' called the boy, grinning delightedly at her. 'I am come to ask you to take tea with us.'

Her heart beat rather fast and she glanced at Inskip. 'Is this by—by his lordship's invitation?'

'No, it isn't, it's by mine,' cut in Wystan. 'Mine and Peggy's. At least, 'course Papa knows about it.'

'His lordship begs you to honour the children with your company,' Inskip said with a smile, 'in order that they may express their thanks for what you did for them on Monday.'

'Eggzackly,' agreed Braxted, grinning. 'Do say you'll come.'

'Oh, Wystan, I don't know. I am actually engaged at this present, and——'

'Oh, *Verity*,' groaned the boy, looking crestfallen. 'You *must*. I even told Peggy and she wants you, too. She said, "Vetty come tea".'

Verity smiled. 'Did she?' She hesitated. Well, she must face it—*him*—sooner or later. 'Very well, I will come. Allow me a moment to let Lady Crossens know and I shall be with you.'

As she hurried back, weaving through the knots of people sitting and standing about in the Assembly Rooms, she instinctively glanced down at her person and remembered that the floral chintz had already been worn in Henry's presence. Well, it would have to do!

She was diverted then as she was intercepted in her path by Sir John Frinton.

'Miss Lambourn! Don't tell me you have deserted poor Cumberland? Upon my soul, I did not look for such usage from you to our illustrious playwright!'

She could not forbear a smile. 'For shame, Sir John! You behaved abominably to the poor man.'

'Alas!' he uttered, a hand exaggeratedly placed upon his heart. 'I have offended you, and I meant only to bring a smile to your sweet face, dear Miss Lambourn.'

'I wish you will not be so absurd!' Verity scolded. 'And do pray let me go. I am in a dreadful hurry.'

His eyebrows flew up. 'Don't dare to tell me you are dying to return to listen to that nauseating claptrap!'

'No, indeed. But I am waited for, and I must make my excuses to Mr Cumberland.'

Sir John's eyes lit with that mischievous gleam. 'Ah! Here is my chance to make amends. I shall carry your excuses to Cumberland, thus saving you a tedious and unpleasant task.'

'Would you indeed?' said Verity, relief flooding her face. 'And Lady Crossens, too, if you please. Tell her I have gone to Braxted Place. It is just that I am in a hurry, and——'

'And Cumberland will keep you as he bores on forever about lost opportunities, et cetera, et cetera.'

He held up a hand. 'Have no fear! I will see to it on the instant.'

Verity thanked him and half turned to go, throwing him a doubtful glance. 'Yes, but you will not say anything wicked to him, will you?'

'I shall be discretion itself,' he assured her, bowing. But as she hurried away, his mouth curled into a smile of unholy glee and he turned to go on his self-appointed errand.

Verity, relieved to have got by so lightly, resolved to make a point of offering her apologies in person the very next time she saw Mr Cumberland. But he could not long occupy her mind, when she was on her way to Braxted Place where the object of all her thoughts awaited her.

The journey was beguiled by Wystan's account of the aftermath of the kidnap.

'The militia went after those brutes, but 'course they'd runned off by then. Kittle ain't been seen since and they guess she's gone with them. Jed says Shottle was thick as thieves with Jim Brigg and Olly Hargate in any event. Seems they've done lots of bad things together.'

'But are the militia not continuing to search for them?' asked Verity, diverted from thoughts of the Marquis and the coming meeting. 'They surely can't mean to let such criminals get away?'

'Oh, they're after them all right. They got good descriptions and they reckon to run them to earth in a day or two.'

'They will certainly catch them,' Inskip put in, 'and they have evidence enough to throw them all in prison for a long time to come.'

'How is that?' Verity asked. 'I mean, we are witnesses, of course, but Wystan is a minor and I only saw Shottle.'

'They found a ransom note in the cottage,' the secretary told her. 'It was in the man Olly Hargate's hand, for it seems he was the only one who could write. They apparently had the intention of demanding ten thousand pounds for the children.'

'Yes!' chimed in Braxted in indignant tones. 'But when they had you, they started to write another, for they thought they could get another ten thousand for you alone!'

'How very stupid of them!' said Verity instantly. 'To suppose that I must be more valuable than the two of you!'

'Well, I don't know about that,' Braxted said, mollified. 'I dare say Papa would have paid handsomely to get you back.'

There was a short, embarrassed silence. Inskip broke it, tactfully veering off the subject of ransom notes.

'We suspect that the plot had been laid a long time ago, for the militia have done some thorough questioning. It seems that Kittle is in fact Shottle's wife.'

'What?' gasped Verity. 'Are you saying she had this planned since she came to nurse Peggy?'

'We think so.'

'But her references?' protested Verity. 'Surely you checked them.'

'By letter only. It is quite usual, you know. But I sent grooms to check the addresses of the two people who recommended the woman, and it transpires that the impression of respectable households was false. For instance, Tannery Lodge proved to be Tannery Cottage, and the inmates—no longer in residence, I may add—common people who could no more afford a nurse than they could a maidservant.'

'How very dreadful!' exclaimed Verity, shocked. 'To think that such deceits may be practised so easily!' A sudden thought struck her. 'Gracious heaven, I do trust you have double-checked on the woman Bradshaw?'

'Have no fear,' Inskip said, smiling. 'I did so before we hired her. You see, his lordship had meant in any event to get rid of Kittle, just as soon as little Lady Margaret should have become sufficiently acquainted with Bradshaw.'

'Oh, so that's what was in the wind, is it?' interposed Braxted importantly. 'I thought Papa gave in over that one too easily.'

'Then all unwittingly,' Verity guessed, 'you precipitated the kidnap, for she must have guessed your intention.'

'Yes,' agreed Inskip. 'Which I dare say is why it was so badly executed. Evidently they had no time to lay their plans sufficiently well.'

'No,' Verity said in a subdued tone. 'I'm afraid they would certainly have succeeded if it had not been for my stupidity—though it all turned out for the best in the end!—for it was something I said that led Shottle to expand his scheme to include me. That must have thrown them out, for I cannot think they expected to have to contend with an adult.'

'That's true,' Wystan said eagerly. 'For with Peggy and me they could have travelled much further and gone a lot quicker.'

Inskip laughed suddenly. 'The wretched villains must have thought Christmas had come early!'

They all erupted into the laughter of relief which came to those who recognise how close they have been to disaster. Not that Verity's lightened mood enabled her to face with equanimity the prospect before her. Her yearning to see Henry, to know he was himself again, warred with the fears evoked the other night by his unprecedented outburst and the collapse that followed it.

Unlike his father, it seemed as if the young boy was not a penny the worse for his adventure. And, by his conversation, it appeared that Peggy too had rapidly recovered. Verity longed to ask about Henry, and searched Inskip's face for a clue, but she could not say anything in Wystan's presence for fear of his asking awkward questions. He had already shown that he was too young to be trusted not to refer to it, if something should put it in his head.

In the event, Braxted led her straight up to the nursery and they did not encounter the Marquis at all. As Verity greeted Peggy and sat down to tea with the children, Bradshaw in attendance, she wondered if Henry was deliberately avoiding her, or whether he was merely keeping out of the way to allow the children time with her.

It was the first time she had seen Braxted Place, and the vast marbled hall and Italianate décor did nothing to ease the uncertainty of her mind. While they were in the relatively unimposing nursery, it did not trouble her, but when Braxted offered to show her around she began to feel more and more depressed.

What had she, Verity Lambourn of Tetheridge Vicarage, to do with all this grandeur? As if Henry's tragic past were not enough, here was his milieu to distance her further.

'And here are all the family portraits,' announced Wystan, turning into the long gallery.

Slowly they traversed the length of it, the boy pointing out his forebears, stopping at one that bore a marked resemblance to Henry.

'That's the one who built this place, my great grand-father. That was before they made him a Marquis, so he called it Braxted Place.'

There were the ancient earls, who had inhabited the medieval manor of Haverigg Hall, and the lords and

ladies who had followed them to the Elizabethan pile
which had been razed to the ground by the Earl of
Braxted, who had become the first Marquis of
Salmesbury, and rebuilt in the latest Palladian style at
enormous expense on the same spot.

Verity began to feel crushed by the weight of Henry's
ancestry, so that he seemed less and less the Henry
Haverigg she had met and learned to love, and more
and more the third Marquis of Salmesbury, a personage
whom she did not know and to whom she never could
be equal—in station, in stature, or in anything else.

Then they paused before a more recent portrait. It
was of a woman, and Verity stared, her heart plum-
meting. For in the sweet face, with its gentle smile, its
dreamy eyes of blue, and the frame of corn-gold hair,
she recognised in an instant the ghost that haunted the
man she loved.

'That's Mama,' Wystan announced, as if Verity
needed telling. 'You see, both Peggy and me are like
her, not Papa. I 'member her very well, you know. She
always smiled like that. Like as if she was thinking of
something secret, something nice.'

He paused, his head on one side, considering the
portrait. Verity found herself unable to say a word.
Face to face with the barrier that would stand forever
between herself and Henry, she experienced such
resentment as she had never known before. She wanted
to drag her nails across the canvas, rip that lovely face
to shreds.

Shocked at the ferocity of her thoughts, she stepped
back from the picture, as if afraid the devil in her might
take her over and make her perform that act of hideous
desecration. She stood trembling and sick to the
stomach while Wystan's light treble grew and jangled
in her head as he began to speak again, the words
echoing and re-echoing until she wanted to scream.

'I asked Mama once why she smiled as if she had a secret, and she said she smiled whenever she thought of Papa. She said whenever Papa laughed, it was because he thought of her. She said they had fun together, they enjoyed each other.'

'*Fun together*. . .fun together. . .enjoyed each other. . .enjoyed. . .fun. . .fun. . .fun. . .'

The word hammered in her ears and she saw them— Henry laughing, the ghost smiling, on and on. The lovely woman smiling that secret smile, smiling. Mouth opening wide, jagged as it began to laugh, turning into a jeering, sneering, undulating gash. The gold hair rippling, flowing about her head, flying high as she opened wide her arms and rose into the air, screaming her evil laughter as she drew the man up to tangle in the invisible web she wove about him to hold him there forever. And somewhere far away, a tiny voice, crying hopelessly, *Henry, Henry*. . .

'Ah, there you are!' said Henry's voice.

Verity snapped out of the vision and her head jerked round. Henry! He was smiling, moving, limping along the gallery towards them. He was speaking, but she did not hear the words. For behind him, her overwrought imagination painted the ghostly form of Lady Margaret, smiling in triumph over his shoulder. . . smiling her secret smile.

'No!' Verity cried out, shaking her head. 'I can't.' She was backing from him. '*Henry, I can't.*'

Spinning on her heel, she sped away, oblivious to the voices calling her.

'Verity, wait!'

'Verity, where are you going?'

'Come back, Verity!'

Away she ran, through the gallery to the great staircase that took her down to the hall below, past the marbled glories, over the mottled floors, to the front door where she very nearly collided with the butler as he hurried to find out the cause of the commotion.

'Miss?' Cradoc said. 'Can I assist you?'

'*Please*,' she begged breathlessly. 'Ask the coachman to catch me up. I must go.'

She went as if to wrench at the double doors, but Cradoc was before her, pulling them open. Out she ran, speeding across the stone patio and down the steps, past the statues that decorated each corner of the three shallow flights of the double stairway.

As she started down the sweeping driveway, she began to slow and discovered that tears were streaming down her face. They continued to fall as she stumbled on, waiting for the coach to take her up and whisk her away from this dreadful place that gave her so much pain.

Inside the mansion, the Marquis kept a tight hold on his son's shoulder.

'But shan't I go after her, sir? I can catch her easy.'

'Let her go, Wystan,' answered Henry wearily. 'Let her be.'

'But Papa——'

'Enough!' He summoned a weak smile. 'She will be back. I promise you. I will fetch her back.'

Braxted's lower lip drooped. 'What if she don't want to come?'

His father was looking at the portrait of his dead wife, quite unaware that this was the first time he had done so without the sliver of that pinprick in his heart.

Was this the trigger? Poor Margaret. If he could have felt this for her, perhaps she would not have died that night.

Then he answered his son, as his hand tightened on the boy's shoulder. 'I don't think I could endure it, if she does not want to come.'

CHAPTER TWELVE

VERITY had pleaded a headache, sending a servant with a message to Lady Crossens, and hiding in her room until she could learn to master her emotion. Her patroness, however, when she showed her brave face at the breakfast table next morning, was not deceived.

'Is your headache better?' she demanded, looking at the girl from under lowered brows.

'A little, ma'am,' Verity answered, toying with a small helping of the ham and eggs with which she had been served.

Lady Crossens snorted. 'Pho! Don't tell me! You are at loggerheads with that Marquis of yours, I'll be bound!'

Verity bit her lip, looking away. 'It—it is not like that.'

'Well, how then is it? Come, child. Can you not tell me what ails you?'

'I would if I could, ma'am. Only there is nothing you can do. No one can do anything.'

'Except *him*, I dare say,' her ladyship shrewdly.

Verity looked up at her. 'No. He—he cannot help it. The past is—is——'

'*Past*,' snapped Lady Crossens. 'Good God, girl, do you suppose a man will pine forever over a dead woman?'

'Please, ma'am,' whispered Verity, wincing.

'You are a fool, Verity! And you know nothing of men. Mark my words. If he is not beating a path to your door at this very moment, you may call me a dunderhead!'

At that opportune moment, there was a knock at the door and the maid came in.

'Well, Dawson?'

'Please, ma'am, there's a gennelman called for Miss Lambourn.'

'Aha!' rasped her ladyship triumphantly. 'Show him up, Dawson.'

'He's already up, ma'am,' grinned the girl.

Verity, who had sat like a stricken statue, now rose to her feet, pale but determined.

'Come along,' instructed Lady Crossens, and opened the door to the parlour.

The Marquis was standing by the window looking out, his brown locks, uncovered, neatly confined in a tie at the nape of his neck. He turned as the door opened, his eyes going past her ladyship to Verity's downcast face behind her.

'You're Salmesbury, I take it,' said the old lady, sailing across the room and grasping his hand. 'I'm Emilia Crossens.'

'How do you do, ma'am?' he said politely, bowing slightly over the hand he held.

'Very well, I thank you. But you have come to see Miss Lambourn, I apprehend, and so I shall leave you at once. Not that I approve of these free and easy modern manners, but circumstances, you know, alter cases!'

'You are so right,' agreed the Marquis, an irrepressible twinkle in his eye.

'At my age I ought to be!' she rejoined, and, marching to the parlour door, she hustled the open-mouthed Dawson before her.

Left to confront Verity, Henry's amusement faded as he searched her set features. The white gown of figured muslin emphasised her deathly pallor. Concern showed in his voice.

'You are almost as pale as I.'

Verity's eyes flew up to meet his, but she checked the response that rose to her lips. Instead she spoke in a quiet, polite manner quite unlike her usual tone.

'Won't you sit down?'

She took a chair herself, and he fidgeted a moment or two, looking at her with a frown in his eyes, then seated himself in a chair near the window. She would not meet his gaze and he found it hard to know how to begin. The silence lengthened and Verity at last looked up.

'I have to apologise, sir, for my abrupt departure from your house yesterday.'

'Verity,' he said in a hurt tone, 'you are addressing me as if we are strangers!'

'I *must*,' she whispered.

'But why?'

She was silent. Henry pushed himself up. At once she rose, too, and moved a step back from him. His face showed his feelings as he stood there, stiff, the black eyes challenging. Verity felt his pain at her rejection, and swallowed on the rising lump in her throat, forcing herself to speak calmly.

'Henry, I know why you have come. But I can't— you must not——'

Her voice failed. Her obvious distress touched him and his stiff pose relaxed, the green frock-coat sitting more easily upon his less rigid frame.

'Why have you turned against me? I want you to marry me, Verity. I thought—was I mistaken?—that we were of the same mind.'

I *was*, she wanted to cry. But she must not. She had decided. She must not weaken. She had doubts, and if in doubt, said the Reverend Harry Lambourn, *don't*. She drew a breath and as of instinct moved a little closer to him.

'Henry, I think we allowed ourselves to be carried away. I never looked for marriage.'

'No, I know,' he said quickly. 'You told me so. It is not, surely, this wish of yours to live by—what did you call it?—the writing of Gothic novels?'

'No, no, I——'

'Because, if so, there is nothing to stop you doing so,' he pursued anxiously. 'At least, not *live* by them. But *write* them, certainly. Indeed, I should take great pleasure in reading them.'

'You can't know that,' Verity protested with a faint smile. 'You may think them quite dreadful. But, Henry, it is not that. Upon my word, that would be *too* petty!'

'And you are certainly not that. *Tell* me.'

'Oh, Henry, it is so hard to explain. I am not of your world, for one thing.'

'What does that matter?' he said impatiently. 'I may be a Marquis, but I am also a man, Verity.'

'I know, I know, and I have never really thought of you in that light. To me you are, you will *always* be only Henry Haverigg.'

He smiled. 'I would not have it otherwise. But if not my rank, then——'

'I said *to me*, Henry,' she cut in quietly. 'To the world, you are the Marquis of Salmesbury. I think I am a poor candidate for his Marchioness. And—and yesterday——'

'Ah, yesterday! You saw my palatial residence, is that it? My God, I never thought to be sorry for the circumstances of my birth!'

'Don't, Henry! It was not that. At least, not *only* that. You see, we had not—*I* had not—properly considered all the implications. Now I have thought of them. Or rather,' she amended, with a twist in her face that cut him to the heart, 'they have been forced upon my notice.'

Henry looked struck. 'Oh, God! It is not my rank, nor my house, nor my estates, is it? That portrait of Meg—the accident—my insane behaviour.' He turned his face away. 'You are thinking of my outburst at the gypsy camp the other day.'

'That is a part of it,' Verity confessed, for she could not lie. 'Oh, don't think I blame you! Believe me, I don't. You were overwrought. I understood.'

'You understood,' he agreed low-voiced, 'and I know you would never blame me. But it frightened you.'

'No, not that,' she said quickly. 'Not in the way you think.'

But it was plain that he did not believe her. 'I can be very like the monster you once spoke of, can I not?' His mouth had a bitter curl to it. 'And a cripple to boot.'

'*No!*' Verity cried.

He shrugged. 'Why deny it? I will never walk with ease again. I will be lucky if I am not confined to a wheeled chair in middle age. Scarcely a satisfactory bargain.'

'Oh, Henry, that is a monstrous way to speak!' Verity scolded angrily, sweeping away from him and back again, as if she could not be still. 'You know your injury has never caused me the least discomfort. It is slighting to dare to suggest I could refuse you for such a reason as that!'

'Then if not that, *why*?' he demanded, matching her anger. 'Please, Verity, let me understand! These items you have mentioned—I don't believe you really care about them. They are excuses. Be truthful with me, I implore you, for I *know* you are not afraid of me, of what I am!'

'Oh, never that, Henry, never that!' she uttered, unguardedly stepping closer, her hands going out.

He grasped them strongly. 'Verity, this—this *thing* between us began that first day. Why do you suppose I came to Tunbridge Wells? Again and again. Oh, I didn't know it then myself, I grant you. But it grew and grew—and you know it!—until there was no gainsaying it. Damn you to hell, Verity, *why*?'

'*Because it is not enough!*' she threw at him wildly.

He stared at her blankly, his anger arrested. 'Not enough?'

'It can never be enough.' She said it quietly, thinking as she did so that it explained all.

To Henry, it was like a blow in the face. His hold on her hands relaxed and he released them. *Not enough*? What more could there possibly be? He shook his head as if to clear it of a fog. He felt empty, drained. Collecting his cane, he began to limp towards the door.

Verity watched him, her heart wrung. She had not meant to hurt him, though she had known she must. Only she had not realised how much, in doing so, she would hurt herself. She felt herself cruel and hated it, as if she had shown him a glimpse of Paradise and then snatched it away. She wanted very badly to run to him, tell him of her love, say she did not mean it. But the portrait rose in her mind. That fatal portrait of Lady Margaret Haverigg, whom Henry had loved and lost, whom she knew she could never replace.

Henry turned at the door. Like an afterthought, he said, 'I had hoped to bring home a new mother for my children. They love you, you know.'

Her throat ached suddenly. Through it, she managed to say, 'They will forget.'

He smiled, a wistful, tender smile. 'Perhaps they may. But will I?' After the briefest of pauses, in a quite ordinary voice, he added, 'The militia have apprehended the kidnappers. I thought you would wish to know.'

Then he passed from the room.

'I think you must have taken leave of your senses!' uttered the old lady fretfully. She had come back into the room on Salmesbury's departure, only to have all her eager expectations destroyed at a stroke.

'It must seem like it, I dare say,' Verity agreed wanly.

'Look at you! I declare, I have never seen such misery! And for what?'

'For *truth*, ma'am! It would not be fair to either he or myself to marry him.'

'Truth! Fair!' snorted Lady Crossens, tacking back and forth across the small parlour like a sail in a choppy wind. 'The truth, my girl, is that you don't know when you're well off! Here is the answer to every young girl's dream, handed to you on a golden platter, and you spurn it for a scruple.'

'Oh, ma'am, it is more than a scruple,' Verity said desperately. 'Much, much more. Must I spend my life in a welter of pain merely because the man who delivers it is a Marquis?'

'Pish and tush!' snapped her patroness crossly. '"Welter of pain"! I never heard such theatrical rodomontade! What more could you wish? Do you not love him? Does he not love you?'

Verity's lip trembled. 'He has not said so.'

The old lady's wrath was arrested in full flood. She stopped in mid-stride and stared at the girl. 'I beg your pardon?'

'He has not said that he loves me,' Verity repeated clearly, though her voice shook.

'But the man is obviously head over ears!' uttered Lady Crossens in a stunned tone.

'Still he has not said so.'

'Pah! *Men*. What a set of brainless idiots they are! You'd think they would realise that all a young girl wants to hear is a lot of romantical whispering. I could wring the ninny's neck!'

'Oh, ma'am!' protested Verity, half laughing. 'You are quite mistaken! I know that he *cares* for me, of course I do. But you don't understand. Perhaps if his wife had died in some other way, some manner that might not have involved him, it would be different. I might hope, in time, to supplant her in his affections. But as things stand—oh, can you not see how impossible it would be? Never to know, never to be sure of his affections. Always to see him sad and grieving any time something happens to remind him of her, of his first, his truest love. Then to see him, at last recognising that he cannot, will *never* forget her in loving me, trying not to show it, perhaps even living a *lie*. Oh, I could not endure it! Better by far we should never begin, than end in such *coldness*.'

Lady Crossens stood transfixed for a moment, caught up in the tragic voice, the pictures conjured up by the vivid words. Then she shook her head fiercely.

'Pish! Pish! Pish! Your trouble, my child, is an overactive imagination. Dear Lord in heaven, anyone would suppose you think to find yourself living in the pages of a three-volume novel!'

Verity coloured, but said in a low tone, 'I know I am apt to exaggerate life, ma'am, at least in my head. But you have not seen him when he speaks of her. God knows I would give anything to be his wife, could I only be first with him! But I cannot compete with a *ghost*.'

The old lady threw up her hands. 'Well, I've done with you! I've no patience. But when you have thrown away your chance beyond recovery, I trust you will remember your family and the future you have denied to them! When I think of all they might have enjoyed under such patronage—your sisters, your little brother, and dear Grace! Yes, and your father, for even he would scarcely applaud such pig-headed stupidity! And if he cannot think of a suitable penance, you may come to me, for I *can*!'

With which valedictory utterance, her ladyship stalked from the parlour, shutting the door behind her with unnecessary force. Verity was left to the doubtful comfort of a hearty bout of tears, but still holding tight to her convictions. For opposition had only strengthened them. Had Lady Crossens had children of her own, she might rather have seen more wisdom in painting the dismal picture of Verity's lonely future, at home with her broken heart—a picture she was desperately keeping at bay for fear that it would break her resolution. Just as she refused to think about Wystan and infant Peggy, unable even to cherish the glad tidings in Henry's last words—that the wicked Shottle and his gang had been captured—because they *were* Henry's last words.

It hardly seemed possible that only a few short weeks ago the sum of her ambition had been to live in a cottage and indulge her taste for the Gothic to her heart's content. Now, with *only* that prospect before her, she remembered old Mairenni's prediction: 'Looking for you'm heart's desire, ye'll find ye have it in yer hands.' Only her hands were empty now, and there was nothing she desired less than to take up her pen and write!

More with a forlorn hope of appeasing her patroness, than with any real wish to seek company, Verity made an appearance in the Assembly Rooms the same afternoon. She was glad to think that there were only a few days remaining to them before they must start for home, for her situation was unenviable.

The story of the kidnap was still talked of, and it had, by some means unknown to her, become common knowledge that she was sought after by the Marquis of Salmesbury. She was obliged to turn off several prying questions with a light laugh, as if it was all a piece of nonsense. But her patroness's smouldering temper was enough to inform everyone of the contrary. So it was that in Sir John Frinton Verity found her only sympathiser.

'A turn along the Pantiles, Miss Lambourn?' he offered, crooking his elbow invitingly, and with such a wealth of understanding in his impish old eyes that Verity was hard put to it to keep from bursting into tears.

'Th-thank you,' she managed to say, and was grateful for the tact that kept him silent until they were strolling along the paved walkway.

'You poor child!' he said then, laying his hand on hers where it rested on his own and squeezing her fingers.

'Oh, don't, please, Sir John,' she begged. 'It is difficult enough to keep my countenance as it is.'

'I see it is. Then I will refrain from such unhandsome comments, and merely inform you that you have certainly made an enemy for life!'

Her startled eyes flew to his. 'An enemy? Not you, I hope?'

'By no means.' He sighed in an exaggerated way. 'But poor Cumberland! You have offended beyond forgiveness, you know.'

'Oh, dear, poor man,' said Verity contritely. 'I did leave him so rudely, I know.'

'Now, Miss Lambourn, you are not going to tell me you were not glad of the excuse? Mind you, he did not take kindly to your having been seized by a fit of nausea in the middle of——'

'A fit of nausea! Gracious heaven, is that what you told him?' demanded Verity, aghast.

'I had to think of some plausible reason,' Sir John said blandly.

'Plausible!'

'Well, you had not found his rhetoric soporific, unlike Emilia and poor, dear Maria Polegate, so I assumed——' Then he began to laugh as Verity broke into voluble scolding.

'I have never in my life heard such——'

'Ah, but here is dear Maria herself,' he interrupted smoothly, successfully diverting his companion's attention as he added, 'And, if I am not mistaken, she is big with news!'

Verity followed the direction of his gaze to find Mrs Polegate hurrying towrds them, her eyes signalling a frantic message.

'Well, Maria?' drawled Sir John as she came puffing up. 'What earth-shattering titbit have you got hold of this time?'

'So dreadful!' gasped the lady, one hand holding her expansive bosom, which was rising and falling comically. 'Horrible! Poor, poor man!'

'Come, come, Maria!' chided Sir John, gently mocking. 'Get your breath back, my dear, or we shall never comprehend a word.'

'Oh—dear!' she got out. 'Yes—but it can't wait.' She looked at Verity. 'You will wish to know *at once*, I am sure.'

Verity went still, her hazel eyes fixed on the lady's face in painful enquiry. Her heart seemed to stop, and the world about her coalesced and became a hazy cloud.

'Dreadful! History repeats itself, you see,' said Mrs

Polegate, not without a certain relish. 'A terrible accident, they say. Took a fall from his phaeton and taken up for dead!'

There was a buzzing in Verity's ears, and she did not hear her own voice croak out the question to which she already knew the answer.

'Who? *Who*?'

'Why, the Marquis, of course!'

Verity was unaware of her own scream as the world went black. The next thing she knew was a spinning in her vision that steadied into faces looking down at her. Voices made themselves heard.

'Thank God, she is coming round!'

'Verity, child! Verity, can you hear me?'

'Give her room, there! Let her breathe!'

A deeper voice bade her lie still, and she came fully to her senses to find herself lying at full stretch on a sofa in the Assembly Rooms, an object of a general curiosity, while beside her knelt an elderly man in whom she recognised one of the resident physicians.

'Rest, please, Miss Lambourn,' he said, one hand encircling her wrist to feel her pulse.

For a moment she was glad to do as he bid her, for she felt quite sick and her head ached dully. She closed her eyes. There was a murmur of voices about her, but she did not question what had happened until she recognised her patroness's testy muttering.

'I don't know how you came to be so foolish, Maria! Could you not have come to me first?'

The image of Mrs Polegate's face sprang into Verity's mind, and, with it, the appalling news she had brought.

'Henry!' she uttered distressfully, and struggled to sit up.

'No, no, Miss Lambourn,' protested the physician, trying to push her back. 'Lie still, I beg of you.'

'I can't, I can't,' Verity cried, pushing away his restraining hand and impelling herself up.

The action caused her a sudden nausea and she was obliged to grip tightly to the back of the sofa, forcing it down. The ladies' voices were again heard, this time directed at her.

'No, Verity, you will remain there.'

'Oh, Miss Lambourn, you must forgive me! Do pray stay where you are a little.'

'Be quiet, Maria! She will certainly stay here.'

Unheeding, Verity willed herself to overcome the waves of sickness and swung her feet to the ground, fighting the many hands that sought to keep her here.

'*Henry*,' she uttered desperately. 'I must go to him!'

'No, no, Miss Lambourn!'

'Please stay, ma'am. You can do no good to yourself.'

'What does that matter?' Verity demanded, her ravaged features going wildly from face to face. 'I must go to Henry! I *must*.'

'Verity, listen to me——' began Lady Crossens in a scolding tone.

But Verity was on her feet, swaying a little, but with a set determination in her face that one at least of the surrounding well-wishers recognised.

'Let her be, Emilia,' said Sir John, laying a restraining hand on Lady Crossens' shoulder. 'Can you not see? Nothing less will satisfy her.'

He pushed through and, with an air of authority that made all give way before him, he took possession of Verity's hand and drew her within a protective arm.

'Come, child,' he said gently. 'I will take you to your Henry.'

'Thank you!' gasped Verity. 'Oh, thank you!'

Sir John turned to Lady Crossens. 'I will bring her safely back, Emilia, whatever the outcome.'

Her ladyship nodded, but her eyes, suspiciously bright, were on Verity's pale cheeks. 'You may as well sit down again, my dear,' she said gruffly, 'until the carriage is called for. I will send someone to fetch you a wrapper.'

Verity only nodded, sinking obediently down on to the sofa again, her mind rapidly numbing as it shied away from the dreadful images conjured up by Mrs Polegate's tale. She was well able to fill in the gaps with her own vivid imagination, but for once the ready visions were shut off, as being too painful to be contemplated at all.

Even so, she hardly heard the doctor, who still hovered over her, proffering a glass of some mixture which she dutifully drank as he instructed. She scarcely noticed how nearly the whole of the Wellsian visiting population took an interest, and how many of them accompanied her as Sir John Frinton led her out to the waiting carriage. Vaguely, as from some distant place, she heard the messages of goodwill, and felt the hands that pressed and the scented cheeks laid against her own. Dimly she recognised that they wished her well and so she smiled a little and whispered words of thanks.

But all her thoughts were of Henry, and she could no more understand now the confusion and fears of but a few hours before that had led her to refuse his suit than had her patroness at the time. If only he were alive and well, she would marry him in the teeth of twenty such Lady Margaret ghosts! What had she been about, to send him away so unhappy, so wretched that he let his ungovernable passion ride him to some hideous doom? For she knew, just as surely as if she had been there, that this was what had occurred. Must she now take poor Henry's burden of guilt upon her own shoulders? God could not be so cruel!

She was grateful for Sir John's calm flow of trivial remarks that kept such thoughts a little at bay. Whether he spoke of the weather or the scenery she did not know, but his voice was soothing. Though her nails dug into her own hands and the knot in her stomach hardened with every turn of the carriage wheels, that calm voice kept her from screaming aloud the fear that welled and welled within her as the miles went by.

It seemed to take forever, but at last the carriage turned into the long drive that led to Braxted Place. Verity leaned forward in her seat, staring intently out of the window, as if she might will the Marquis to appear there before her eyes.

As Cradoc opened the vast double doors to an imperative knock, two small hands seized him by the coat.

'Cradoc, where is he? Where have they taken him?'

'Miss?' asked the man in a puzzled voice.

'*Where is he*?'

Then the frantic hands released him, and Verity was speeding through the hall, calling out, 'Henry! Henry! Where are you?'

Cradoc made to follow her, but was halted by the man who had accompanied the girl. 'Let her be, man. She will find him for herself.'

The butler stood still, but stared after the girl as she flew up the grand marble stairway, her feet making even lighter work of the journey back over the way she had trodden only twenty-four hours ago, when she had run from this house like one crazed.

'Henry! Henry!' echoed her voice, carrying across the hall.

She did not hear the doors that opened, nor see the heads that popped out. Inskip came quickly into the hall to join the butler and Sir John.

'What is it, Cradoc?'

'I don't know, Mr Inskip. It's Miss Lambourn. Ripe for bedlam, I reckon! This gentleman brought her.'

Inskip glanced at Sir John, who bowed slightly and gave his name. 'She heard of the accident. Nothing would do for her but to come and see for herself how it was.'

'Good God!' ejaculated the secretary, and started off after her up the stairs. But by the time he reached the gallery, and opened his mouth to call, Verity was already approaching its other end. He stopped, watching her gravely, but there was the tiniest of smiles at the back of his eyes.

Verity did not know where to go, where to look. She paused uncertainly, her anguished gaze fluttering to the corridor ahead, and then up the next flight of stairs above her as she heard someone clattering down them.

'Wystan!' she cried out, as she recognised Braxted flying towards her.

'Was that you shouting, Verity?'

She did not answer, only seized his shoulders and shook him. 'Take me to your papa!'

The boy gazed up at her in perplexity. 'He's in his room.'

The grip left his shoulders, and she dashed a hand over her heated brow. 'Take me there!'

'But, Verity——'

'No questions!' she begged hoarsely. 'Take me, Wystan, for the love of God!'

'Come on, then!' he shouted, catching a little of her excitement, and sped off down the corridor that led from the long gallery.

Verity was in no mood to take in the labyrinthine route, nor to realise that her frantic calling would not have been audible on this side of the house. She only urged Wystan to hurry, every time he tried to ask her what was the matter.

It did not occur to her that the calm of the household argued against the tale she had heard, so urgent had become her need to reach Henry. Only when Wystan stopped at a door to knock, and she impatiently thrust him aside and flung it open for herself, did she pause to think.

For there, standing in his shirtsleeves before a dressing-table, with his valet in attendance, miraculously unharmed, stood Henry Haverigg, his startled eyes turned towards the door.

'Henry!' she cried out, and the wrapper dropped from about her shoulders as she ran across the room, her arms stretched out. 'You are alive! Oh, *Henry*!'

Henry received her in a comprehensive embrace that almost knocked him off his legs. Incredibly he kept his balance, holding tightly to the body that had unexpectedly descended upon him.

'Verity! My angel!' he uttered in tones of astonishment and delight. 'What in the world brings you? My God, my God, have you changed your mind?'

'They s-said you were dead!' Verity sobbed, raising her head from his shoulder and gazing adoringly into his face. 'Oh, Henry, it was all my fault! I should never have been so utterly, utterly foolish. But I was so confused! Oh, Henry, Henry, say you forgive me?'

Henry's black eyes searched her face. 'My darling, I am all too ready to forgive you anything at all, but I don't know what you are talking of!'

Verity drew a little away so she could the more easily stare at him. 'But the accident! They said you had fallen from your phaeton and been taken up for dead!'

'Oh, that.' He laughed in relief. 'Is that all? Good God, that was nothing! I took a fall, yes. Into some very muddy ground, let me tell you. I have just taken a bath and changed my clothes, as it happens.'

'But they said——'

Henry smiled. 'Come, now, Verity. You know how pale I am. No doubt the countryfolk who saw Hoff heave me into the phaeton thought I was at my last prayers. My doctor, Claughton, was not at all pleased with me, but I am very much alive, as you can see. A little bruised perhaps, but nothing serious.'

'Oh, thank God!' Verity uttered, collapsing on to his chest and crying weakly.

She was obliged to stop, however, because the Marquis chose this moment to kiss her, having first signalled to his open-mouthed son and his disapproving valet that they would do better to leave the room.

'Come, lend me your arm, and we will sit down,' he said presently, indicating a sofa that was placed before the window, from which an extensive view of the gardens was obtained.

'But where is your cane?' Verity enquired, slipping her arm about his back so that he might lean on her shoulders.

'You are my cane,' he told her caressingly, as he unselfconsciously gave her his weight.

She thrilled to the words, and to the feel of his hip as it thrust against her in its forward pull, the intimacy more dear even than the tender kiss with which he thanked her.

When they were settled in comfort, Henry removed her bonnet and gave her his handkerchief.

'I can only say thank God for the exaggeration of countryfolk,' he told her happily, 'since it had the effect of bringing you here to rescue me.'

Verity dried her eyes. 'It is very well for you to make a joke of it, but I know you were driving carelessly, for you were in one of your black moods!'

Henry grinned. 'Miss Lambourn, if you wish to be an arbiter of my conduct, there is a penalty to be paid, you know.'

She bit her lip, but the smile crept out. 'I dare say I may guess what *that* is.'

'I dare say you may, since you are far from stupid. And,' he added, the black eyes wickedly quizzing her, 'although you may not have noticed in your agitation, you are now hopelessly compromised by your presence in my bedchamber!'

Startled, Verity looked about her, becoming aware for the first time of the opulence of her surroundings, the huge four-poster bed that dominated one side of the room. She made an instinctive move to rise and was firmly restrained.

'No, you don't! We will remain here until I have your promise to marry me.'

Verity turned to him, her eyes moist. 'Oh, Henry, of course I will marry you! I can't think why I was making such a fuss. When I thought you were. . .' Her voice failing, she could only seize his hand and hold it tightly.

'My darling, I think I must have a very ignoble soul,' Henry told her ruefully. 'To have you restored to me is like—like being released from an iron cage! Yet I can find in myself a perverse satisfaction that you felt something of the devastation I experienced this morning, when I believed I had lost you.'

'Devastation!' echoed Verity in staring disbelief. 'Dear Lord, I thought they had *torn out my heart*! Henry, Henry, I love you so desperately!'

Henry's eyes blazed with passion, and he seized her in his arms again in a kiss so forceful that the thought flitted through her dizzying brain that she would swoon again. Flame seemed to erupt inside her and she clung to him, responding to the violence of his lips with a longing deep within her for that which she now knew would soon be fulfilled.

When at last he let her go, he was smiling at her with so much tenderness in those black eyes that Verity wondered how she could ever have supposed he did not care enough. His next words confirmed that he did.

'Verity, do you know that you are the most wonderful thing that has ever happened to me in my whole life?'

'No,' she said baldly.

Henry blinked. 'What? Don't you know how I love you?'

Verity shook her head. 'No. You never said so.'

He looked blank. 'Did I not?' A little laugh was surprised out of him. 'Perhaps you are right. To me it was so obvious.'

'Not to me,' Verity said firmly. She lifted a finger to trace a line down that pale cheek, no longer afraid to speak of the thing that had driven her into such deep despair. 'You see, I had *Margaret* to think of.'

He frowned as if the name meant nothing to him. 'Margaret?'

'Yes, Meg. Your *wife*.'

Recognition flashed in his eyes, but he drew her closer within his embrace and put up a hand to caress her cheek. 'Yes, I see.'

'I could not believe you might love me as intensely as you had loved her. It seemed as though the manner of her loss would always keep you from me.'

Now he stared at her in amazement. 'Good God, now I don't see at all! Are you telling me that is why you refused me?'

Verity nodded, a little shame-faced. 'I was silly, I know, but——'

'No, you were not silly,' Henry interrupted. 'It was a natural conclusion for you to make. It is I who was the fool, not to see how it must appear!' He seized her hands, holding them tightly between his own, and his black eyes locked on to hers as if by this he might convince her better of what he was about to say. 'My darling, you don't understand. Meg and I were never *in love*. I cared for her, yes, of course I did. But not like *this*.'

Verity gazed back at him blankly. 'What do you mean? You were *married*.'

He smiled. 'My innocent, Meg and I were destined for one another almost before we were out of our cradles. It was all *arranged*, long before either of us knew anything of the matter.'

'What?' uttered Verity faintly, as ignorant of this aspect of aristocratic affairs as she was of the rest of his public life.

'*Yes*,' he insisted. 'She was the daughter of the Earl of Templand and Lady Margaret in her own right. Rank and birth are of the first consequence in these matters, and we both had wealth, too. It was an admirable match and we were both very dutiful. Fortunately, our respective parents saw the wisdom of allowing us to become acquainted and we saw much of each other as children. They took no chances, nevertheless, for our engagement was announced at Meg's début and we were married soon after. She was only just seventeen. I was little more than a year older.'

'I think that is terrible!' Verity said, appalled.

He shrugged, faintly smiling. 'Perhaps. It is quite usual for persons of our order, however, and we saw nothing amiss. We had no choice, but we made no objections either. It was duty.' He grinned suddenly, and kissed the hands he still held. 'But I already have an heir, and I am now at liberty to please myself.'

Verity was too much caught up in this revelation to be diverted by the pleasantry. She released her hands only so that she could grasp his arms.

'Then, Henry, when she died——'

The pale face shadowed a little. 'When she died, I was responsible. I grieved for her, more perhaps for her loss to the children than to myself. But it was for the *waste* that I suffered most! It was I who cut her off in the flower of her youth, and I must ever live with that knowledge. If I had not found you, I cannot think I would long have survived it.'

'Don't speak that way!' Verity scolded, but she softened the words with a kiss, raising her hands from his arms to cup his face between them.

'I love you,' he said softly, putting his lips to hers and with them gently caressing her mouth.

But in a moment Verity pulled a little away. Still she was not entirely satisfied, not entirely convinced.

'But Henry, had Meg lived. . .what then?'

An expression of faint distress flickered over his face. 'There, my sweet, you have perhaps one of the unkindest twists of fate. Or perhaps the kindest. Who knows? For if Meg had lived, we would have gone on in quiet content, accepting each other's vagaries, sometimes with impatience perhaps, even growing a little apart as we grew older.'

He slid his arm about Verity's back and with his other hand cupped her head, tipping it back so that her dark curls rioted about her while he roved her features with his eyes.

'And then I should never have known what it is to love a woman to the point of screaming madness, to love her to the depths of my soul, and to know that in all the world there is nothing I could desire more than to walk with her beside me through the remainder of my life.'

'Oh, Henry!' Verity whispered, and closed her eyes as she leaned forward to receive his kiss.

Behind them the door burst open. They came apart as if sprung, turning their heads to see who had caught them so indecorously entwined.

'You're going to be married!' yelled Braxted from

the doorway, hitting the air with a triumphant fist.
'Inskip told me, and anyone can see it's true!'

Held in his other hand was his little sister. Tugging
her along, he skipped towards the sofa.

'I brunged Peggy to see for herself. See, Peggy,
they're going to be married, and I knowed it.' He
began to chant. 'I knowed it! I knowed it!'

'I no-dit! I no-dit!' sang Peggy, her little face beam-
ing as she reached the couple on the sofa, putting up
her arms in mute invitation.

'I hope you will like it, Peggy,' Verity said, lifting
the infant on to her lap, her countenance wreathed in
smiles.

Wystan looked from one to the other of them. 'It is
true, isn't it, Papa?'

Henry could not keep the happiness out of his face.
'Yes, it's true. Verity has consented to be my wife—
and your new mama.'

'Hurrah!' Then the boy put his arms akimbo, staring
at his father with an air of great seriousness, and
added, 'And about time too!'

Instantly, Peggy swivelled about on Verity's lap and
poking her father in the ribs, summed it up neatly.

'Time *too*. . .time to 'ug?'

THE DANBURY SCANDALS
Mary Nichols

Having been brought up in the Reverend Cudlipp's
household, Maryanne Paynter was both astonished and a
little frightened to be suddenly taken up by Viscount
Danbury. Discovering herself to be related to
aristocracy changed her life completely, and even more
mystifying, it brought her into contact with Adam
St. Pierre, who also seemed to have some connection
with the Danburys. The uneasy peace between France
and England in 1814 seemed to be part of the mystery,
where past Danbury scandals could affect the future.
Where could Maryanne seek refuge–with her new
cousin Mark, or Adam?

TWO
HISTORICAL ROMANCES

&
TWO
FREE GIFTS!